anything
he wants

anything
he wants

sara fawkes

ST. MARTIN'S GRIFFIN ❧ NEW YORK

This is a work of fiction. All of the characters, organizations, and events portrayed in this novel are either products of the author's imagination or are used fictitiously.

www.stmartins.com

ISBN 978-1-250-03533-2 (trade paperback)
ISBN 978-1-250-03532-5 (e-book)

First Edition: December 2012

10 9 8 7 6 5 4 3 2 1

For my very first fans—hi, Mom and Dad!

Acknowledgments

I wouldn't be where I am without my readers. Seriously! I'm so thankful to have the people in my life I've met through the process of writing this book, those who've helped me shape the story and encouraged me along this path. I am forever grateful for the assistance of so many people: Carl East, Virginia Wade, Delta, and all my EFers; my editor, Rose Hilliard, and St. Martin's Press; my agent, Steve Axelrod; and so many others who have contributed their time and experience, helping me grow in my career as a writer.

Mainly though, I have to thank my readers. You guys are absolutely incredible and were instrumental in getting me here. Thank you so very, very much, and know that I'll always be *your* fan.

1

The high point of my workdays lately was seeing the gorgeous stranger every morning.

I hurried through the lobby toward the elevators as fast as decorum and my heels would allow, passing ladders and service crews working on the old building's antiquated electrical systems. The dark-haired stranger arrived at the elevator like clockwork, at 8:20 A.M. every day, and this morning proved no exception. I jockeyed my way through the crowd until I stood close, but not conspicuously so, to the stranger and stared at the elevator doors while pretending to ignore him. It wasn't a game, although it sometimes felt that way. Men that handsome always stayed several steps outside my sphere of influence and this man was no different.

Didn't mean a girl couldn't dream.

The doors opened and I moved with the small crowd onto the elevator, making sure my floor was pressed. The old—or "historic," as some liked to say—building was in the midst of a full renovation. Everything was being upgraded to new, more modern settings, but for now they still had the older-style elevators. Smaller and slower than current models, the metal box nevertheless did its job as it chugged up to the floors above.

I rearranged the large satchel in my arm, sliding a glance sideways and catching his eye. Does he know I watch him? Flushing, I turned my gaze forward once again as the elevator opened to let another string of people off to their floors. My stop was still eleven floors away; I did data entry as temp work for Hamilton Industries. The company spanned most of the upper levels but my small cubicle was tucked away in a forgotten corner near the middle.

I loved the clean-cut, suited look, and the dark-haired man was always impeccably dressed in suits and ties that probably cost more than what I made in a month. Everything about him screamed high society, far out of my league, but that never stopped my fantasy life from including him. The handsome stranger was part of my dreams, the face I saw when I closed my eyes for bed. As I'd had nothing between my legs not run by batteries in well over a year, my fantasies were getting pretty kinky. I took a moment to think about them now and a slow smile spread across my face. It didn't take much to get me going, but the image in my mind of being pushed against a wall and ravaged . . . Oh yeah.

Passengers continued to disembark and as the elevator doors shut, I pulled myself out of my reverie as I realized that, for the first time, I was actually alone with the stranger. Clearing my throat nervously, I smoothed down my pencil skirt with my free hand as the old elevator continued its trek up to my workplace. Breathe, Lucy, just breathe. Desire curled in my belly, fueled by thoughts of all sorts of naughty things in elevators. I wonder if this one has cameras. . . .

I heard a faint rustle behind me, then a thick arm appeared beside me and pressed a red button on the panel. Immediately the elevator ground to a halt and before I could say anything, arms appeared on either side of my head and a low voice next to my ear murmured, "I see you on this elevator every morning. Your doing, I take it?"

Shocked into silence, I could only blink in wide-eyed confusion. Should I pinch myself? Is this really happening?

As I was pressed against the elevator doors by a hard body behind me, the cool metal against my suddenly hard and sensitive nipples elicited a breathy moan. "What—" I started, immediately forgetting whatever I was going to say as I felt his hard length press against my hip.

"I can smell your arousal," he growled, that low sexy voice making my stomach tighten. "Every morning you get on this elevator and I can smell your need." One hand moved down and entwined with mine as he dipped his head toward my neck. "What's your name?"

My mind went blank for a moment, forgetting the simplest of answers. Oh God, that voice is pure sex, I thought wildly, lifting my hands to brace myself against the hard surface before me. His voice was low and had a lilt I couldn't place, and my chest grew tight with need. "Lucy," I finally managed, hoping my brain was done short-circuiting.

"Lucy," he repeated, and I drew in a shaky breath at

hearing my name said in that too-sexy voice. "I need to see if you taste as good as you smell."

There was no request for permission in his voice, only an implacable demand, and I rolled my head sideways to allow him access. His lips slid across the soft skin behind my ear, tongue flicking out to touch me; his teeth nipped the lobe and I moaned, pressing back against him. He rotated his hips and my breathing sped up, needy pants a staccato in the silence.

"God, you're so fucking hot." His hand trailed down the side of my body, across my hip and down my thigh until he found the hem of my skirt. His hand then retraced its steps back up, skimming lightly across the smooth skin of my inner thigh, pulling the material of my skirt up toward my hips. Unthinking, I spread my legs to give him access and gasped loudly as fingers slid along the outside of my soaked panties, pressing against my aching core.

Was this really happening? My body bucked, trapped between the metal doors and the hot body behind me. It was like every fantasy I'd ever had was being played out in person, and I was helpless to stop my conditioned response.

His fingers pulsed, sliding across my clit with increasing frequency, and my hips moved of their own volition, craving more of his touch. I cried out when his teeth sank into my shoulder, then his fingers slid beneath the thin cotton and lace and stroked my wet skin, pulling at my tender opening in a way that had me moaning loudly inside the elevator.

"Come for me," he murmured in his low Vin Diesel voice, lips and teeth running along the exposed line of my neck and shoulder. His fingers pushed deep inside, thumb flicking my hard nub, and with a strangled cry I came hard. My forehead rested against the hard steel of the door as I shuddered, suddenly boneless.

Below the numbered panel to my right, a telephone rang out.

I stiffened in shock, the blaring tones cutting through my murky haze. Lust gave way to mortification and I pushed against the door to free myself. The dark stranger stepped back, allowing me space, and pressed the red button again. I hastily rearranged my clothing as the elevator chugged back up the shaft; a few seconds later the telephone stopped ringing.

"You taste even better than I imagined."

I turned, helpless against that voice, to see him licking his fingers. The look he gave me made my knees weak, but the ringing phone had woken me up and I fumbled blindly for the floor buttons, pressing every button within my reach. This only seemed to amuse him, but when the doors opened to an empty hallway two floors below mine, I stumbled out. No people were in sight on this floor, to my relief—I wasn't sure I could take more attention right then.

A quick whistle behind me drew my attention and I turned to see the stranger pick up my satchel and hold it out to me. It had slid out of my arms, forgotten, to the floor while we were . . . I cleared my throat and took it with as much dignity as I could muster.

He smiled, the simple expression changing his entire countenance. I stared, dumbstruck at his utter gorgeousness, as he winked at me. "I'll see you again," he said as the elevator doors shut, stranding me temporarily on the lower floor.

I took a deep breath and fumbled with my clothing, tucking my blouse into my waistband with shaky fingers. My panties were a lost cause—I'd have a wet spot on my dress all day if I continued to wear them. Focusing on that and not the growing embarrassment of my actions, I searched and found a bathroom nearby in which to clean myself up.

A few minutes later, clean but vulnerable without any underwear, I took the stairs up two flights to my floor. The halls leading to my area were packed with last-minute arrivals, and I made it to my cubicle without any problems. I was a minute late clocking in on the computer but nobody seemed to care as I got right to work, drowning myself in my job to try to forget my shocking display earlier.

2

The day passed in a mental jumble. No matter how I tried to focus on my work, I couldn't make myself concentrate. I found it necessary to double-, then triple-check my work to make sure I'd done it right. The temp data entry assignments I was given were tedious and brainless, but nevertheless I kept messing them up. My mind would flash back to the elevator, the handsome stranger and the first semipublic orgasm I ever had, and when I got back on track I couldn't remember what lines I'd entered in the computer.

This was so unlike me. I'd always been a sexual creature but had never been the type to know what to do about it. The boys never asked me out; I wasn't invited to parties or the like even in college. The few boyfriends I'd had, if they could be called that, hadn't stayed around long. My life at the moment was boring, mostly out of necessity—college loans didn't pay themselves, and living near the city made things even tighter—but I couldn't find much connection with most men. They wanted to go party, I wanted to read; they were *Sports Illustrated*, I was *National Geographic*.

Dating, while the least of my worries at the moment, was definitely not a strong point.

Despite my attempts to forget the whole situation in the elevator, by lunch I desperately wanted my vibrator and a swift kick in the rear. My actions and instant response to the stranger were troublesome, regardless of my fantasy life. It couldn't happen again no matter how much I may have wanted a repeat. I needed this job, even if it was monotonous, and I couldn't afford any more distractions. But my job didn't require much brainpower to begin with and I couldn't stop remembering how soft his lips were, and how his teeth across the skin of my shoulder sent shivers down my spine. His large hands had held a dual promise of strength and tenderness that my body refused to forget.

It was a long day.

Barely managing to get my quota of files archived and turned in by the end of the day, I contemplated taking the stairs down fourteen flights but finally opted for the elevator, which I made sure was stranger-free. I cut through the underground parking garage while the bulk of the crowd headed for the taxis out front. Few people were able to park under the building; certainly not a new temp, even if I did have a car. But cutting through the garage was a much faster route to the subway station two streets away, and nobody had told me the shortcut was off-limits.

I headed down the single flight of steps and out into the chilly afternoon air of the underground garage. The squeal of tires came from somewhere in the multilevel complex but I saw nobody else, just lines of cars. Rubbing my arms, the bite in the air promising cold temperatures as soon as the sun set, I turned toward the guard shack, wishing I'd brought something to slip over my arms. It was late spring but the weather had taken a colder turn over the last few days and I wasn't dressed appropriately.

Someone grabbed my arm and jerked me sideways into the shadows beside me. Before I could make a sound, a hand clapped over my mouth, and I was dragged back into a small alcove half hidden from the rest of the garage that was reserved for motorcycles. I struggled but the arms holding me were implacable, like iron across my body.

"I did tell you I would see you soon." The voice was familiar and deep, and I recognized it immediately. It had been running through my head all day long in fantasies I'd tried in vain to stamp out.

As soon as I heard his voice a wave of relief washed over me, followed quickly by confused anger. Why on earth do I trust him? Frustrated by my own apparent stupidity, I stomped down as hard as I could on the instep of the stranger's foot. He grunted but didn't release me, instead spinning me and pressing me up against the cold concrete wall. His body molded itself to my back, hands holding my wrists against the concrete. "You can fight," he murmured, running his lips along the back of my ear. "I like that."

His casual dismissal annoyed me. I threw my head back, trying to hit him in the face, but he ducked out of the way with a chuckle. Another attempt to stomp his foot with my pump was foiled when his leg snaked between mine, leaving me unable to struggle that way. The fingers around my wrists, softer than iron manacles but no less firm, set fire to my skin without giving me any room to move.

"Let me go or I'll scream," I said in an even voice, trying to turn my head to catch his eye. It frustrated the hell out of me that I was neither afraid nor as angry as I knew I should be; the man was once again prompting the wrong feelings for the situation. I had to be brain damaged if I thought I could trust the man when I didn't even know his name!

He leaned forward, pressing his face against my hair and taking a deep breath. The appreciative rumble deep in his throat reverberated throughout my body. "I couldn't stop thinking about you all day," he murmured, not acknowledging my threat. His thumbs made light circles on my wrists and my body clenched at the almost tender motion. "How quickly you responded to me, your smell, your taste."

I swallowed, trying to ignore the sudden flutter in my belly. No, I thought desperately, I can't be turned on by this. The sight of him looming over me, however—his hard hot body pressing against my back—was making my head whirl and limbs ache to wrap around him. Dammit. "Let me go," I said between gritted teeth, trying to ignore my body's traitorous reactions. "This is wrong, I don't want . . ."

He laid a soft kiss on the skin behind my ear as I trailed off, a stark contrast to the unbreakable grip in which he held my wrists. My breath caught in my throat as lips and teeth dragged down my neck as his hips rolled against my backside, his hard length sliding along the crease. "I would never take a woman who doesn't want me," he murmured, moving to whisper in my other ear. "Say 'no' and I will leave you alone forever." He ran his lips down the side of my throat, giving my shoulder a gentle bite as he waited for my answer.

By now I was shaking, but not in any kind of fear or distress. When one of his hands left my wrist and skimmed along the underside of my arm I didn't move, reveling in the sensations his touch produced. His hand moved up the back of my thigh under my skirt, fingernails raking the skin, and a finger slid between the firm lobes of my backside. He gave a growl, squeezing my butt with both hands and spreading the cheeks, then pressed between them with the hard bulge still locked behind his pants. A moan slipped from my mouth as I arched my hips back, using the wall as leverage to get closer.

The hands left me and I was flipped around to face him. I had a brief close-up glimpse of a familiar handsome face and green eyes, then his lips crashed against mine in the hottest kiss of my life. I responded, arching closer so I was flush against his body. I slid my hands across his torso, moving them up and through his hair, but he grabbed my hands and stretched them high above my head. A leg between my thighs pushed me higher and I ground my hips, rubbing myself against the rock-hard thigh. Breathy moans escaped my lips as he moved his mouth lower, sucking and nibbling on the sensitive skin of my neck.

"I want to feel your mouth on me," he murmured, gliding his lips up my neck and jawline. "I want to see you on your knees, that perfect mouth around my cock . . ."

This time when I tried to free myself he didn't stop me, instead he stepped back and set me on my feet. My hands went immediately to his waistband, sliding down the zipper. He reached down to help me, and as he pulled his member free of the pants I sank down on my heels and flicked the tip with my tongue. He tasted clean, and the sharp intake of breath above told me he liked what I was doing. His need was my own; I felt a fresh wave of heat between my legs as I moved my head forward, sucking the head deep.

"God!" His body shuddered and, suddenly bolder, I wrapped a hand around the thick base and pulled him farther into my mouth. My tongue rolled along the base and flicked the tip, then I started bobbing my head over the thick member. His hips jerked, thrusting in time with my mouth; a hand came to rest behind my head, pulling insistently, but I controlled the pace. I undid the button of his pants and reached inside, cupping his balls with my free hand. He shook above me, dick jumping in appreciation, then both hands dug into my skull, pulling me closer and silently demanding more, deeper. This time I obliged, releasing the base and pulling him in as far as I could, bobbing and weaving with my head and tongue. My free hand slid down between my legs, gliding through my wet folds and pressing against the throbbing nub.

"Are you touching yourself?" I heard him grit out above me. The thrusts into my mouth grew more frenzied as I sped up my own ministrations, the hard length in my mouth muffling my cries. The stranger was silent for the most part, but the few moans he did let free when I swirled my tongue or massaged the tip with the back of my throat were gratifying to hear.

Part of my brain, a very small part, wondered what on earth I was doing, but I tuned it out. I had gone far too long without anyone noticing me; even my coworkers ignored me. So for a man this beautiful to see me, let alone approach me in any fashion, was a heady notion. I didn't allow myself to wonder why he chose me or what would happen next—right now I only wanted to feel. Fingers dug into my scalp and my own orgasm rushed to meet me even as his balls contracted, close to their own finale.

Hands pushed me away, back against the concrete wall, and I disengaged with a surprised pop. The man before me bent down and wound his arms around my torso; I was lifted into the air and thrust back against the wall, a hard body settling between my legs. I turned startled eyes to the handsome stranger's face, now only inches from mine, then I felt his member probing my entrance. He pressed inside and I bit back a cry from the intense pleasure. Muscles that hadn't seen action in too long were stretched, my own juices giving him an easy entrance. His lips crushed mine, swallowing my cries as he pounded me back into the concrete wall.

The orgasm I'd been coaxing along with my fingers rocketed to the surface with the rubbing and stretching and grinding. My scream was caught by the stranger's lips as I came hard, waves of pleasure rolling through my body. I kissed him wildly, nipping at his lips and raking my fingernails down the jacket arms of his suit. My response brought out a similar wildness in him and he pounded into me, releasing my mouth and latching on to my shoulder with his teeth. My cries, fainter now after the orgasm, still echoed off the walls in the small alcove.

He gasped against my skin, then he pulled out and came on the ground beneath me, his free hand rubbing out the last of his orgasm. Sandwiched between his hot body and the hard concrete, I finally noticed the chill of the cold stone and the sound of cars deep inside the complex making their way toward the exit. The chill against my wet thighs served as a wake-up call to what I had allowed to happen; I pressed feebly against the hard shoulders, my body still limp from my orgasm.

The stranger stepped back, still supporting my weight with large hands beneath my backside, then slowly lowered me to the floor. I wobbled in my heels, gripping his arm for support before stepping away. The enormity of what I had just done—again—sent my mind reeling. I shivered, only partly from the cold, then jumped as something warm and heavy covered my shoulders. I glanced up briefly at the now jacket-less stranger but was unable to utter any words of thanks. He helped hold it for me as I slowly pulled the dress coat over my arms. While not a cold-weather jacket, it remained warm from his body and cut the worst of the chill, which helped immensely.

"Let me take you home."

The moment I heard the words I shook my head, stepping away from him. My body burned with shame and I couldn't bear to look at him. "I need to catch the train," I mumbled.

A finger came under my chin and tilted my head up until

I was looking into the strong lines of that handsome face. Even after riding the elevator with him so long, I'd never been this close, and the sight took my breath away. Dark skin, whether through genetics or being kissed by the sun, only served to accent deep green eyes framed by black lashes and dark brows. His thick hair was nearly as black, falling in strands across his brow, tousled now thanks to my handiwork. A light shadow along his jaw, the skin prickly to the touch, seemed to complete the picture and made my heart skip a beat. His stony expression didn't quite match the concern in his beautiful eyes as he peered down at me, thumb caressing my chin. "Please," he said softly.

My body still responded to his touch; I wanted to lay my cheek against the rough skin of his hand. Tears pricked my eyes at the silly sentiment—was I really so desperate?—and I stepped back again, pulling from his grip. Clearing my throat and forcing myself not to act like a simpering twit, I looked him in the eye. "I need to catch the train." Keeping my head high even as shame made me want to crawl away and hide, I started walking away but then faltered. "Your jacket," I murmured, and started to shrug out of it.

He held up a hand to stop me. "Keep it." A bemused smile flickered across his lips and it seemed for a moment I had his full attention . . and approval. "You need it more than I do right now."

The air was chilly and I knew I looked a mess; the coat hung on me but at that moment I needed the cover. Murmuring my thanks I walked quickly out of the alcove and started toward the exit. I lifted a shaky hand to my head; my hair was loose but seemed to be in order. I'd need to find a mirror quickly as I was certain I looked a fright.

I heard the sound of a car pulling up behind me and stopping. Against my better judgment I glanced back to see a chauffeur step out of a long black limousine and open the passenger door, then the handsome stranger ducked inside. I stood there, staring like an idiot, as the driver closed the door and pulled out toward the exit. The windows of the car were tinted so I couldn't see inside as it passed by me, and I watched as my erstwhile ride pulled past the guards and out into the loud traffic outside. *Who on earth is this man?* I wondered, then shut off that line of thought and headed out of the empty garage.

I ducked inside a nearby café and locked myself inside the bathroom to clean up. My skirt and blouse fared well enough, flattening back to some semblance of order. Smoothing down my hair proved impossible, the dark blond strands refusing to cooperate after being so deliciously manhandled, so I dug around inside my bag for a hair tie and did a loose ponytail. I didn't bother reapplying my makeup, but did clean up the smudges around my blue eyes so I at least looked presentable. Fifteen minutes later I ducked back out, my satchel hanging by its strap over a bare arm and the dress coat draped over the bag; despite the chill, I felt strange wearing it. I caught a later train than usual but most of that time was a haze, my brain repeating one thought over and over again.

What the hell was I doing?

3

The next morning, I arrived at work half an hour early and made sure the elevator I took did not contain the stranger. Nervous as I was that someone might comment on my actions the previous day, it was a relief to be ignored as usual by the people around me. The building at that hour held a fraction of its usual occupants, and I hurried to my desk to avoid any unwanted confrontations with certain green-eyed individuals.

I'd spent most of my evening and night trying to figure out whether or not I should go to work the next morning. The recklessness and downright stupidity of my actions haunted me all night, making me go so far as to question my sanity. This isn't who I am. I'd never been so thoughtless about my actions, and a desperate libido wasn't enough of an answer for me.

I'd started searching out job opportunities, something I could turn to if my present situation went sour, but the market was as tough as ever. The proper half of my brain demanded I quit this job, but the logical portion maintained I needed the money. My bills were coming due and I had no savings that would allow me time to search out a better employment situation.

Oh, Lucy, how far you've fallen.

Once I got to my desk I spent my time on work that allowed me to avoid having to log in to the computer, as I didn't want my early arrival noticed by management. My coworkers arrived, chatting among themselves as they passed by my tiny cubicle, but I stayed in my little corner for most of the day, content to be ignored. The day went by uneventfully until almost four in the afternoon when my boss poked her head around the walls of my desk. "Follow me, please, Ms. Delacourt."

My manager's presence startled me. I saw her almost every day but, after my initial interview, she had all but ignored my presence in the office. That she chose now to talk to me had the world spinning and my stomach curling into knots. Her tone brooked no argument, however, and with a hurried "Yes, ma'am" and a brief pause to get myself together, I pulled myself up on trembling legs and followed after her.

She bypassed her office door and then strode out the door of our office area to the hall outside. I followed after her silently, afraid to ask what this was about for fear of learning the whole building knew about my sexcapades the day before. I could think of no other reason I'd be called out, and I doubted they'd take me out of my section simply to fire me.

We rode the elevator up silently, and my apprehension

grew as we neared the top of the building. My manager never once spoke to me and was impossible to read—not that I tried too hard, afraid of what I'd find. The moment the elevator doors opened I knew I was in an entirely different world. Gone were the lifeless narrow corridors as I stepped into a wide passage lined with dark wood paneling that had the company name HAMILTON in bold letters across the wall. The wide entryway led toward a reception desk at the opening of a large open room. Office doors lined the walls and two large glass-encased conference rooms sat in either corner of the large area. There was a rich old-world sense about everything, dark woods and gold accents mixing with modern lighting and artwork.

"Mr. Hamilton is expecting us," my boss said to the lady at the desk, who nodded and picked up a phone as we passed.

I stumbled at her words, my legs suddenly refusing to work. Why were we in the corporate section of the building? I'd never read up on the company; it was a temp job, meant only to be a short-term employment gig, but I knew this wasn't just any floor. It had a Donald Trump feel, more a reception area than an office. There was no way, however, that they'd send me here if they knew what I'd done.

Confusion and trepidation continued to climb as I followed my supervisor at a cautious distance. She headed toward one of the offices and knocked before poking her head inside. "Mr. Hamilton will see you now," she said, motioning for me to enter.

I stood there, staring mutely at my manager for a moment,

then slowly moved toward the door. I gave her one last confused glance as I walked through, then came to a halt inside as renewed horror washed over me. Oh no, no no no . . .

"Thank you, Agatha, that will be all for now."

Nodding once, my supervisor pulled the door closed as I stood, aghast, inside the large office. My mouth worked soundlessly as I stared at the familiar figure sitting behind the desk. My eyes fell to the nameplate on the desk. "Jeremiah Hamilton," I said, my body numb with shock.

The dark-haired man behind the desk raised cool eyes to appraise me. "Ms. Delacourt," he said in reply, gesturing to a chair in front of his desk. "Please take a seat."

My heartbeat sped up as I heard his voice, confirming my worst fears. Unable to speak, I moved to the chair he'd motioned me toward, movements jerky and hesitant, and sat down. He ignored me, running through something on the tablet in his hand. As we sat in strained silence I glanced around the large office. Windows covered the wall behind the CEO's desk from ceiling to floor, giving a panoramic view of the streets below. The desk was a dark wood and sturdy, covered sparsely with a laptop computer, the nameplate, and a Newton's cradle, the steel balls unmoving. The chair I sat in was plush and thick with rolling castors at the bottom.

"Ms. Lucille Delacourt," the stranger said, startling me. Jeremiah Hamilton, I reminded myself, still unable to get my brain around my current situation. "Currently a temp data clerk out of the Executive Management Solutions employment agency, hired one month ago by Agatha Crabtree.

Correct so far?" At my jerky nod he continued. "I see you used your passport as identification." He glanced up at me. "Passport?"

Talking was difficult with a suddenly dry mouth, but I still tried. "I always carry them with me."

He raised an eyebrow. "Them?" the CEO asked, his expression probing for more information, but I only shrugged, words failing me.

There was a moment of silence before he resumed speaking. "Grew up in upstate New York, attended Cornell University for three years before dropping out. Menial jobs since then and you moved to the city three months ago. Why did you drop out?"

The summary of my life was cold and brief, the words piercing through me. The question at the end sailed right past me; it was the generous pause that made me look up into his expectant face. "What?" I asked, cursing inwardly for not listening.

"Why," he repeated, "did you drop out of college, Ms. Delacourt?"

His tone demanded an answer but it was complicated and personal, bringing up memories I still struggled with nearly three years later. The question was an invasion of my privacy and I knew I didn't legally have to answer, but I found my lips moving anyway. "My parents died."

There was a long pause this time as I stared at my hands, trying not to cry—a difficult task, given the nerve-wracking situation I'd gotten myself into. *Would they be ashamed of where I am now?* I wondered, swallowing back tears. They had sacrificed so much to let me get ahead, most of which I hadn't discovered until after their deaths. Losing the house I'd grown up in, the one that had been in the family for two generations, because of the huge mortgage they'd taken out to pay my tuition, had been a sickening blow. I'd tried so hard to keep it from falling into the bank's hands, but . . . Swallowing the lump in my throat, I struggled to regain my composure.

"I'm sorry for your loss," Jeremiah said after a long moment of silence. He cleared his throat, and I heard him lean back in his leather chair. "What brought you down to New York City?"

I thought I detected a note of concern in his voice but still couldn't bring myself to look at him. Even though the question was personal and none of his business, I still answered. "I lost my family's house and had to move; an old college friend in Jersey City said I could live with her."

"I see." Jeremiah scratched his chin for a moment. "Do you know why I've asked you to come, Ms. Delacourt?"

It was the question I dreaded and couldn't possibly answer. Swallowing, I raised my head to meet his green eyes but my courage failed me. "No?" I replied, more a question than an answer.

He opened his mouth to say something, paused, then tried again. "Let me tell you how your day would have gone today prior to our meeting." He folded his arms on the desk before continuing. "You would have worked until half an hour before closing, when you would have been called into your supervisor's office. She would have explained that your temp work contract was terminated and today was your last day. You would have been given your last paycheck and escorted out of the building."

For the second time that morning, the bottom dropped out from under my feet. "You're firing me?" I asked in a faint voice, unable to believe my own words. Anger bubbled up at the unfairness of my life. "Is this because we . . ."

Jeremiah held up a hand to stop my words and shook his head. "The decision on the layoffs has been planned for a month now. We no longer need most of the temps in your department." His eyes narrowed as he added, more to himself, "I signed the directive earlier this week before I knew who you were."

"Nobody's hiring right now," I whispered, forgetting my looking for another job was supposed to be secret. No reason to hide that now. The anger was difficult to sustain as I realized I'd have to weather another blow after so many in my life recently.

"I looked at your file and you did good work," Jeremiah continued as I stared, numb, at the top of his desk. "We would give you an excellent recommendation for any future job inquiries."

At a loss for words, unable to think of what to say, I looked up and stared at the CEO. "Why did you tell me this?" I mumbled. "Why bring me up here?"

"Because I have another offer for you, a job if you're interested. I'm in need of a personal assistant."

I blinked several times, taken by surprise at the offer. I peered into his face but it was like granite; I couldn't tell at all what he was thinking. Suspicion curled in my belly as I asked, "What kind of personal assistance?"

"Anything I want."

I took a deep breath at the words, my mind taking me to all sorts of places within that phrase. He couldn't mean . . . surely he's not implying what I think. But something in his eyes, despite the relaxed business demeanor, implied it was exactly what I was imagining. His gaze promised all sorts of wicked things—or maybe it was my mind trying to make my fantasies a reality. I needed to be sure. "About yesterday, when we, um . . ."

Jeremiah leaned forward and rested a strong chin on his fingers. "Yes," he said simply, the one word answering all my questions.

I tried to get indignant at the proposition, tried to find some way to protest and maintain some shred of dignity, but I was too practical. Right now I desperately needed a job and here was an offer, and I couldn't afford to let it pass not knowing when I might get another. My heart constricted as I remembered how, for nearly two years, I'd poured every dime I'd earned into keeping my family's house, only to lose it and wind up with nothing anyway. Without any immediate family willing or able to help, if it hadn't been for a former classmate offering to let me stay with her, I would have been on the streets. What was meant to be a temporary solution, though, had progressed longer than either of us had planned; between the creditors constantly calling and the high price of living in the big city, I never seemed to have a penny to my name.

That didn't mean, however, that I was just going to say yes. "What are you offering?" I demanded, raising my chin and hoping he didn't see the flush that suffused my body. *I can't believe I'm actually considering this!*

A slow smile tipped one corner of his mouth. "Full benefits, a raise in pay, and all travel expenses paid." He wrote something on a small Post-it note and passed it over to me. "This should be sufficient for a starting salary."

The sum on the note made me faint—I could have my student loans paid off in only a few months, and have more than enough money to go back to college within a year. My jaw wouldn't work as I fumbled for words, unable to think of what to say. It's an opportunity, part of me insisted, while another part, the one that usually sounded like my parents, screamed at me to RUN! I sat in silence a moment, pondering my options, then drew in a shaky breath. "I want this in writing."

Something told me that hadn't been the answer he was expecting; he cocked his head sideways and his eyes crinkled, the only sign I saw of humor. That gorgeous face remained otherwise stoic as he nodded. "Very well," he said, "but first I need to interview you further for this position." He leaned forward and set his chin on steepled fingers. "Stand up, bend down, and put your elbows on the desk."

4

I froze, the earlier phrase, "anything I want," echoing through my head. After a tense moment where I warred with myself and lost, I rose to my feet and moved toward the desk, bending down to place my elbows along the edge of the dark wood. Nervously, I watched Jeremiah as he stood and came around the desk. "Stay like this until I tell you to move again. How many words can you type a minute?"

The question surprised me, but I'd been drilling myself lately on questions for job-hunting and knew the answer. "Eighty."

"What strengths would you bring to this position?"

He disappeared behind me, breaking my concentration. I could turn my head to see him but kept my gaze on the desk as I answered the commonplace interview question. "Attention to detail, and dedication to get a job done no matter what."

A chuckle came from behind me at the obviously rehearsed answer. "Where do you see yourself in five years?"

I started to reply but was startled into silence as a hand slid up my thigh, sneaking beneath my skirt and over my ass before pulling away. I swallowed, my breath ragged, but still managed to respond. "Finishing law school preferably, or in a job I love."

That got me a low "Hmm," but silence otherwise. My pulse increased and I closed my eyes, trying to keep myself under control. It was just like on the elevator—one touch and I was lost, my body craving his contact.

"What would you consider your dream job?"

Fingers slid between my thighs, running along the thin cotton of my panties, and a moan escaped my mouth. My hips pressed down, seeking more contact, but again the hand disappeared, and I bit back a groan. The respite allowed me to gather my thoughts to answer, although it was difficult. "Someplace where I matter, and can help people."

"Good answer," he murmured, then the hand was back, pressing at the soft flesh between my legs, turning me into a writhing mess. My palms pressed down on the desk, nails digging into the cool wood as I felt a rush of heat in my belly. A hand smoothed over my back and down one hip as the fingers continued to tease and torment me. I kept my trembling arms on the desk as something hard pressed against my backside. The fingers finally moved beneath the panties and pressed inside me, sliding easily along the wet folds. I choked on another cry, trying and failing for silence.

"My office is soundproof and the door is locked," he murmured, answering a question I hadn't thought to ask. Fingers penetrated deep inside me, causing my body to quake.

"Before we go any further, however, we need to get rid of these."

The thin cotton panties I wore were pulled down my legs and, without thinking, I stepped out of them as they hit the floor. A shoe pressed against the inside of my foot, widening my stance as his hips pushed against my backside. The fingers between my legs never let up their exploration; my breathing was rough as Jeremiah lifted the skirt to bunch at my waist, his bulge thrusting against my backside.

His thumb, which had previously been massaging the hard bud between my legs, slid back to my rear opening. I surged forward in shock, the desk and his hips holding me prisoner as the thumb eased around the tight hole. The idea of a man being interested back there had never occurred to me; I wasn't so naïve as to be ignorant of the idea, but it had never come up before. Thinking proved difficult, however, as he continued to manipulate my body until I was trembling with need.

Lips pressed against my neck. "Eventually," he purred in that deep voice, the word a promise, as he caressed the opening once more, then moved his thumb back to my clit. By now nearly every breath was a moan as I tilted my hips up, desperately needing to be filled. His fingers teased and tormented but never let me fall over into orgasm.

Something shifted behind me; Jeremiah lowered his body along my bare bottom, then teeth grazed the skin over one buttock as hands spread my cheeks. Before I could even comprehend what was coming, I felt for the first time in my life a tongue against my most intimate of places, licking up the crease, then pushing inside my weeping opening. I surged forward against the desk with another loud cry, and couldn't stop myself from making another as he controlled my body's responses with his tongue and fingers. The unfamiliar and exotic feel, unlike anything I'd ever experienced before during my limited activities, pushed me over the edge. I came loudly, my nails scratching against the hard surface of the desk and my body bucking uncontrollably.

I laid my head on my hands as I heard the crinkle of the condom wrapper, then a moment later the hard length of his cock slid between my ass cheeks. The fingers were pulled out only to be replaced by a thick presence that forced its way inside my tight opening. I moaned again as he pushed inside, while one thick arm reached around my waist and pulled me tight against his body. He pressed me down against the desk as he slid out then in, stretching and electrifying the tender skin. Still riding the wave of my orgasm, his movements left me panting and frantic, pushing back against him wildly.

"Fuck, you're so hot," he murmured in my ear as he thrust hard, earning another cry from me. I braced myself against the edge of the dark wood as he pounded into me, his thrusts shaking my entire body. One hand lifted to my neck, tilting my head back against his shoulder and partially restricting my breathing; it didn't stop the breathy moans I made as another wave washed over me and my body shuddered for the second time in as many minutes.

My head fell to the side and teeth grazed my neck, running along the line of my shoulder as his hand pulled away the material of my blouse. The soft feel of his lips across my skin was a direct contrast to the hard pumps of his hips, but I reveled in the experience, allowing him to set and control the pace. Two orgasms left my body limp, drained from the experience, but Jeremiah held me up easily in his strong arms. I arched myself back against him even though my skin was almost too sensitive for his thrusts, the pleasure too much.

Like before, his teeth sank into my shoulder as he shuddered, his hard thrusts almost lifting me from the floor. He let out a ragged grunt and with one last stab, he shook against my back, coming inside me. The hand around my neck released and blood rushed to my head again, making me dizzy. He laid me carefully atop the desk, resting his hard body atop mine as we both struggled to catch our breath.

After a moment he pulled out and stepped away, leaving me alone against the cool wood. It took a moment before I finally became aware of how exposed I was, but I still spent another minute catching my breath before I lowered my skirt. I was wet enough that sitting in the chair would stain my skirt so I wobbled in my heeled pumps, using the desk as a brace.

"That wraps up this interview. By the way, you're hired."

Still breathing hard, I turned my head to look over at Jeremiah Hamilton standing at a small coffee bar on one side of the office. His suit and dress pants were back in place, as impeccable as if nothing had just happened. The look on his face was probing and inquisitive, but I couldn't tell what he thought to discover. I tried to feel shame, anger, outrage at my wanton actions and his taking advantage of my situation, but all I could come up with was a deep exhaustion and a sense of security.

I am so screwed.

A hand at my elbow turned me gently, and a glass of water was pressed into my hands. "Go clean yourself up," Jeremiah said as I took a sip of the cool liquid, his voice as soft as I'd yet heard. "I'll make arrangements and we can leave once you've come back."

My brain wasn't firing on all cylinders so I thought perhaps I had missed something. "Arrangements for what?"

"You said you carry your passport with you?"

I blinked, back to being confused. An odd question. "Um, yes, I do?"

He nodded as if that answered everything. "Perfect. Then you'll come with me today and can serve as my escort."

I took another sip of the water, still baffled by the direction of this conversation. "Your escort where?"

"Paris. We leave in an hour."

5

Limousines were roomier than I remembered. Of course, the last time I'd been inside one was my high school prom and it had been packed to the gills with friends and their dates.

I snuck a glance at the handsome man across from me in the backseat of the limo. He ignored me for the moment, focused on the tablet in his lap and leaving me to my own devices. My leather handbag sat in my lap and I hugged it close, still reeling over the day's events. Was I really on my way to Paris?

The last two days had been crazy. I still couldn't believe that Jeremiah Hamilton, CEO of Hamilton Industries, a multinational business conglomerate that rivaled anything Trump ever produced, sat across from me in the dark limo. It still hadn't fully sunk in that I was heading to the airport to fly with him to Paris. As his personal assistant. With a forthcoming contract whose stipulations revolved around the phrase "anything he wants."

As far as ranking among the Worst Days Ever, this was in

the top five. Definitely a tie for first on Most Mind-boggling Day Ever.

Manhattan rush-hour traffic being the normal tangle of pedestrians and vehicles, I didn't pay much attention to our route, too caught up in my thoughts. I noticed traffic decrease, however, as we left Manhattan, and belatedly realized we were heading toward New Jersey. It wasn't until the limo began passing planes behind a tall fence that I looked out the window and saw with some surprise the sign for Teterboro Airport. The New Jersey airport wasn't as big as its New York City counterpart and while I'd never flown through there, I knew it served a large number of private flights and airplanes. I'd only ever been through JFK so the smaller airport was something new. I saw a number of small charter planes parked along the asphalt, the kind taken by tours and the very rich.

Well, I suppose today that's us. The thought sent a wave of chills up my spine and I shivered, rubbing my arms. Oh God, what was I getting myself into?

"You're sure I won't need clothes?" I asked for the third time as we pulled into the airport terminal. I hadn't been allowed to bring anything with me aside from personal effects already in the office—namely, what was in my purse and the work clothes I was still wearing. The skirt and blouse were clean but hardly enough for any kind of overseas trip.

"They will be provided for you," Jeremiah assured me. "Your contract will go over all of this."

It was the same answer I got anytime I asked him a question about this surprise trip. At this rate, my contract would be longer than Tolstoy's *War and Peace*. The flippant thought did nothing to settle my nerves. I haven't signed anything yet. I can still leave, find another job.

The sudden image of me flipping burgers for a living made me shudder and a wave of sorrow washed over me. Is that where I'll end up? Could this really be my last chance? I looked up to see Jeremiah watching me. There was no emotion on his stoic face, yet his penetrating gaze made me feel like he could read my mind. Frustrated, unwilling to let him see my indecision, I clenched my jaw and refused to look away first.

The door opened, breaking our staring contest. I grabbed my bag and climbed out past him, but thought I saw humor on his face as I passed. *So he likes conflict,* I thought as we were hustled into the building. *Good, because I'm not going to crawl and beg for respect.*

An image popped into my head of me on my knees in front of him, looking up into that gorgeous face, and I felt a flutter in my belly. Aw, dammit.

The speed with which we passed through security was a novel experience. The most grueling part of the process was security poking through my purse and finding the underwear from yesterday I'd forgotten was still there. My whole body heated at that discovery but they remained professional. Once security cleared us, we moved through the small waiting area and were taxied across the tarmac to our waiting flight.

Long and sleek yet a great deal smaller than what I was used to flying in, the airplane wasn't anything like a commercial jet. There was no other way I'd ever get to travel in something like this; normal girls like me never so much as saw the inside of one of these planes unless they were flight attendants or pilots. The interior was as posh as the outside promised, with leather seats twice as wide as anything I'd ever seen. The pilot allowed us to take our seats before closing the door and retreating into the cockpit. Impressed by my surroundings, I started playing with the various gadgets and implements attached to my seat. It even had its own private phone under one thick armrest, which I found amusing.

A thin tablet slid onto the table I'd unfolded, the same one I'd seen Jeremiah working with earlier. Startled, I glanced over to see Jeremiah seated in a nearby chair. "What's this?" I managed, my amusement dimming.

"I drew up your contract in the limo, but you'll need to sign it before we take off." When I hesitated, he leaned in to catch my gaze. "You knew this was coming."

"No joke." The sarcastic reply belied my nervous tension. Was I signing my life away?

"A car will take you home if you wish to leave." He pulled a silver stylus from his jacket pocket and held it out to me. "The choice is yours."

I snatched the stylus from his fingers, clenching it in my fist so I wouldn't betray my shaking as I scanned the document. I'd grown adept at deciphering legalese during college but the wording was fairly straightforward. The paper put a more legal spin on the phrase "anything he wants" but the message was the same, even including a nondisclosure agreement. On coming close to the end, however, I did trip over one stipulation we hadn't discussed. "Fifty thousand dollars?" I squeaked, looking up in surprise.

He nodded. "If you are still in my employ in six months, you're entitled to a bonus," he said, quoting the contract almost verbatim. "It, along with any weekly paychecks due, won't be taken from you should you terminate the contract after that time."

So even if I quit, I'll still get something out of this. Seeing it in writing helped my mind come to terms with this absurd choice. The contract, while vague on my specific duties, gave a professional vibe to the whole situation and made me feel, well, less slutty. Who knows? . . . Maybe this was a standard contract among the rich and famous. I'd hardly know otherwise.

Still, I hesitated. *I can still leave,* I thought, staring at the stylus in my hand. *I can end this silly charade, take a taxi back to my apartment. . . .*

. . . and then what?

One of the biggest worries I'd had since moving from my hometown to live with an old college acquaintance was the sudden high cost of living so close to New York City. The foreclosure on my family's home had left me all but destitute; I had no options to live anywhere else, and saving money, despite my best efforts, had proven ineffectual. My current living arrangements had been meant to be temporary, and I knew from my friend's recent attitude that I was quickly using up what welcome I had left. My only hope was to pay down a little more of my student loan debt, and then I'd be in the position to begin paying rent. Until then, I was perilously close to living in a shelter, a thought that made my blood run cold.

Jeremiah regarded me patiently, his pitiless stare almost a welcome change. Since my parents died, I'd struggled not only to pay the bills but also with people's views of my situation, and I was tired of being "that poor orphan girl" in the eyes of others. The CEO had made it abundantly clear what this contract entailed—my "interview" had been me splayed across his desk as he took liberties with my body that left me a moaning, panting mess. The memory made me want to cringe and hide; I'd never been that kind of girl and yet a stranger had seduced me not once but three times in a twenty-four-hour span. The contract in front of me represented financial independence, but only in exchange for another, more personal form of freedom.

I have no other choice.

I read through the contract twice, the enormity of my decision weighing on me, then with shaky fingers I signed my name digitally across the bottom and handed back the tablet. Jeremiah reached up and pressed the attendant button. Immediately the engines began gearing up, and I made sure I was buckled in. I gripped the chair tight and tried to ignore my own unease about the flight and the man seated across from me.

"You don't like flying?"

I kept my eyes closed and feigned sleep as the engines geared up and propelled us down the runway. The process was smooth and not as loud as I'd imagined for such a small plane, but I didn't breathe easy until we were in the air.

We were still climbing when Jeremiah took off his seat belt and stood, heading to the main area behind me. I kept my eyes straight ahead, determined to ignore his presence, until a hand carrying a glass of clear liquid appeared before me. "I don't drink," I said.

"Not even water?"

I didn't find his amusement charming but took the drink from his hand with a mumbled "Thank you."

"There's food in the bar if you need something more substantial."

"I'm not hungry, thank you."

My stomach chose that moment to growl loudly, exposing my outright lie. "Okay, fine, maybe a little."

His lips compressed and I had the feeling he was trying to keep from smiling. "You really had no idea who I was, did you?"

Suddenly not in the mood for conversation, I huffed out a breath and shrugged. "Apparently, you're not as popular as you seem to think."

He took my sarcastic words in good humor. "And how popular am I?"

Squirming in my chair, I looked up to see amusement crinkling the edges of his eyes. He does stoic really well, except for his eyes. They were the most beautiful green I could ever remember seeing on a man, vibrant against the olive complexion and dark hair. Realizing I was staring, I cleared my throat and struggled for an answer to his question. Witty rebuttals escaped me, however, and I shrugged, taking a quick sip of my water.

I ignored his chuckling. "You may want to rest," he said, "this is going to be a long flight."

As he went to the rear of the airplane I stayed in my seat, reclining and snuggling into the large chair. Unfortunately my stomach, now aware of food nearby, wouldn't let me rest. I managed to stall maybe half an hour, busying myself with the various gadgets around me, before finally getting up and heading back to see what was available.

When I passed my boss he was sitting in one of the wide chairs, a glass of dark liquid in his hand. I could feel his eyes on me as I went into the kitchen alcove and poured myself some orange juice before peeking at the food. I snagged a pre-made chicken sandwich with ingredients that made it sound like fine dining, and ate in the small room.

The man made me nervous; I couldn't trust myself around him. Whenever he was nearby I kept imagining erotic scenes I'd only read about in romance novels and saw in my fantasies. That had been fine when he was a stranger on an elevator I saw once a day. Now I needed to get him out of my head, but easier said than done; he had become a prominent fixture in my fantasy life and my body wouldn't allow me to forget that. Even the hopelessness of my current situation couldn't stop my reaction to his presence, the same reaction that had gotten me into this mess in the first place.

Grabbing a bottle of water, I turned to leave the little kitchen area and ground to a halt when I saw him standing beside the opening. He moved toward me and I backed up a step, only to bump into the countertop. "I, um," I stammered, "I should get back to my seat . . ."

His fingers were toying with a button on his shirt. "Could you help me with this?" he asked, indicating his shirt and ignoring my statement. "It seems to be stuck."

I blew out a disbelieving breath. Seriously? His words came across as a lame line, almost absurd given the situation, but another line I'd heard earlier that afternoon popped into my head. *Anything I want.*

I snorted. So now I'm dressing him, too? This wasn't what I thought I'd signed up for but with a small huff, I reached out and took the button. His fingers brushed mine and I tried to ignore them along with the tightening in my belly.

Surprisingly, the button really was caught but it took only a few seconds to untangle. I released his shirt when I finished, leaving the button open, but he captured my hands before I could step away. "Check the others, perhaps?"

I glanced up into his eyes then quickly down again. *This is stupid,* I thought, trying for anger as my hands were pulled back to his shirt. I was going to be a lawyer, someone who stood up for the little guy; this isn't what I took out massive college loans for, to be a glorified seamstress . . .

Jeremiah stared down at me and I tried hard to ignore his gaze—easier said than done. Giving him a brief glare that was mostly bravado on my part, I started unbuttoning his shirt. The material was thin but strong, not silk but something similarly expensive. I didn't make it to the third button before my hands began to tremble, not from fear but from his proximity. It didn't take me long to realize there was nothing beneath the shirt but skin. The more buttons I released the more torso was revealed, dark skin against a white shirt that refused to stay closed on its own. He took a step closer, looming above me, and my whole body began to quake. *Oh my God.*

My life up to that point hadn't involved many men outside of family and a few study buddies. High school, then college, had been all about academics; I had always been more interested in books and studying than forming any relationships with the opposite sex even if they had been interested. Life after my parents died had been a blur; there was never time to do more than work at various jobs and worry about my future. If anyone had been interested I certainly never noticed, but I definitely noticed the man in front of me now.

Fighting the urge not to touch the smooth skin beneath my fingers was a losing battle. He took a small step sideways and I unconsciously moved, too, turning slowly with him as he pulled off the shirt and threw it over the chair beside us. I was breathless as my eyes roamed the body his shirt had previously covered, then the flutter in my belly became full-blown sparks when his fingers skimmed up my arms. I didn't even realize we were moving, too caught up in his proximity and touch, until my back pushed up against something hard—a wall. My hands tightened against the firm muscles of his abdomen as I looked up to see him watching me with an intensity that left my knees weak. There was no thought of resistance as he pressed his body against mine and lowered his head to take my lips.

What started out soft, barely a brush of our mouths, morphed quickly into something much more passionate. Helpless against his assault, I moaned into his mouth and skimmed my fingernails down his taut body, responding to his kiss with a fire I didn't know I had. My touch served only to enflame him as he pressed closer, his tongue coming out to briefly flick my lip and tease my mouth open. His large hands roamed down my body, settling on my waist, his fingers digging into my hips and backside, pulling me closer against his wide frame.

My hands came up around his neck, tangling in thick dark hair, as desperate for his touch as he seemed to be for mine. One leg wedged itself firmly between my legs and I gasped as it pressed against parts of my body that were swollen and begging for more. The hands clutching my hips tightened and I was suddenly lifted, pressed against the wall and supported only by his body and grip. My hips wrapped around his waist as his lips left mine, teeth skimming down along the soft skin of my throat as he thrust his hips against me. A small cry burst from my throat, then again as his teeth latched on loosely to my shoulder through my blouse and he rolled his hips again.

My hands fumbled for his face and I kissed him again, making panting moans into his mouth as he continued to rub himself against me. My skirt was almost up to my waist and his fingers crept toward the apex of my legs, pressing against the thin barrier of my panties toward my aching core. I moaned into his mouth, nipping his lip and arching my hips down against his hand, desperate for more.

"Perhaps you can help with my pants button, too?"

The low words took me a moment to process but managed to cut through the haze of lust. I broke off the kiss, realizing what I'd almost allowed to happen—again—and looked into his eyes. The hot need there still made my insides melt, but when I pushed weakly at his shoulders he stepped back, lowering me gently to the floor. My skirt was bunched around my hips, and I hurried to correct it as I skittered sideways out of his reach.

"You should get some rest, it's a long flight to Paris."

I looked back at him. He stood there looking good enough to eat, seemingly as comfortable half naked as he was wearing those buttoned-up expensive suits. Why am I walking away from him again?

Principles. Morals. Oh yeah. Dammit.

Giving him a jerky nod, I forced myself to turn around and walk back to my seat. Grabbing a pillow from a nearby cubby, I sat down in my seat and pushed the chair so it was reclining backward. I didn't think I'd be able to sleep but managed to finally fall into a fitful slumber as the sun passed below the horizon, the orange glow extinguished by the earth.

At some point I awoke to find it was dark outside the windows and a blanket had been laid over me, the edges tucked in around my body. I frowned, certain it hadn't been there when I sat down, and looked behind my seat to see Jeremiah fast asleep in another chair nearby. His shirt was once again buttoned, the suit jacket folded neatly in the chair beside him. He took up more space in the chair so wasn't able to tuck himself up like me, but seemed comfortable reclining back.

Sleep had softened the hard expression on his face; he looked different, younger, more relaxed.

I wish I could hate him, I mused, but there was no anger in the thought. The man in that chair had all but blackmailed me into signing a contract that allowed him whatever liberties he wanted to take, yet there had been moments of tenderness that shone through. *He never did anything I didn't want,* I thought, fingering the blanket around me. I wonder which is the real man: the hard CEO who interviewed me bent over his desk, or the man who covered me with this blanket.

I shelved that conversation for another day, exhaustion making my eyes heavy. Yawning quietly, I pulled the blanket up to my chin, nestling in the comfortable chair, and slid back into a sound slumber.

6

"Do you have anything to claim?"

Considering I wasn't allowed to bring anything with me . . . "No."

The man checked my passport again, then handed it back to me, motioning for the next person as I walked past the desk. Bold letters displayed above me told my location in several languages and I stopped and stared. *I'm really in France.*

Jeremiah stood nearby and as I drew abreast, he laid a hand on the small of my back and steered me through the small crowd. I saw a line of people waiting for the new arrivals as we made our way out to the main terminal. A large bald man with a blond goatee stood next to a far wall, and strode forward to meet us halfway to the doors. "Lucy," Jeremiah said, "this is Ethan, my chief of security. He'll take you to the hotel."

We shook hands but it was clear my presence wasn't the man's priority; his eyes remained fixed on Jeremiah. "Celeste is still here." Ethan's voice had a Southern twang, light but noticeable. "She won't leave for another three hours."

Jeremiah nodded. "Perfect. See to it that Ms. Delacourt here gets to the hotel."

"What about you?" I asked as he started to walk away.

"I have to deal with the vultures." To Ethan he added, "Try not to be seen."

I watched him walk away toward the glass doors leading out. *That's it?* I thought, confused. *I'm being given over to the chauffeur and secreted out of the airport?* It occurred to me I should be happy to be out of his presence but, suddenly alone with another stranger in a strange country, I found I missed the stoic man.

"Okay, let's go."

I followed Ethan silently, sneaking glances back toward my boss. As Jeremiah exited the glass doors I saw a commotion outside as several people rushed toward him. Flashes of cameras and the garbled din of voices flowed to me as we exited farther down from the action, ignored by the crowd. "What's that about?" I asked, struggling to keep up with Ethan's long strides.

"Paparazzi." Ethan held the door open for me as we exited the terminal a ways beyond the throng. "His attendance at the gala this weekend is high profile enough to earn press coverage."

Gala? I got into the back of the large SUV waiting at the curb. Another man who had been waiting behind the wheel exited the vehicle so Ethan could take his place, and we pulled out. "Is he going to be okay?" I asked, looking through the rear window at the swarm of reporters.

Ethan snorted. "This is nothing, and he did it mostly to

divert attention so we could leave unmolested. He won't be far behind us."

Indeed, I saw him move through the crowd as a limo pulled up and breathed a small sigh of relief. *I could never do that,* I thought, thankful in hindsight for the reprieve. The thought of all those cameras in my face, following me everywhere . . . I shuddered just thinking about it.

There were a million questions running through my mind but the man driving didn't seem the talkative type so I kept them to myself, instead enjoying my first real view of Paris. The European city had always been someplace I longed to visit; my parents had been history buffs and that had rubbed off on me as well. Paris had always seemed so far off and exotic, a totally different world in which I could immerse myself. While still in high school, I had secured a promise from my parents that, when I graduated and got my bachelor's degree, they would pay my way to the French city. That wish had never materialized—their deaths my junior year of college had derailed my planned life, forcing me on a radically different path from the one I'd always imagined— but my love for the city remained. The glimpses of the Eiffel Tower between the buildings made me smile, some of the stress of the last couple days draining away.

I'd been so young back then, unable to see just how stretched thin my parents were financially. Reluctant to look a gift horse in the mouth, it never occurred to me to ask where they found the money for my Ivy League education. Not until they died suddenly, leaving me to pick up the pieces, had I finally realized how much was on the line. There had been life insurance but barely enough to cover funeral expenses and lawyer fees; after that, every penny I made went into trying to save the house, only to lose it anyway. The memories were an aching hole in my heart, but seeing Paris finally served as a balm for some of that pain. *I wish you guys were here to see this with me.*

I had no idea where we were going, but when we finally stopped and a valet opened the door for me, my jaw dropped as I stared in shock at the hotel. "We're staying here?"

I didn't get an answer and, honestly, the question was rhetorical anyway. I stared up at the magnificent Paris Ritz, finding it incomprehensible that I would be sleeping there. Another Parisian establishment I'd only seen online and in magazines, pictures hadn't done the structure justice. While not as big as I'd thought, it was as grand and stately as I'd always dreamed and I was itching to see the inside.

A redhead in a pale fitted dress suit made her way toward us, heels clacking on the stone ground. She seemed pleased to see Ethan but paused when she saw me. The big driver gave her hand a kiss, a romantic gesture that seemed at odds with his gruff demeanor. "Celeste, this is Lucy Delacourt, Mr. Hamilton's new personal assistant."

The confusion immediately cleared from the woman's face, although she still seemed surprised by the news. "Pleased to meet you," she said with a warm smile, extending her hand in greeting. "I'm Celeste Taylor, the head of operations for Hamilton Industries." Her handshake was firm and businesslike, her smile a welcome relief after the stoicism I'd seen so far. "It's been a while since Remi has taken another assistant."

Remi? "Yes, well, I'm new." It was difficult to know how much I should say so I decided to keep it professional. "I was hired yesterday afternoon."

Celeste's eyebrows rose almost to her hairline. "Well, he certainly moved quickly this time." Her gaze softened. "This must all be so strange to you."

This first bit of genuine sympathy almost made me cry. I wanted to thank her but managed to refrain from throwing my arms around her shoulders, and instead swallowed back my gratitude. "Yesterday I was a temp barely getting by. Now I'm, well . . ."—I gestured to the hotel around me— "It's a bit overwhelming."

"Yes, I imagine so." She looked around the car. "Do you have any luggage with you?"

"Uh . . ." I couldn't figure out how to explain that bit of detail. Who flies across the Atlantic without bringing any clothes or luggage for the trip? Me, apparently, but I didn't know what to say without bringing up embarrassing details.

Celeste cocked her head to the side at my uncomfortable silence, eyes narrowing. She took a step back, examining me from head to toe, then nodded. "Ah, I see why," she said with a knowing smile.

I looked down at my clothing, not understanding her meaning. They were still clean, although rumpled a bit from the trip and my sleeping in the chair. "Why, what's wrong with what I'm wearing?"

This got a laugh from Celeste. "Oh, it's not my opinion you should be worrying about," she said, shaking her head and grinning. "If Remi doesn't like something, he'll do everything in his power to change it. He's a steamroller, used to getting his own way in matters. You don't have to say anything, I can already see it happened to you." She motioned toward the door of the hotel. "Come inside, it's chilly out here."

I followed her up the walkway while Ethan stayed out by the curb, fielding a call on his cell phone. "When did you meet Mr. Hamilton?" I asked.

Celeste gave me an amused look at the use of the man's formal title. "We went to school together years ago, although I moved out west almost immediately after graduation. Got a divorce, moved back to start anew, couldn't find anything. Almost gave up hope, then Remi found me." She shrugged. "I started out as a manager, then when he restructured the entire company after his father died I was given a choice: take the COO position or I was fired. Like I said," she added, rolling her eyes at me, "a steamroller."

"Sounds familiar." The doors were opened for us by hotel employees and I stared in wonder around the entryway. "This place is even better than I imagined."

"Wait until you see the suites." She glanced at her watch. "My plane doesn't leave for almost three hours. Want me to show you around?" When I grinned at her, she took my arm. "You have to see the pool first. Always takes my breath away."

"So are you and Ethan . . . ?" I trailed off, not wanting to imply anything, but Celeste nodded.

"I was already working as COO when Jeremiah partnered with Ethan to run the fledgling security company. I was used to a bit of freedom, so when suddenly there were more hoops to jump through just to get inside the building, I resented it.

All the protection seemed like overkill, and I was probably the most vocal detractor." Celeste smiled. "Then there was the fact that Ethan was always underfoot, asking if I needed help or an escort. When the new head of security insisted on walking me to my car anytime I needed to so much as get my purse, I tried to put my foot down but was overruled."

"Sounds like he was stalking you," I commented, voice dry.

"No no, it wasn't like that. Ethan kept everything on a strictly professional level and, well, I never really thought anything more about his actions. This job keeps me busy twenty-four/seven and I didn't think I had time for a relationship, so it never even occurred to me . . ." The redhead rolled her eyes. "Honestly, I probably never would've noticed him beyond being an annoying security detail had he not saved my life."

My eyes grew big. "Really?"

Celeste nodded. "I bucked tradition somewhat by preferring to drive the business car myself, rather than have a chauffeur. So I was walking out of the office one night and was jumped by a group that tried to throw me into a van. It was late and I was sure nobody was there to help me, then suddenly this big bald guy is there, beating my attackers to a pulp—that was the first time I really and truly noticed him." She shrugged, a rueful smile tilting her lips. "He then assigned himself as my permanent driver and the rest is history."

"Wow," I murmured, "how romantic!"

"Yeah, maybe," the redhead demurred, then slanted a look at me. "So, how did you land the most coveted job in the country? Anytime Hamilton Industries puts out calls for interns, we have applicants coming out our ears."

By that point we had reached the indoor pool, an extravagant sight surrounded by pillars and a recessed ceiling. "This is gorgeous," I breathed, momentarily ignoring the question and sharing a grin with Celeste. "The rest of the hotel is like this?"

"Yup," she replied, grinning. "The rooms are even better, no two are alike. Wait until you try the food, it's outstanding!"

What did I do to deserve this? I wondered, staring at the over-the-top opulence. The lavish surroundings only served to accentuate my situation as a fish out of water. I couldn't believe my luck, or that I was even here, yet staring at the lavish displays and ornate fixtures brought out my own insecurities. The world had been so different only a few years ago, then everything I'd loved and taken for granted had disappeared. Staring at the opulence surrounding me, I felt a similar fear creep over my heart. Will this chance be pulled away just as quickly?

Celeste glanced at her watch. "I need to get going," she said, a note of regret tingeing her words. "Even private planes have a schedule to keep."

My shoulders slumped at the words. I barely knew the woman, but was nevertheless disappointed to see her go. The last two days had been hectic and stressful, and Celeste's presence, however brief, had been a welcome balm. Extending my hand, I said, "Have a safe flight."

She took my hand in a steady grip, then leaned in close. "Look, be nice to Jeremiah, okay? He can seem like a jerk sometimes but he has a big heart for those he cares about or decides to protect."

Her words startled me. Be nice to him? "He's my boss," I said stiffly, not sure how to respond without sounding petulant. "I have to respect him."

She started to shake her head, paused to think for a moment, then nodded ruefully. "That's close enough, I guess." Leaning close, Celeste added in a lower voice, "It's been almost two years since he had a personal assistant; the last one, hmm, left on bad terms. As his assistant, however, you'll be accompanying him to functions and serving as his escort. Most of the press are used to these arrangements and should leave you alone but be aware you may get some attention. It's inevitable."

Did he treat them all like me? I was surprised to find that the mention of previous assistants irritated me. Then Celeste's warning about unwanted attention sank in and I remembered the swarm of paparazzi outside the airport. My skin crawled at the thought of being surrounded by the photographers, and suddenly this whole venture seemed like a very bad idea. Then again, when had I ever thought the whole situation was anything but a strange trick of fate?

"Ah, speak of the devil."

I turned to see the tall figure of Jeremiah enter the hotel. He had a small wrapped box under one arm and was speaking privately with Ethan near the entrance. They had a similar vibe I found interesting and I mentioned it to Celeste.

"Well, they were both in the military together . . . maybe it's that."

"Military?" I never would have pegged him for a soldier.

It seemed there was a great deal I didn't know about the man I was now working for.

Celeste nodded. "They were both Army Rangers until Remi's dad died and left him in charge of the family business. Nasty business, that. I came in right afterward and helped with the fallout."

I wanted to ask more but both men made their way toward us and the moment was lost. Celeste smiled and stepped forward, taking Jeremiah's outstretched hand. "Looks like I'm no longer needed for this little soirée tonight."

Jeremiah raised Celeste's hand for a brief kiss before letting go, but beside him I saw Ethan flinch at the gesture. The redhead stepped back, then looked up at the tall bald man beside her. "Ready to go, babe?"

I blinked as Ethan's stolid face softened into a smile. Celeste gave me a wave and they walked off, the big man's hand at the small of the COO's back. Only then did I notice the gold band on his left hand.

"They've been married almost a year now." At my startled glance, Jeremiah quirked an eyebrow. "The question was written all over your face."

I ducked my head at his sardonic tone, clearing my throat. "What now?" I asked, sparing one last glance for the retreating couple. The stress was back as I realized I had no idea what he wanted.

"Celeste showed you around the hotel?"

"A bit, yes." I couldn't stop the smile that lit my face. "It's absolutely incredible. Pictures never did it justice."

He gave an amused chuckle. "Wait until you see the rooms."

7

I sank into the warm water, gripping the sides of the huge porcelain bathtub so I wouldn't slide under the surface. Foaming hills of bubbles tickled my nose as I settled into a comfortable position and I grinned, blowing them so they danced in little puffs through the air. The deep tub was surprisingly comfortable, I noted, breathing a sigh of relief and fiddling with the water knobs with my toes.

Jeremiah had sent me upstairs to the room, saying he had to take care of a few things before joining me. I had followed the hotel worker who showed me to my room and when he'd open the doors, I'd been rendered speechless. The interior of the suite was the most over-the-top, gaudy place I had ever seen, with its gilded mirrors and paintings, white panels trimmed with gold, crystal chandeliers and lamps, and rococo moldings and filigree along each corner and open panel. Tapestries lined the walls and every inch of the room screamed *Look at me, I'm expensive,* hitting you over the head with its overstated elegance and extravagant, lurid design.

I absolutely adored it.

While the hotel host had been showing me around I'd barely been listening, too busy exploring on my own. The suite included several sitting rooms with furniture that looked expensive but very uncomfortable. Every amenity I could think of, and several I'd never have considered, was provided. I thought I'd died and gone to heaven when I saw the bathroom with its tall ceilings and mirrors, marble countertops and floors, and a tub almost as big as a hot tub sitting in the middle. My host had time to point out the closet of linens and robes before I shooed him out as politely as possible and drew myself a bubble bath. My mother used to collect old-fashioned perfume bottles, and it delighted me to see the hotel used these for bath oils. I chose a lavender scent before stripping out of my work clothes, grabbing a robe, and locking the door.

I allowed myself to enjoy the warmth and mellow scent of the water for a while before setting about actually bathing. Using my toes to fiddle with the hot water knob kept the bathwater warm as I thoroughly scrubbed my skin. I took my time but eventually my wrinkled hands convinced me to leave the bath, the bubbles only a white film atop the water. Slipping into the robe and wrapping my hair in a towel, I poked around the countertops and drawers to see what other treasures were hidden in the bathroom.

Three sharps raps against the locked door made me jump in surprise. "I'd like to see you out here." Jeremiah's deep voice carried through the thick wooden door, his words a command that was expected to be obeyed.

I froze, the tension I'd managed to wash away now back with a vengeance. A quick glance around the ornate room made me realize with dawning horror that I had no clothes besides the robe and towel; I'd left them in the bedroom now occupied by my boss.

Swallowing, I took a look at myself in the mirror. My face was scrubbed of all makeup, shiny and clean but naked without my usual mask. Underneath the towel wrapped haphazardly around my head, my hair was a mess and still too wet to brush.

I can't let him see me like this, he'll kick me out of this hotel!

I hastily pulled the towel off my head and called out, "Just a minute," so he wouldn't think I was ignoring him. *Why do you care what he thinks?* a rational side of my brain tried to ask as I fumbled with my wet hair and smoothed out eyebrows that desperately needed a brow pencil. *Don't you want to stay away from him anyway?*

Maybe, but I'd at least like to look decent while I'm walking away.

Tousling my longish hair into some semblance of order and straightening my robe, making sure the belt was tied snug, I walked over to the door. Pausing for a moment, I gave myself one last look in the mirror—*seriously, you're never this vain!*—before unlocking the door and striding out.

Jeremiah stood across the bedroom beside a small silver cart with domed dishes. The faint aroma of food wafted to my nose, making my mouth water. He looked up as I approached, his eyes taking in my robe and wet hair. "How did you like your bath?"

I resisted the sudden urge to gush, shrugging one shoulder. "Not quite what I'm used to."

His steady gaze made me want to fidget as though caught in a lie, and it took a great deal of self-control to keep myself still. He turned to push the cart toward the table and suddenly I could breathe again. *Stop letting him get to you like that.* My responses to him were silly but I couldn't help feeling threatened, as if I were the prey to his predator.

"I have something for you."

That got my attention. "Breakfast?" I asked, my eyes falling to the dishes beside him. My tummy rumbled in anticipation.

"In a moment, perhaps." He straightened and looked me dead in the eye. "Take off your robe and come here."

Everything inside me went cold. I hugged the robe around me, trying to stave off the inevitable. "Why?"

He said nothing, and I looked up to see him watching me. There was no emotion in his gaze; as far as he was concerned, I was to disrobe and go to him merely because he said so. Because I'd signed a document saying I would do what he said. At the time it felt like he'd given me a choice, but now I felt like I'd fallen for a carefully orchestrated ruse. The glittery trappings around me did nothing to disguise what they were: a cage, designed to keep me off balance and at his mercy.

Finally, finally, I got mad. "Why me?" I gestured around the room. "Why all of this?"

He cocked his head to the side. "Why not you?"

He was turning my questions back around at me and that

pissed me off. "I was nothing in your life, hands to type data, then to be tossed to the streets when I was no longer useful. So why am I here?"

His lips thinned but he said nothing. Moving across the room to a large marble table, he picked up a crystal carafe and poured himself a glass of the amber liquid it held. "My career consists of me looking for potential," he said, swirling the liquor around as he regarded me dispassionately. "It's my job to find businesses that I can buy or sponsor, fix up, then sell for a profit."

"So what am I, a project?"

A tip of his head sideways confirmed my suspicions. "You were ambitious, clever as a college student, used to a certain kind of existence. Life dealt you a hard hand, brought you lower than you thought possible." He saluted me with the glass before taking a sip. "You would never have turned down a chance to get back on your feet, no matter what the cost."

"So give me a job," I said, the sarcasm dripping off my tongue. "You didn't need to strip me of my dignity, make me . . . The elevator, the garage—"

The thump of the glass on the serving tray shocked me out of my anger. "You rode that elevator every morning," Jeremiah said in a low voice, staring at the crystal carafe, "giving me those little glances, getting close but not too close." His eyes met mine, and I sucked in a breath at the fire I saw there. "I knew your scent, knew when that need rolled across you. Those secret little smiles, not knowing what was going through your head . . ."

My breath caught as he trailed off, the fingers clenching

the top of the glass white with strain. *I don't believe you.* "I'm nobody," I said, my own words driving daggers through my heart.

His free hand clenched into a fist against a hard thigh as his jaw tightened, then his body relaxed. He strode up to me and I fell back a step, trying in vain to hold the last of my anger as a shield. Being so close to him was intimidating; my heart thudded in my chest as I looked to the side, unable to be strong any longer.

A finger came under my chin and lifted my head until I was staring up at him. His face was as implacable as ever but his voice was mild as he repeated his earlier request. Demand. "Take off your robe."

The words reverberated through my body, his proximity doing strange things to my mind, and I found my hands untying the belt to my robe. The soft material slid back off my arms and onto the floor, pooling at my heels. Fully exposed to him for the first time ever, I closed my eyes against his perusal, a tear squeezing out between my eyelashes.

When he put his arms around me I stiffened, but his hands stayed on my shoulders as he turned me around. "Look at something," he said, and when I didn't immediately open my eyes he repeated, "Look."

A large oval mirror stood in front of me, and I cringed at my reflection. "What do you see?" he prompted.

Flabby tummy and thighs, big hips, boobs that need a bra to look good. "Me." I'd always been my own worst critic: my blond hair looked limp from the long flight overseas, and my pale skin stood in stark contrast to his darker complexion. Never in my life had I felt comfortable naked, and this time was certainly no exception. Looking in the mirror proved difficult as the contrast between his dark, masculine beauty and my normalcy left me miserable.

I saw him frown in the mirror. "Do you know what I see?" he said, tilting his head to study my reflection. "I see a beautiful face," he murmured, running a finger down my cheek and along the side of my neck. "Soft skin, the right curves." He leaned in close to the side of my head and breathed deep. "You also smell good enough to eat," he added, his words almost a growl.

My breath caught, his words making my belly tighten. One large hand covered my breast, fingers tweaking one nipple, and this time I gasped aloud. His grip on my shoulder tightened as the hand circling my breast dipped lower, skimming across my belly and leaving a trail of fire in its wake. "So beautiful," he murmured, and my head fell back onto his shoulder as the hand splayed over my hip, fingers digging deep into my skin. I watched him in the mirror, my heartbeat loud in my ears, as that hand smoothed over my mound, not sliding lower but feeling its shape.

Abruptly he stepped away and let me go, leaving me confused and off balance. "Don't move," he said, his voice a whip, and I froze. My instinctive obedience disturbed me but I stayed standing as Jeremiah picked up the box I'd seen him carrying in the lobby and handed it to me. "I was going to save this for later but now is a better time."

Suspicious, I took the package and opened it, pulling back the tissue paper. My eyes widened as I ran a finger along a pair of nylon stockings and beneath them, the satin straps of a sheer white bustier. Speechless, I looked up at my boss then back down to the contents of the box, not sure how to respond.

Jeremiah took the box out of my hands gently when I didn't do anything for several seconds. "Turn around."

As I did what he said, he pulled out the skimpy articles and then, to my further surprise, began dressing me. First the white bustier, which he laced up behind me; it covered my breasts and belly, with straps that hung down to my thighs. I stepped into the tiny panties, then the thigh-high stockings, to which he connected the straps from the bustier. There was something incredibly sensual about the whole affair despite how professionally he went about it. I'd never in my life worn lingerie like this, certainly not for a man, and it was an interesting experience. *I'm too fair to wear white*, a cynical part of me thought, but I kept that observation to myself.

When he finished, he took me by the shoulders and turned me around so I was facing the mirror again. "Now what do you see?" he asked, leaning close to my ear.

I blinked. Wow, so this is what you get with high-end lingerie. The white fabric managed to hide what I'd always hated and accentuate what I never realized I had. My hands ran down my waist—modestly cinched by the laces at my back—and over my hips to finger the satin straps running down my legs to the stockings. The whole ensemble wasn't overly restrictive but tight enough to pull parts in and push certain things up—namely, my chest, which I'd never considered particularly impressive. *Looking good now,* I thought, gliding my fingers across the firm tops of each breast.

Suddenly remembering he'd asked a question, I cleared my throat to answer but didn't know what to say. I locked eyes with him in the mirror and he nodded, obviously seeing my answer there. "Glad we see eye to eye," he murmured, running his hands up my arms and across my shoulders. "Now that we have that squared away . . ."

A hand twisted in my hair and my head was wrenched back. I gave a small cry, my hand covering his in surprise as I looked back at him. His face had grown cold as granite, green eyes intense, but his voice was smooth as silk. "I don't like being contradicted. When I tell you to do something, I expect it done immediately or there will be consequences." The hand in my hair tightened. "On your knees."

8

I knelt quickly to the ground, the added pressure of the hand on my head forcing me to my knees. The garter straps against my back thighs and butt pulled tight, an interesting feeling but still eclipsed by the discomfort of the hand twisted in my hair. My head was tilted back and I watched as Jeremiah examined me from high above. "You enjoy this, don't you?" he murmured.

God yes! That traitorous part of my soul was on fire again, reveling in the forced submission even as I wondered what I'd gotten myself into. His hand left my hair and traveled down my cheek. "So beautiful, on your knees before me. You must see why I'm hard thinking of your mouth around my cock."

I shivered at the crude word, watching as his fingers skimmed over the bulge in his pants only inches from my face. Rolling my head sideways, I looked at our reflection in the large oval mirror. We weren't even doing anything—yet—but the way he stood over me, chin high and body straight as I knelt at his feet . . . My insides were melting, pooling between my legs to make me ready to take him. Craving his touch, I pushed against his hand like a cat, and was rewarded by his thumb stroking my forehead.

"I dreamed of you on your knees, that gorgeous mouth sucking me off." A finger ran across my forehead again, smoothing back the damp hair. "Would you like to help me come, little cat?"

"Yes," I breathed, then grunted in shock as he grabbed my hair again.

"Yes, what?"

"Yes . . ." I wracked my brain for an appropriate response. "Sir?"

He made an approving noise, then his hands left me, moving to unfasten his pants and pull himself free. "I won't promise to be gentle," he grit out, his voice harsh with need, "as I've been thinking too much about this, but I do promise to finish whatever I start."

I wrapped both hands around his hard length, sliding them down to the base then back up experimentally. His hips jerked so I did it again with similar results before leaning forward and flicking my tongue over the head. I traced the ridge where it met the shaft before sucking him into my mouth, rolling the head with my tongue. I pumped my fist again, skimming the bulbous tip with my tongue and sucking at the soft knob, then removed my top hand and pulled him deeper.

He laid his hands on my head, not forcing me but as a reminder of his presence. I bobbed my head over him, my hand stroking his shaft as I drew him deeper and deeper. The sounds coming from above me, low grunts and truncated breaths, were gratifying to hear. *I can make him lose control,* I thought, the idea giving me motivation to double my efforts. When I thought I had a handle on my movements, I released the base of his shaft and pulled him in as far as he could go.

A choked cry came from above, fingers digging into my skull. The thick head tickled the back of my throat, forcing me to withdraw or risk gagging. Wrapping my hand around the base, I began my efforts again but the hands on either side of my head pulled at me, his hips thrusting into my hot mouth.

"Hands behind your back." The words were a rough order. I paused only a moment before complying, twisting my arms behind me and locking my wrists. I prayed he would be gentle with me.

I should have known better.

His first thrust hit the back of my throat and my eyes watered immediately. "Hands behind your back," he barked again when I instinctively reached back around, "or I'll give you no choice and tie them."

It took every ounce of willpower I possessed but I forced my hands back into position, interlocking my fingers and hanging on for dear life. He repeated his thrust, this time not as deep, allowing me room to breathe. He continued like this, pushing himself in and out of my mouth, and I slowly began to get used to the movement. Indeed, pretty soon I was able to improvise, growing used to the tempo enough to use my tongue. I pressed against the base as it passed over; his plunging grew shallow, allowing me more space to maneuver and play. The small sounds coming from above, bitten-off groans and sharp intakes of breath, were sexy as hell and a good indicator that I was doing something right. When I flicked his tip with my tongue, forming a tight seal and sucking him deep, the gasp I heard above me made the corners of my mouth turn up.

His fingers dug into my skull, directing my head as his hips thrust him deep in my mouth. Any time I felt like gagging or had difficulty breathing he slowed down the pace, and I thanked him as best I could. My eyes flicked sideways to watch us in the mirror and the raw need I saw on his face— *I'm doing that*—was a powerful aphrodisiac. The throbbing between my legs increased, my tiny panties no match for the slickness running down my inner thighs. *I need him inside me soon or this is going to be too much.*

Apparently he thought the same because he pulled out and stepped back. My saliva glistened on the taut skin in front of my face. "Stand up."

Not sure whether he meant I could move my hands, I maneuvered myself upright until I was standing, arms still locked behind my back. There may have been approval on his face but he grabbed the back of my neck, his grip firm but not tight, and marched me to a round marble table with a thick wood base. "Lay across and grab on to the sides until I say you can let go."

I eyed the large table dubiously. It looked solid enough but the stone had to be cold and I wasn't wearing much. From somewhere deep inside my soul a small voice cried out, *You can still say no, it's not too late.* Body suffused with raw desire, I made my choice, however, and leaned down, grabbing the far edges firmly, and was relieved when it didn't move an inch. Jeremiah's hand left my neck, trailing down my back and across my bottom, giving one cheek a firm squeeze. "Spread your legs."

I did as he said and his hand trailed lower, following the line of the thong between my buttocks. I shivered as his fingers caressed the thin panties and me beneath them, and tilted up my hips for more contact.

"Are you on birth control?"

The unexpected question pulled me out of the haze of lust for a moment and I nodded. Irregular periods more than any kind of sex life were why I got the shots; I'd never really needed them for any other reason than that.

In reward for my answer his fingers slid beneath the band of the small panties, pressing against my damp skin, and I moaned. He circled my entrance with deft fingers, then up toward the hard bud that throbbed with every beat of my heart. My breaths came in pants but he didn't go farther, his hand merely exploring. "Would you like me to make you come, little cat?"

I nodded vigorously, his fingers making my breath catch. A chuckle came from behind me and lips pressed against the small of my back, just below the bustier. "You'll have to work for it . . . are you willing to do that?"

Before I could make any response, his thumb slid back through my folds and pressed firmly against my rear opening. I surged forward in shock but the table prevented any escape from the foreign invasion. I trembled as his hand caressed both my entrances, the alien sensation a puzzle my body couldn't quite figure out.

"Many women enjoy backdoor play," Jeremiah murmured behind me, his fingers continuing their surface explorations. "Some actually prefer it as the forbidden gets them off." He leaned in close, his body molding to mine. "Some men also prefer this entrance, the tight fit and taboo as much of a turn-on as the sex itself." His lips were behind my ear as he added, "Guess which kind of man I am?"

I moaned helplessly, trapped between the cold marble table and his hot body. His fingers kept working on the hard nub between my folds, causing my hips to jerk and breathy pants to escape my lips. The two sensations at once made it difficult to differentiate which was the turn-on; his thumb would rub over both and I'd crave more. Confusion was difficult to sustain as the sensations threatened to overwhelm me. So when Jeremiah's thumb pushed inside, stretching the tight muscles in a way I never would have remotely considered sexy, I moaned and tilted my hips back against his hand.

His laugh was deep and sexy, washing over me and making my skin tingle. Those fingers redoubled their pace, finding places inside myself that left me shaking and bucking against him, my moans loud and unabashed. "You are so fucking hot," he whispered in my ear, rolling his hips against my backside. Still naked from the waist down, he slid his hard member between my thighs alongside his hand before repeating the motion. The insides of my legs were moist with my own juices and the roll of his hips against my backside was sexy as hell; my grip on the edge of the table tightened until my knuckles were white. My cries were long wails, the sensations and growing urgency making my body tense in anticipation.

"You'll come when I say, only when I say."

I whined, this time in protest, and his hand fell away. The sudden absence was like a cold bucket of water—an unwelcome interruption no doubt punishment for my complaint. To my delight, however, the space was quickly filled by another sway of his hips as he slid his hard shaft between my thighs and a hand came up to clamp behind my neck. He didn't push inside, merely sliding along the wet folds. "Please," I moaned, lifting my hips to grant him better access.

"Please, what?"

His voice held amusement although I couldn't see his face, but this time I was sure I knew the answer. "Please, sir."

"What would you like, little cat? Do you want me inside you, that gorgeous ass of yours spread to take me deep? Should I ride you hard, force you to come with my cock pounding deep?"

That deep voice, gravelly and rich and right next to my ear, could melt stone. He slid across the hard bud between my legs and everything rushed back; I was so close, it wouldn't take much. . . .

I felt his bulbous tip nudge at my aching entrance at the same time hands spread my butt cheeks, fingers running along the puckered skin. He pushed inside both openings at once and I almost sobbed, the pressure and stretching a welcome relief. He wasted little time, his hips picking up a steady tempo even as his fingers worked my back hole. Within a minute I was moaning with each thrust, my cries echoing off the marble table and ornate mirrors in the room.

As his thrusts grew more forceful, banging the tops of my thighs repeatedly against the edge of the marble slab, I looked up into the large wall mirror above the mahogany dresser in front of me. It gave a clear view of the man behind me, and although I heard very little from him, I saw the raw need on his face. His mouth opened in muted gasps, the long arms reaching to my neck straining against the white shirt material. The corset back of the bustier with its strings and white lace was hot; it was impossible to believe it was my body reflected in the mirror.

Very quickly, however, it became all about the various sensations, the building explosion I desperately sought. He was pounding into me now, each thrust slamming me into the table, which, for all the abuse, remained steady. I wailed, my orgasm rushing to meet me. "Please, I can't stop. Sir, please!"

The hand between our bodies disappeared and Jeremiah increased his strokes, jerking hard inside me. Fingers on the back of my neck squeezed, throaty cries and guttural groans coming from close behind my head as fingers slid around front of me, gliding over the beating core between my legs. "Come then, I want to feel your body's reaction around me."

There was no way I could have stopped myself. My orgasm flooded over me like a wave of light; I cried out, my hands gripping the table like a vise, body shaking. Jeremiah's thrusts hit places inside me that had the waves rolling on and on, but then I heard a guttural, hoarse cry from above and he jerked over me with only a couple of last erratic thrusts. I laid there for a moment, panting and thankful for the cool surface of the marble beneath my too-hot body. Jeremiah laid his forehead against my shoulder blades and we stayed that way for a moment, struggling to catch our collective breaths.

Finally he pushed himself off me and pulled out, running a hand along my spine as he stepped back. "You can let go of the table now."

Easier said than done. My hands were stiff and difficult to free and as I tilted upright I flexed them to return feeling. Leaning against the table for support, I gave myself time to catch my breath as Jeremiah rearranged his clothing then walked over to a nearby seat. He picked up a small paper bag with some big swirly name I didn't recognize and brought it over, setting it gently on the table beside me. Leaning in close, he placed a surprisingly soft kiss to my forehead, then nudged me gently toward the bathroom. "Go, clean up and put these on. Keep the lingerie on underneath, I want to know it's there beneath the clothing."

My legs were like jelly but I took the bag and wobbled to the bathroom, remembering to grab my purse before locking myself inside. Setting the bags on the floor, I stood in front of the sink mirror and stared at my reflection in the tall mirrors. My blond hair was a mess, still damp from the bath, but the tousled look seemed to fit the rest of my outfit. I ran my hands down the stiff white fabric, turning so I could see the corset strings across my back. I'd never before worn lingerie this fine—heck, I'd never really worn proper lingerie ever—but staring at the flare of my bottom beneath the white lacy contraption, the strings barely covering the tiny thong that hadn't been much protection . . .

I looked good. It was a novel concept for me and I admired my reflection in the mirror. Then I sobered. I'm not going to end this farce, am I? Whatever games Jeremiah Hamilton was playing had gone too far; I'd allowed myself too many liberties to play the innocent in this game any longer. So what does that make me, a well-paid office assistant, or a glorified mistress?

The question disturbed me and I tried to block it from my mind. Taking a few minutes to clean myself up thoroughly, I discarded the tiny panties before turning to see what was inside the bag he had given me. A trendy pair of pants, a simple yet silky blouse, and a pair of red flat shoes made up the clothing portion, while a brush and other toiletries lined the bottom. The clothes, as far as I could tell, were the right size even though I knew my curvy figure wasn't exactly the norm in Europe. He'd obviously done this before, to know exactly what was needed. I didn't care to explore why that thought annoyed me. The revelation brought up more questions I didn't want to ask right now, so I pushed them aside and hurried to make myself presentable.

Twenty minutes later I emerged, fully clothed and refreshed, to see him waiting beside the table with the domed dishes I'd seen earlier. They contained a simple selection of fruits and crepes, with real whipped cream in a chilled metal dish. Looking at the clock I saw it was still morning and I thanked the powers that be I had managed to sleep on the plane. "What's the plan for today?" I asked, remembering Ethan mentioning something about a gala.

He took my hand and lifted it to his lips before popping a handful of grapes into his mouth. "Eat while you can," he said, watching me pile the fruit onto the thin crepe wrap. "Today, your work really begins."

9

Paris was as dazzling at night as in daylight, but I was too nervous to notice.

I smoothed the expensive dress with my hands, watching through the limousine windows as the city flashed past. The flutter in my belly at that moment had more to do with fear of what I was getting myself into and less to do with the man seated next to me, one large hand maintaining a possessive grip on my thigh.

Only forty-eight hours ago I'd been struggling to get by, worrying how homelessness was only a single paycheck away. Now decked out in a dress and shoes that cost three months of my previous salary, and on my way to a charity gala alongside one of the richest men in the world, that person seemed light-years away.

I'd pinch myself to see if I was dreaming but, after doing that all day, I was pretty sure this was real.

"You look nervous."

The softly spoken words made me swallow. I stared at the

hand on my leg, watching a thick thumb lazily caress the material, but couldn't bring myself to raise my gaze farther. "I'm terrified," I admitted, but couldn't say more as my emotions jumbled all the thoughts in my head.

Jeremiah made a low murmur, acknowledging my answer, and we fell back into silence. The Eiffel Tower glittered on the dark horizon, a bright beacon over the still-busy city, but even that sight couldn't shake me out of my current doldrums.

"Where would you most like to visit in France?"

The question surprised me. I looked up to see him watching me, green eyes thoughtful. "Excuse me?" I asked.

Jeremiah pointed out the window at the passing city. "Most people want to see the Eiffel Tower, or visit the wineries, or any other number of activities. What is one thing you'd like to do?"

I didn't consider the question relevant to this particular moment, but I knew the answer anyway. I'd known it since childhood. "See the beaches of Normandy."

He blinked slowly, and I got the impression I'd managed to surprise him this time. "Really?"

I smiled at the bemused question in his eyes. "My grandfather was an RAF fighter pilot, and my dad always loved World War II stuff; I grew up watching movies and documentaries, anything about the subject. Guess his love rubbed off."

"RAF?" Jeremiah asked, interest sparking in his beautiful eyes. "Was your grandfather British?"

I shook my head. "Canadian. He died before I was born, but my father always said he told the best stories." I found talking about my father painful, but strangely cathartic. I'd avoided even thinking about my parents for nearly three years, but now the memories allowed me to smile and relax. "He loved watching war documentary marathons on the history channels during military anniversaries. Mom always called him a useless lump those weekends, but she let him have his shows. He had a picture on our mantel of him on Utah Beach long before I was born, posing next to some of the old wreckage still on the sands."

I looked up to see him watching me with a strange expression, almost yearning. His face closed off immediately, settling into its normal neutral mask, leaving me to ponder what exactly I'd seen. Why would a billionaire envy me my piddly little life? "What about you?" I asked, praying I wasn't prying. "Did any of your family fight in that war?"

Jeremiah shook his head. "My father was too young and I doubt he would have gone anyway. Our family made their first million from the war movement, however."

I cocked my head, detecting a hint of bitterness in the statement. "They built ships and weapons?"

"No, they sold the necessary raw materials to the government at a huge profit. When the war was over, my family was richer than ever."

The anger in his voice confused me. Was he ashamed of his family's conduct? "Not everyone could fight in the war," I said. "My paternal grandfather was a fighter pilot but my other grandpa failed the entrance physical and had to stay behind. He ended up assembling ships and torpedo boats."

Something flickered in his eyes. "I didn't mean . . ."

I put a hand on his thigh. "I know. I just meant that your family helped in the war, too, no matter what the motivation. That is nothing to feel guilty about."

Something told me the CEO had never considered the situation like that. How hard it must be to be ashamed of your own family, I mused, because that was the impression I got from the conversation. I glanced up to see Jeremiah staring silently at me, his eyes probing. Suddenly self-conscious, I cleared my throat and fiddled with the purse in my lap. The hand on my knee crept up my leg and around my waist. Then he suddenly hauled me sideways until I sat face-to-face with him. I swallowed at the penetrating look he gave me as his fingers pushed an artfully curled strand of blond hair from my neck. "You look beautiful tonight."

That deep voice rumbled through me, setting my body on fire. I flushed and cast my eyes sideways, only to have him take my chin and gently pull my head back so I again faced him. His eyes searched my face then his hand followed, lightly tracing the edge of my brow line and jaw. "I'll be the envy of every man there."

I swallowed, breath stuttering in my throat at his passionate gaze. The hand behind me dipped lower, cupping my backside through the green fabric as his fingers and eyes traveled down my body to the low neckline of the dress. I sighed, body yielding to his unspoken demands, reveling in the moment.

The day had flown by like a crazy, impossible dream. My boss had taken me to some of the trendiest (and most expensive!) shops in the city to look for a gown. It had taken three stores before we found what I thought was the perfect dress; apparently Jeremiah thought so, too, because he bought it on the spot when I stepped out of the dressing room. The green sleeveless number made me feel sexy, accentuating my curves in ways I'd never imagined possible. He then whisked me away to a salon for the rest of the transformation. Attendants used an airbrush for applying the makeup, something I'd never experienced before. Though I would have loved to see the process, they denied me the wall mirror, facing me away from it during the whole procedure. Afterward, however, they twirled me around and, even though I never really cared much for makeup, the result impressed me. They'd lightened my long blond hair several shades, and the makeup made my skin appear flawless.

The hand at my back crept up to my neck, grasping tight. He pulled me close in what I thought would be a kiss, but he stopped just short. "Tell me," he said, his other hand sliding beneath the high slit in the side of the gown, "are you already wet for me?"

Always. I swallowed, heart racing as his fingers crept toward my inner thigh. He played with the top of my thigh-high stockings, then moved up again toward the apex of my legs.

The dark green dress had necessitated different lingerie from the white set Jeremiah had gifted me with earlier that morning. He had picked the ensemble out, then, when we returned to the hotel room later in the afternoon, had insisted on stripping me out of my clothing and dressing me in the new underwear. The whole thing had felt incredibly erotic, but Jeremiah made no demands on me despite the erection

I'd seen tenting his pants. His approval, however, had warmed other parts of me; it felt good to be seen as desirable.

The memory itself made me hotter, and I gave a panting moan, opening my legs to his questing touch. His fingers slid along my panties, pressing against me without actually touching, and I shuddered. I heard his deep chuckle as he did it again, then raised his chin to kiss my forehead. "Looks like we'll have to wait," he murmured, and I gave a mewl of disappointment as he set me again firmly beside him. "Tonight, however, you're mine." The promise in his voice made me shiver in anticipation.

We turned off the street, heading toward a well-lit building. A throng of people milled about the entrance, and I tensed again. Jeremiah squeezed my leg, and I forced myself to relax, grabbing my purse beside my feet. The car pulled to the entrance of the building and slowed to a stop, then I heard the chauffeur get out.

Showtime, I thought, hands wringing my purse. While there were not as many people as I feared—some had already entered the building—more than enough remained to set my heart racing.

The door opened, and Jeremiah emerged first, holding out his hand as I scooted toward the car door. Lights flashed as I stepped out, very conscious of the clingy dress and high heels. Jeremiah's arm was solid as he guided me effortlessly through the line of people, giving me firm ballast to which I clung. While I knew how to walk in heels, the attention we received had me feeling like a bumbling idiot. I focused on not falling or otherwise making a fool of myself, and breathed a relieved sigh when we reached the entrance and the cameras and babbling press faded into the background.

Jeremiah had given me little information—maybe deliberately—with regards to the gala. I knew only that it took place at the Port de Versailles and would benefit charity. The sheer number of people already there, and the way they moved, gave me the impression that we had not arrived anywhere near the start of the festivities. A quick peek at the events schedule pressed into my hands confirmed my suspicion, and there was also much more going on than what I saw. Scanning the scheduled events, I pointed at one name. "You didn't tell me you were a guest of honor."

Jeremiah lifted one shoulder in casual dismissal as he guided us into the central area. A classical band played music at the far end next to the stage, and a few people swept across the dance floor, but most clustered in groups spread throughout the room.

"Ah, my friend, I'm glad you could make our little soirée." A short balding man stepped toward us and grasped Jeremiah's hand in a vigorous handshake. He was wearing a tuxedo, complete with bow tie, and had a strong French accent. "I trust you only just arrived?"

"Hello, Gaspard," Jeremiah said by way of greeting, a small smile playing over his lips. His approval seemed genuine; he obviously had a fondness for the Frenchman. "Thank you for the honor of the invite."

Gaspard laughed. "Forever modest, when so often it is you who funds these little endeavors."

I blinked and slanted a look at my boss. He seemed

unperturbed by the praise, and I realized it was likely the truth. I didn't know he gave to charities. Indeed, there was a lot I didn't know about the man standing beside me, and my own ignorance was beginning to frustrate me.

"Who is your lovely companion tonight?" Gaspard asked, drawing my attention back to the present.

"May I introduce Ms. Lucille Delacourt, my newest assistant. Gaspard Montrose is the man responsible for this whole affair."

"Enchantée, mademoiselle." Gaspard took my offered hand and laid a light kiss on the knuckles. I felt Jeremiah's hand on the small of my back clench, fingers digging into the fabric of my dress.

"Enchanté, monsieur," I greeted in return, then gestured to the large room. *"Cette salle est merveilleuse."* This place looks marvelous.

Gaspard's face lit up. *"Ah, mais vous parlez en français!"* Ah, you speak French!

"Un peu; je suis née au Québec avant de déménager à New York." Only a little, I was born in Quebec before moving to New York.

"Ah, French-Canadian." Gaspard beamed at me, obviously pleased, and I returned his smile. "Welcome to Paris, *mademoiselle.*"

I could feel the weight of Jeremiah's gaze, but ignored him, scanning the schedule. The booklet listed various charity presentations during the day but it was winding down for the evening, leaving only dinner and the final ceremonies.

"Ah, before you go in, Jeremiah, there's one thing you

should know." Gaspard leaned in close to the taller man and said in a low voice, "Lucas is here tonight."

Jeremiah stiffened, and when I looked up his face was like stone. Gaspard looked apologetic about the news. "I don't know how he received an invitation, but it was legitimate and he was allowed attendance."

I busied myself with my dress, curious as to who they were talking about but trying not to seem nosy. Jeremiah's jaw clenched, a muscle ticking in his cheek, then his face smoothed out. "Thank you for the news, Gaspard."

The Frenchman nodded and turned to another arriving couple as we swept past. Now that we were no longer in front of the press, I felt much more comfortable, walking normally but still had to work to keep up with Jeremiah. His long strides carried us into the hall, and I suddenly felt the weight of eyes on us. I clenched my teeth and tried to ignore the intrusive stares.

"You never told me you spoke French."

I'd been expecting a comment on my exchange with Gaspard and, despite a nervous flutter in my belly, managed a small smile of triumph. "You never asked."

My reply was cheeky, but I looked up to see him contemplating me, a bemused look on his face. "So during your interview when you said you had passports, plural . . ."

I nodded. "I have two: one Canadian and the other American. My mother is American but she moved up there after marrying my father. I grew up in Quebec, then moved back to New York when my grandma, my mom's mom, died. I was fourteen."

"You live an interesting life, Ms. Delacourt." Again I saw the approval on his face, and it warmed me to the tip of my toes. Surprising him was likely both a difficult and a risky proposition, but this time I came away unscathed.

I felt eyes watching our movement through the room, but nobody approached us, which I found odd. Jeremiah seemed to know exactly where he was going, and I tried to keep up. Our pace didn't allow much time for anyone to approach, and I wondered what was so important.

Unfortunately, I wasn't given the chance to find out. We stopped near the dance floor, surrounded by groups talking and laughing among themselves. He took my hand, the same as Gaspard only moments before, and laid a soft kiss across my knuckles. Unlike the Frenchman's, however, this one sent tingles through my body; his eyes captured mine, and I knew he was aware of my reaction.

"I need to speak to someone in private," he murmured, his voice barely audible above the ambient noise. "I won't be more than a minute; stay here until I get back."

Then without another word he turned and walked away, disappearing through the cluster of guests.

10

When I was in fifth grade, I received my first, and last, major role in a school play. I practiced my lines at home and with the other students until I knew them forward and back. Even the dress rehearsals in the large gymnasium went without incident, the empty area safe from critics. I'd been proud to get my part, small but crucial, right up until the night of the first performance. Faced with a gym full of strangers, I froze, my lines disappearing from my head, unable to move or speak under what felt like a condemning tide.

Suddenly alone in that great exposition hall, in a foreign land not knowing another soul, that same freezing terror turned me to stone.

The beautiful hall, with its well-dressed patrons and high-class atmosphere, took on an almost sinister quality now that I was left to my own devices. The schedule crumpled in my hands as I peered about, trying to decide where to go. Staying put as Jeremiah said wasn't an option; I needed to get out of that sudden crush of bodies the same way I'd needed to leave that stage all those years ago.

"Lucy Delacourt?"

Hearing my name startled me from my turbulent thoughts. Looking around to see who had spoken, I saw a dark-haired woman in a long yellow gown approaching me. She seemed familiar, then a surprised smile tilted my lips as I recognized her. "Cherise?"

"Oh my God, it *is* you!" The smaller girl clapped her hands together in delight, beaming at me. "I thought I saw you come through the doors, but couldn't be sure until I got closer."

Still amazed to see someone I actually knew, I threw decorum to the wind and pulled the girl into a quick hug. Cherise had shared dorms with me for our first two years of college at Cornell, and while we hadn't seen much of each other during classes—she was premed and I was prelaw—we'd still hung out on weekends with the other students. I didn't question what providence brought her here, I just thanked whoever was watching over me for a familiar face.

"What are you doing here?" I exclaimed as we parted.

"I'm here with David actually." Her big smile widened in pride. "We help run a clinic down in Borneo and he's here trying to raise donations."

"You two finally got married?" When she nodded I just grinned. Cherise and David had been high school sweethearts when I'd met them in college. Both had big dreams of saving the world, and they seemed to be on their way. "So you're both doctors now?"

"No, I actually switched to business when David went into med school. It worked out well as I now help him run the business side of the whole operation. I get to be out in the field with him anyway, so it works great for me!"

Cherise brought with her the upbeat, infectious joy her friends had always luxuriated in. Her obvious pleasure in seeing me lifted my somber mood from moments earlier, and I finally relaxed. The bubbly brunette got an impish look to her eyes. "So spill: Was that really Jeremiah Hamilton with you at the door?"

I flushed at the question. *There's no reason this needs to be awkward*, I admonished myself. "He's my boss," I replied, shrugging my shoulder as if it were nothing.

"So are you two . . . ?"

"No," I replied, shaking my head emphatically. "I'm his new personal assistant, which I only just found out means I have to accompany him to these functions. This is all so new though." I didn't lie, but I still felt bad leaving everything else out, especially when I saw Cherise's disappointment at the news.

"Weren't you going to be a lawyer?" she asked, looking puzzled.

The question was a sore spot, but not something she would have known about. When my parents died, we were both college juniors and rarely saw each other. I'd inadvertently cut ties with most of my college acquaintances while I tried to get my life together, something that was still an ongoing process. "It didn't work out," I said, then in an effort to change the subject I looked around behind her. "Where's David?"

"Out in the crowd, mingling with the rich folks and trying to get more donations. Our presentation didn't net as much as we needed, so he's trying to get a few more sponsors." She rolled her eyes. "He's so much better at that than I am. It's weird walking up to a stranger and just asking for money."

"Funny," a heavily accented voice said nearby, "as this is what I see in front of me."

I looked over to see a tall, slim, blond woman standing beside me, eyeing Cherise with smug superiority. I had no idea how long she'd been standing there, but when Cherise's face fell my hands curled into fists. "Excuse me," I said bluntly, indignant at her treatment of my friend, "who are you?"

She turned her cool gaze to me, blue eyes giving me a once-over. "I am Anya Petrovski. I understand you are Mr. Hamilton's new personal assistant." She studied her nails. "It is a position with which I am well acquainted."

The woman didn't offer her hand, and I wouldn't have taken it anyway. I neither liked the emphasis she put on the word "position," nor did I appreciate her knowing smirk. Annoyed at having my "business relationship" with my boss mocked by this woman, I used my anger as a shield. "If you'll excuse me, Ms. Petrovski, I was already talking with—"

"You will find that when you work for wealthy men, people will selfishly approach you only for your contact." Anya gave Cherise a condescending glance. "You must guard yourself against even such clumsy attempts."

Beside me, Cherise stiffened at the veiled insult. "This is a charity function, if you haven't noticed," I countered, coming to Cherise's defense. "If she wants me to help her raise money, it's my choice to do so."

Anya lifted a shoulder. "The venue only legitimizes the petty begging attempts."

My whole body tensed in outrage, and I was set to go off on the haughty, blond woman when Cherise backed away from us. "If you two will excuse me," she said stiffly, "I need to get back to my husband."

As she turned to leave I reached for her arm. "Cherise . . ."

"It's okay, Lucy, I'm happy to see you but . . ." The smaller girl gave the haughty Russian beauty an uncharacteristic glare. "When your business is done with this, this woman, come find us," she said before walking off, head held high.

"Why did you do that?" I said, rounding on the beautiful blond woman. "She was a friend."

Anya shrugged, but her cool eyes seem amused by my anger. "She means nothing to me. I have only been sent to collect you."

My hands clenched again. Surrounded by strangers, and in a foreign environment, I didn't want to draw any undue attention to myself. But I found it hard. The fact that my struggle obviously amused the Russian woman made my decision to keep calm, at least on the outside, even more difficult. "By whom?"

Her smirk widened. "My employer."

I bit my cheek to keep from saying the first words that came to mind. "Please tell your employer I'm indisposed for the rest of the evening."

"I really must insist." Anya linked her arm through mine

and attempted to steer me around. "Mr. Hamilton does not appreciate tardiness."

"What?" Her words surprised me, shock making me take a few steps before digging in my heels. "Jeremiah sent you?"

She responded with a jerk of her chin behind me, and I swiveled my head to see Jeremiah's profile between the guests. He sent this harpy to collect me? My lips pursed in annoyance as I grudgingly allowed myself to be led through the crowd, loathe to make a scene but really wanting free of the sanctimonious blond woman's grasp.

Several military figures surrounded our target, their uniforms a similar dark green but decorated differently to denote varying ranks. As we drew nearer I realized I'd made a grave error: this was not Jeremiah, but now there was no way to get free. A familiar yet foreign dark head turned in our direction and a set of cool blue-green eyes lit up as they saw us approach. Long slicked-back hair framed a familiar-yet-not face, olive skin bisected by a small white scar across his nose and one cheek. Dressed in all black and holding a wineglass loosely in his fingers, the familiar face lacked the cool rigidity to which I'd grown accustomed.

What have I gotten myself into?

"Gentlemen, if you'll please excuse me. We can discuss our business further tomorrow."

Even his voice sounded similar, but he had a slick quality and cynical air about him, much different from Jeremiah's stiff control. The stranger's carefree expression as he gave me a once-over disconcerted me, as I'd grown used to the stoicism I associated with the familiar face.

"And who do we have here?" he asked, lifting my hand to his lips. The way he kissed my fingers was different from Gaspard's earlier. Whereas the older Frenchman had been gallant, this was more personal than I'd prefer. His eyes held mine, his lips lingering perhaps a bit too long across my knuckles, and despite my best intentions I felt a flutter in my belly. Annoyed with myself and my response, I snatched my hand away, and watched as amusement flashed in his eyes.

"This is Lucy Delacourt, the new assistant to Jeremiah." Anya's accented voice held the same snide tone as before, but her demeanor seemed more deferential. She sidled next to the man, and wormed her arm through his—almost possessively. "Meet Lucas Hamilton, the true heir to the Hamilton business." I couldn't miss the air of entitlement in her statement, and Lucas didn't deny the claim.

So this was the Lucas that Gaspard had warned Jeremiah about? I frowned at the two gorgeous people. The predatory nature of their gaze had part of me wanting to flee, but I stayed, crossing my arms instead. A kernel of anger smoldered in my belly at being thrown into this unaware, without backup.

Lucas ignored the gorgeous woman hanging on his arm, cocking his head to the side and studying me. "You seem tense, love," he said, addressing me in a smooth voice. "I don't want a beautiful woman such as yourself disappointed by my company."

Beside him, Anya tensed, and the angry look she gave me spoke volumes as to her jealousy. While it felt good to watch her come down a peg, I had no desire to continue this conversation. Something told me I was way out of my league here. However this went, I doubted I'd come out ahead. "I thought you were someone else," I said stiffly, not bothering to mention that I was dragged to see him. "If you'll excuse me . . ."

As I stepped back to leave, the band behind me struck up a new tune, a livelier number that had several couples walking to the dance floor. Lucas stepped forward, shaking off Anya's grip on his arm. "Would you care to dance?" he asked, holding out a hand toward me.

Anya stepped forward, obviously having something to say about the offer. A sharp look in her direction by the man before me, however, and Anya stopped, simmering in place as she glared at me. *Why am I suddenly the bad guy?* I wondered, irritated by the entire game. "No, I'm sorry," I said stiffly, trying to maintain my poise, "but I really need to find my—"

"Really, I must insist." Before I knew it he had a hand around my waist, and was leading me out onto the floor. I balked immediately, digging in my heels. *Why is everyone insisting I do what they want tonight?* I thought, annoyance bubbling to the surface.

"We're quite visible here," he murmured, leaning in close. "You don't want to cause a scene now, do you?"

I hesitated, suddenly mindful of the strangers around us, and that momentary hesitation gave him all the time he needed. He swept me out onto the floor and into his arms before I could think to say no again, gliding us across the dance floor as smooth as silk. I tried to pull away, but his vise-like grip allowed me no escape. "Let me go," I said, my rising anger bleeding into my voice.

"And ruin a perfectly fine opportunity to dance with a beautiful woman? I think not." He seemed amused at my resistance; I danced stiffly in his arms, but my gracelessness didn't faze him a bit. He pulled me close to his hard body, arms like iron; my feet barely touched the ground, my weight supported almost entirely by his arms.

"We seem to have gotten off on the wrong foot. Tell me why: do I smell bad?"

The absurd comment caught me off guard, and I struggled not to be amused. Involuntarily, I breathed in his scent: spicy and sweet like cinnamon, and I couldn't tell if it was cologne or his natural fragrance. Annoyed at my reaction, I retorted, "I don't appreciate watching my friends get belittled, then being dragged to meet someone under false pretenses."

Lucas tipped his head to the side, acknowledging my blunt comments. "Anya can be tempestuous; indeed, it was once part of her charm. Perhaps we can begin again. I am Lucas Hamilton. And you are . . . ?"

I frowned at his collar, refusing to meet his eyes in defiance. "You already know who I am."

A finger under my chin lifted my gaze. "But I'd like to hear it from your lips," he said softly, sweeping me in a big arc across the dance floor.

Butterflies exploded in my stomach, and my jaw clenched. Damn my body and its silly reactions. His hands were burning coals against my skin, eyes like magnets. Just like his brother.

Reminding myself of Jeremiah allowed me some measure of control over myself—I didn't need another man to make me go weak in the knees and lose all willpower. One was quite more than enough. "What do you want?" I asked firmly.

Instead of disappointment at his seduction attempts being ignored, his gaze sparked with renewed interest and no small bit of amusement. "Besides a dance with a beautiful woman?" He shrugged a shoulder. "To make my stick-in-the-mud little brother jealous."

I pursed my lips, gut tightening. *At least he's finally being honest. I think.* "I'm not interested in playing games, Mr. Hamilton." I struggled slightly in his grip, jostling a nearby couple. "I'd rather not make a scene, but if you won't let me—"

"What if I answered any questions you might have about my brother?" At my startled look, Lucas gave a wry smile. "My brother is one who keeps his secrets close." He swayed me closer, mouth dipping close to my ear. "Aren't there some things about your boss you are dying to know?"

I ground my heel into the toe of his wingtip shoes. Lucas winced and pulled away but didn't let go, continuing to twirl me across the wood floor. That infuriating mouth tipped up in the corners as I scowled at him. He knew he had me.

I was curious.

There was so much I didn't know about my new employer, and it kept me feeling off balance when I was around him. The way Jeremiah watched me, his gaze piercing through my mind, I constantly felt like he could read my very thoughts. The idea of knowing something, anything, about him that could tip those dizzying scales in my favor was as tantalizing as water to a man dying of thirst. Still, I didn't appreciate the smirk on Lucas's face. "Anya used to work for Mr. Hamilton? Um," I stuttered, "the other one. My boss."

His lazy smile grew. "She was his last personal assistant," he drawled, eyes watching me intently.

I struggled in vain to keep my reaction from showing. That harpy? What did he see in her?

I didn't realize I'd said the words aloud until Lucas threw back his head and laughed. The sound startled me, and I flushed. We drew a few glances from the couples around us, but the dancing continued. "She wasn't always this way," he said, humor lacing his voice. "Actually, she used to be a very sweet girl, much like yourself."

"What happened, then?" I asked, determined not to fall prey to any more of his lines.

He lifted a shoulder. "I seduced her away from him, then turned her into my spy. When he discovered this and threw her out, she came to work for me."

The arrogance in his voice was a bitter gall, and I tried again to free myself. Surprisingly, he loosened his grip as if to let me go, twirling me under his arm. He remained impervious to my glare, an infuriating smile fixed on his face, but I still held his attention. "Next question?"

I was dancing with a snake, but I couldn't see any way out at the moment. A quick scan of the room showed no relief coming to my aid, so I forged ahead. "What did Anya mean about the rightful heir business? You and Jeremiah are brothers, right?"

"Ah, straight to the heart of things." He twirled me again, blue-green eyes deep in thought. "What do you know so far?"

Not much, aside from what Celeste had revealed earlier. "The Wikipedia version. He was in the military, got out, and took over the company . . . had a rough go in the beginning."

Lucas dipped his head. "A decent summary, if lacking in the pertinent details."

I paused, thinking. "What exactly does Hamilton Industries do? How does your family make money?"

He quirked an eyebrow but still answered my question. "Investment mainly, usually in other companies that then give us a large portion of their profits. The corporation at this point serves to maintain and grow the money that's already there, but there are many companies and people under its proverbial umbrella. We always . . . ." He faltered, trailing off, then continued. "Tell me, how was your relationship with your father growing up?"

The bizarre question blindsided me. My mouth tightened, and I searched his face for any ulterior motives, but the question seemed genuine if more personal than I preferred. "Good," I said cautiously, "why?"

"Ours wasn't." Lucas's previously jovial expression shadowed. "Rufus Hamilton was impossible to please, especially if you were in any way related to him. Of course, we didn't realize this until we were much older and his demands had already warped our sensibilities. I'll give you the short version:

I went the route expected of me, to take over the family business, while Remi rebelled the only way he knew how and joined the military without my father's consent. It was the one time he managed to thwart our father's plans, and that success ate away at the old man."

He paused, and the silence in the conversation stretched. "Obviously something happened," I said, prompting him for more information.

Lucas snorted, his gaze far away and cynical again. "Yeah. The old man died." He looked down at me, and his lips tightened; another twirl, which I began to realize was how he gave himself time to think. "Rufus really couldn't have timed it better if he'd tried; heart attack took him out in the middle of a board meeting, and only days before Jeremiah was set to go back. He surprised me by turning up at the reading of the will—my little brother hadn't left on good terms—but I was even more shocked when our beloved father left the bulk of his estate to his younger son, Jeremiah."

The controlled fury in Lucas's eyes as he spoke warred with the sneer that twisted his lips. He was looking off in the distance again, lost in memories he obviously didn't like. "Jeremiah got everything, including majority shares in the company, with the stipulation that if he refused to take over, the entire company and all its holdings would be liquidated and scattered. That would have meant the loss of thousands of jobs and the collapse of a carefully built infrastructure spanning decades, all to get back at the son who had managed to outmaneuver him."

The callousness of the whole affair boggled my mind. "So

willing Jeremiah the entire company was meant as a punishment?" I asked.

I felt a brief shiver, as my voice jolted Lucas out of his memories. The dark expression disappeared, replaced by the smug amusement I began to understand was a mask. "Our dear Remi was always looking out for the common man," Lucas remarked, twirling us spiritedly around the dance floor. "It's why he joined the army, you know; he wanted to help others. So, when the executor read the will, lawyers and board members surrounded Remi, impressing on him the gravity of the situation, how many lives he would ruin if he turned it down, et cetera, et cetera. Given my little brother's predilection for being the hero, it was a no-brainer what he would choose."

"What about you?" I asked, genuinely curious. If Lucas told the truth at all, then his father had cheated him out of his inheritance through no fault of his own. While it didn't erase all my dislike for the man, it did put it into perspective.

"I survived." His gaze traveled over my shoulder, and a wicked smile curved his lips as the song came to an end. "Doesn't mean I don't enjoy my bits of fun when they come along."

I squeaked as he shifted me around, one arm looping behind my back, then bent me over until I was paralled to the ground. Grabbing his shoulders, I stared wide-eyed up at his beautiful face only inches from my own. "Let's give them a show, shall we?" he murmured, then brought his lips down onto mine.

I stiffened, fingers digging into his dark suit. His mouth

took full advantage of my shock, tongue and teeth playing with my bottom lip. The kiss was brief and, while it still brought butterflies to my stomach, I managed to keep my wits about me. As he pulled me upright, my arm was already in motion. My hand cracked along his cheek, momentum giving the slap strength. The blow stunned us both—I couldn't believe I'd done it and apparently neither could he. I saw open surprise in his gaze, and perhaps a smattering of respect enter his eyes as he released me.

"What's going on here?"

11

I breathed a sigh of relief at Jeremiah's familiar voice, but the look on his face when I turned wasn't the least bit comforting. I tried to move toward him, but Lucas gripped my hand tight, pulling me up short.

"Brother," his voice boomed, unnaturally loud now that the band had concluded their song. "Fancy meeting you here. Care to join me and my lovely companion for a drink?"

I tried again to wrench my hand from his grip, but Lucas held fast. Turning an apologetic gaze to Jeremiah, I was disappointed by the accusatory look I received in return. *Why is this suddenly my fault?* I thought, indignation bubbling up. *You left me to fend for myself!*

The confrontation attracted the attention of nearby attendees. Their prying eyes watched the drama unfold, but not a one moved a muscle to intervene . . . leaving me stuck smack in the middle. The two men seemed more intent on each other than me although neither allowed me my freedom. Lucas still held my hand, and Jeremiah blocked any avenue of escape.

Together like this, I found it much easier to tell the two brothers apart, and I couldn't believe I'd mistaken one for the other. Jeremiah looked a caged bull, his broad frame hunched over and ready to charge. His impassive mask had slipped, and now his eyes blazed like the sun. In stark contrast, the leaner and slightly shorter Lucas stood back on his heels, a patronizing smirk on his face. There was a malicious twinkle in his eyes; he was obviously well versed in taunting his younger brother.

"What are you doing here?" Jeremiah all but growled, his eyes darting between his brother's face and our still-entwined hands.

"Perhaps I wanted to help the less fortunate, or to visit with my long-lost brother. After all, our last meeting was so dramatic."

"You stole thirty million dollars!"

Lucas waved a hand in the air. "So I have been told," he remarked blithely, then looked at me. "Come, my dear, drinks are on me."

He pulled me forward a resistant step, and then Jeremiah stepped in the way, blocking his brother's escape. "I could have you arrested in two minutes," his low voice rumbled, faint enough that only those close by could hear the words. "Even in France they wouldn't hesitate to extradite you, Loki."

"Ah, little brother has been checking up on me!" Lucas smirked and opened his arms wide, but there was a mocking gleam in his eyes. "You do miss me."

Following the conversation between the two siblings was difficult, causing more frustration to well up inside me. Both men seemed to have forgotten I was there while whatever problems lay between them were playing out in front of those around us. Along the edge of the dance floor I saw Anya watching us, a triumphant smile on her hard face, and wondered if she had been the one to point out my location in Lucas's arms to my boss.

Beside me, Jeremiah seemed to grow bigger, his expression darkening. "If you weren't my brother . . ."

"You'd what? Beat me to a pulp? Ruin my life?" The taunt in Lucas's voice was clear, and loud enough to be heard by those watching. "Too late, brother, someone beat you to it. Oh wait, no, that was you."

Jeremiah took a small step forward, and his brother held his ground. "Loki . . ."

"Enough!"

My voice cracked like a whip, the word piercing the tension. Both men started, then turned their furious stares on me. I myself was too angry to back down, however, and looked first at Lucas, raising my captured hand to almost eye level. "Let. Go."

There was a barely perceptible relaxing of his grip, and I snatched my hand back, stepping away. Jeremiah reached for my arm and I sidestepped him as well, much to his surprise. "Don't," I said, glaring at him.

He scowled back, clearly disliking my sudden defiance. "Ms. Delacourt," he started, but I shook my head, meeting his angry expression with my own.

"You left me to fend for myself, and that's exactly what I intend to do." I spared a glance for Lucas, who was watching me with amusement, then looked back at Jeremiah. "It seems you two have some things to discuss, so I'll leave you alone."

My boss clearly didn't approve of my sudden independence, but right then I couldn't have cared less. I felt the weight of several onlookers' gazes, but stiffened my spine and walked away. The stupefied looks of the two men followed my exit; I could feel their gazes burning holes into my back. Unfortunately, I was not at all in the mood to appreciate the dubious victory I'd no doubt pay for later.

Few women at the function wore yellow dresses; so it didn't take me long to locate Cherise. She looked surprised at my presence, but before she could greet me I spoke up. "I want to help you."

David stood beside her, and he squinted at me. "Lucy?" he said in surprise, and I realized Cherise hadn't told him yet about seeing me.

"Tell me everything you can about your operation." Fire burned through my veins; I hadn't felt this alive in years. "I'm going to get you your funding."

In college, one of my professors once mentioned in passing that I'd make a good lobbyist. Though never my goal, I recognized the accuracy of his observation. I found taking up the burdens and issues of others easier than dealing with my own; I never had problems approaching strangers on another's behalf. Years had passed since I'd last done anything like this, but my frustration needed an outlet and I threw myself into campaigning for my friends.

Over the next hour I charmed and cajoled my way through the crowds, translating when necessary and doing everything I could to help them. The process was surprisingly simple—the very nature of the event had already primed the attendees to write checks, and I had only to convince them why a little clinic in Borneo deserved their largesse. I dredged up every rusty social skill I'd ever learned, and flitted through the assembled group, sending them to David and Cherise before moving on to the next possible donor. Although I'd always been someone who was more comfortable being a wallflower than a social butterfly, I threw all caution to the wind and somehow managed to make people listen to me.

I caught glimpses of Jeremiah through the crowd, and could feel the weight of his gaze, but I ignored him as best I could. Easier said than done—even from a distance the man had the uncanny ability to throw me off balance. Still, I continued my crusade, and he didn't approach, giving me space—for which I was grateful. Neither Lucas nor Anya made another appearance, either, which also pleased me.

After an hour of moving from group to group, Cherise approached me and pulled me to the side. Grinning from ear to ear, her body all but vibrating with excitement, she said, "I don't believe it, but we've made nearly one hundred thousand so far!"

My mouth dropped open, and I had to stop myself from

giving her a big hug. "Will that be enough to last you guys awhile?"

"Enough?" She looked incredulous. "We could continue for several years with this at our current location—and not charge the locals a dime. Oh, thank you!" Cherise didn't seem to care about decorum, either, because she threw her arms around me in a quick but fierce hug. "You're incredible!"

"I would have to agree with that assessment."

Swallowing, I turned to see Jeremiah standing behind me, regarding us with a curious expression. He only had eyes for me, and when Cherise released me from her hug he held out a hand in my direction. "May I have the honor of a dance?"

My mouth worked silently, and I glanced at Cherise. Her grin had a knowing look about it, and when I hesitated she all but pushed me into my boss's arms. "The man asked you to dance," she said, eyes twinkling. "I think we can handle it from here."

No longer having an excuse, I stared at Jeremiah's offered hand. He had requested, not demanded, and he seemed content to wait me out. Looking into his green eyes, I realized I'd forgiven him some time ago for abandoning me, but I didn't feel like he should get off lightly. "You won't leave me alone on the dance floor, will you?" I teased, taking his hand.

Rather than the annoyance I feared I'd see, Jeremiah seemed almost amused by my question. "I promise not to let you out of my sight for the rest of the evening."

A promise in his tone sent chills across my skin as he led me to the center of the room. His touch was light as he gathered me into his arms on the dance floor, a stark contrast to his brother's earlier rigid grip. "I apologize for my conduct tonight," he murmured.

My eyebrows shot up. He was apologizing? To me? "Apology accepted," I replied, then let out a quick breath. "Your family is a bit dysfunctional, I see?"

A wry smile tipped one corner of his mouth but he didn't reply to the question. "You two were talking earlier," he said instead, a question in his voice.

"He answered some of my questions about you." When he tensed, I hurried to explain. "He said your father essentially forced you to take over the company. Is that true?"

"Essentially," he finally said after a long pause, but didn't elaborate.

"Celeste said you used to be an Army Ranger," I said after another moment of silence. His lips thinned, but I persisted. "What was it like?"

"Best thing I've ever done with my life." He slipped into silence again, but I could tell that he was thinking. "Originally, the military was meant only as a way to get away from my family, specifically my father. Once I got in, though, every aspect of that life fit me perfectly. I would have gone career if . . ."

If the choice hadn't been stolen away from you. As bitter as the argument had been between the two brothers earlier, I knew Lucas had told the truth. Jeremiah's own nobility had forced him to leave behind a life he loved to save his family's company and all the lives of those connected to it. I leaned forward and laid my head on his shoulder; he stiffened in my arms, and I wondered briefly if I'd be pushed away, then his body relaxed and he pulled me closer. He smelled divine, like chocolate and cherries; the skin of his neck was close enough that I only had to turn my head to see if he tasted as good as he smelled. . . .

Forcibly reminding myself that I was in a room full of people, several of whom were probably watching us, I lifted my head off his shoulder but didn't back away. Jeremiah must have somehow read my intentions; he pressed against me, a hard bump poking my belly. A dull ache filled my belly, body tingling from my heels to my fingertips, and I swallowed a small sigh. His reaction to me acted as a drug all by itself, a powerful aphrodisiac that made me want to pull him someplace private to do naughty things. I saw the same desire reflected in his eyes as our gazes locked; his grip on my lower back tightened, pulling me in closer to rub against the hard shaft, and I felt a rush of heat between my thighs.

Someone tapped a microphone, then a familiar French voice came over the speakers. "We would like to take the opportunity to thank some members of our audience for their contributions tonight."

"I think they mean you," I murmured. There were definitely eyes on us now as the band ended the song, but Jeremiah didn't release me for several more seconds. Finally he stepped away but didn't let go, raising my hand to his lips.

I swallowed, heart skipping a beat. Celeste had told me that the press and general public believed he only took his assistants as platonic companions, but it would be hard to convince any onlookers of that tonight. Heck, I was getting confused, with too many mixed signals bouncing around my head. *One day at a time,* I thought as he released my hand and headed to the front of the gathering crowd. *This can all end in an instant, and I'll be back in a crappy Jersey apartment.*

Even with as much power as he wielded in our relationship, both business and personal, I knew I could walk away at any moment. While perhaps not enough to put us on even footing, the option gave me some stable ground in my suddenly topsy-turvy life, but the thought made my heart ache. Jeremiah wasn't the type to play games, but he was difficult to read sometimes.

"You're thinking too hard, my sweet."

I started, body tensing at Lucas's voice only inches from my ear. "Go away," I muttered, not taking my eyes off Jeremiah. He continued moving toward Gaspard, who began giving an introductory speech in French, and I was nervous what Jeremiah would do if he saw Lucas beside me.

"All in good time. I just thought it rude to leave without bidding farewell to such a beautiful lady."

I snorted in disbelief. "Go bother Anya, I'm sure she's used to it by now," I snapped, careful to keep my voice low, and heard a low chuckle in return. Most of the guests were ignoring us, for which I was grateful. "If you want to get back at your brother," I hissed in a low voice, "leave me out of it."

"Oh, but it's so much more fun this way."

Fingers grazed my hip, and I immediately lashed out, kicking backward with my heel, grazing a shin. The hand quickly disappeared, and I had a moment of triumph until I heard him chuckle again.

Jeremiah had taken the stage by then, and I prayed he wouldn't look this way. "You're going to get me in trouble," I said.

"Oh, you'll probably enjoy it," Lucas all but purred, and I shot him a dark look. A self-satisfied smirk sat on his lips as he regarded me with unabashed interest. I rolled my eyes, determined to ignore him, and turned back to the stage . . . only to have Jeremiah's intense gaze rivet me in place. Damn it.

"Oh dear, looks like he's spotted our little tête-à-tête." Fingers brushed the hair back from my neck, and I flinched sideways. "I wonder what's going through his mind right now."

Judging by the look on his face, my boss and erstwhile lover was not amused, and I found myself in a quandary. My hand curled into a fist but I knew doing anything at this point would only bring me unwanted attention, and further amuse the snake at my shoulder. Jeremiah continued to glare in our direction, and Lucas, while no longer touching me, seemed determined to stand as close as he could manage. I could only guess what was going through Jeremiah's mind.

Up on stage, Gaspard came partially to the rescue. Noticing his guest's inattention and my current situation, the Frenchman clapped an arm across the billionaire's shoulders and managed to briefly distract him. I breathed a sigh of relief, one weight momentarily lifted. The two men shook hands for the cameras, signaling the end of the segment.

"Ah, there's my cue to exit." Lucas leaned in close, chest brushing my shoulders, and planted a quick kiss on my cheek. I jerked away but knew from the cloud covering Jeremiah's face that he'd seen. "Au revoir, chérie," Lucas murmured before disappearing, leaving me to face the advancing bull all by myself. It was useless to try to plead my case, so I stayed silent as Jeremiah came up beside me.

"Let's go."

His low tone brooked no argument; his hand on my lower back steered me effortlessly through the crowd. I turned back to see that Gaspard already held the audience's attention; few bothered watching our escape, for which I was grateful. Our exit from the large hall gave me the relief I'd been craving. I no longer had to worry whether I would trip or otherwise make a fool of myself in front of a crowd. The earlier euphoria from helping Cherise and David had worn off, and I felt exhaustion nipping at the edges of my consciousness.

Jeremiah fixed his flinty gaze on the doors leading out of the building, and I had the impression he was deliberately ignoring me. That made me nervous, as I didn't know what it ultimately meant. The ease we'd shared while dancing had vanished, so I stayed quiet, vowing to e-mail my good-bye and best regards to my friends as soon as I had the chance.

The limo was waiting for us outside the main exit. We dodged the few remaining paparazzi and climbed inside the dark vehicle, the driver closing the door behind us. I took the edge of the bench seats on one side of the vehicle across from Jeremiah as we pulled out, heading back to the hotel. I watched nervously as he shut the dark glass partition between us and the driver.

I glanced toward the shrouded front of the long car, and in my moment of inattention he moved suddenly, pushing me back onto the long bench. Squeaking in surprise, I clamped my lips tight as he towered over me, one hand on my right shoulder keeping me pressed against the leather seat. His eyes trailed down my torso, then up to my face, and I swallowed at the fire I saw in his eyes.

"Open your legs to me."

My lips parted in shock. Breathing became difficult as he skimmed his free hand down the side of my body, running his palm along the thin material. The dress parted along the high slit and his fingers slid beneath, stroking my inner thigh.

"About your brother," I said in a shaky voice, sudden nervousness making me desperate to explain myself, "nothing happened; I thought he was you and . . ."

"No."

I fell silent at the word. Jeremiah paused, body tense. "I don't want to hear about my brother again tonight. Please," he added, the word ground out. When I nodded my understanding he relaxed a hair. "Now, where were we?"

His palm slid between my knees, prying them apart in increments as he pushed his way up my leg. My breath caught, belly tightening, as his fingers tugged at the garter strap along my thigh, smoothing beneath it to the belt around my hips. My legs pressed together involuntarily, and his hand stopped. "Open your legs."

The words surrounded me, a sensual net, and I swallowed. My body had already begun vibrating, breath coming in pants. Part of me almost feared what he would do to me—not that I expected anything painful or demeaning, but that I'd lose all control of my body. Perhaps that was the point. With a shuddering sigh, I forced the muscles of my thighs to relax and let my knees fall apart.

"More."

Swallowing, again I complied, opening myself to him. He shifted above me, removing his hand from my shoulder to brace against the couch. I gasped when a finger pressed through the thin line of panties against my core, and arched my body into the contact. He gripped my hair, holding me steady as his hand rubbed and prodded. My breath came in shuddering gasps as he leaned over me, his face pressed close.

"You're mine," he murmured, eyes ablaze. He sped up his ministrations until I was moaning, the grip on my hair tightening. "I want to hear you say it."

"I'm yours." I struggled to get the words out; my body quaked and pulsed like a heartbeat. Eyes fluttering closed, my whole being focused on the sensations his hands provoked. The ache between my legs spread; I slipped out of my heels for traction, tilting my hips toward his hand.

"Again."

"I'm yours, sir."

The grip on my hair tightened, and my eyes sprang open, my breath coming in gasps. His eyes searched mine, for what I couldn't tell, but I couldn't think to hide anything. All I wanted was him, and I tried to let him see my desperation. The walls of my opening pulsed, demanding attention, and I silently begged him for more.

His grip on my hair eased, and he shifted again, his gaze no longer as intense but just as demanding. "I want to see you come," he murmured, lowering his face close to mine.

The words made me melt, his deep voice surging through my body. The deft fingers down there moved effortlessly underneath the panties, and I moaned loudly as they slipped through my folds and caressed my weeping opening. The car beneath me rocked slightly, reminding me where I was, but its movement only added to the sensations. A thick finger dipping inside, while his thumb flicked my aching bud, forced breathy moans from me.

"Only I am allowed to do this." Jeremiah accentuated his words by teasing a spot inside me with pinpoint accuracy; my hips shot off the seat, and I groaned. "No other man gets to touch you unless it is with my permission. Is that clear?"

I choked on my answer, waves of pleasure coursing through my body. I was rocketing toward an orgasm and couldn't think straight. The hand in my hair tightened, and I managed to reply, "Y-yes."

"I can't hear you."

I cried out, the sensations almost too much. "Yes! Please, sir!"

"Eyes on me." I locked gazes with him, the power of his stare pinning me to the seat. His thumb rubbed harder as his finger hooked me from inside, rubbing my opening with expert precision. "Now, come," he said, and with a wail I joyously dove off the edge. Body shuddering uncontrollably, I clutched at his dress jacket, everything in me exploding. The last ounce of strength fled my body, and I melted into the leather beneath me, trying in vain to catch my breath.

Jeremiah released my hair, and sat back in his seat, leaving me sprawled along the bench seat. I managed to close my legs, but couldn't do anything more; pulses still rocked me, and my limbs felt like jelly. The car slowed and turned, pressing me back against the seat, and I started as a hand came to rest on my knee. Swallowing, I looked out the tinted window to see the bright façade of our hotel looming above.

12

We made the short trip up to our suite in silence, tension thick in the air between us. I had barely kicked off my uncomfortable heels, enjoying the freedom to wiggle my toes, before a thick arm snaked around my waist. He pressed his hard body to me, trapping me against the wall; a thigh wedged itself between my legs and, before I knew what was happening, Jeremiah's mouth covered my own in a scorching kiss. Still reeling from the limo ride, I wrapped my arms around his neck, fingers digging through his thick hair as I moaned against his lips.

Hands cupped my backside, and he lifted me high, and once more wedged me tightly between his body and the wall; I gripped his shoulders to steady myself, but he held me secure, lowering his mouth to run lips and teeth down my neck. He ran hands down my thighs, then wrapped my legs around his waist. I moaned as I felt his hard length press against my already throbbing core.

"Mine," he murmured, the low rumble moving through

me like a flood. Capturing both of my wrists in one large hand, he pinned them above my head as his lips again found mine, sucking and nibbling. His free hand kneaded the soft flesh of my breast, thumbing the nipple, and I pushed into his touch.

His need and unabashed passion set me aflame. I moaned against his mouth, arching my body against his, trying desperately to get closer. He rolled his hips, pressing them against me, and I gave a small cry. His teeth played with my ear and dragged down the side of my throat, and I was lost to all else.

Belatedly, I noticed we were moving, but it didn't sink in until the world tilted and I landed on my back on the huge bed. Jeremiah wasted no time in covering me; he didn't seem to care about the expensive dress, slipping a rough hand down the front. The fervor of his passion made me hotter as well. I wanted, needed, more. I tried to touch him but he grabbed my wrists again, holding them beside my head as he sucked and nibbled my neck.

"Roll over."

I quickly obliged, and felt the zipper of the dress glide down my back and over my bottom. He peeled the layer from my skin, then trailed his lips down along my spine. I arched up like a cat, desperate for the soft touch, and heard the jangle of his belt. Excited by the sound and what it represented, I pushed my backside up to rub against his crotch, and to my immense satisfaction heard his small indrawn breath.

Hands wrapped around my wrists again, pulling them up toward the headboard. Cool leather wrapped around them as Jeremiah deftly secured me to the brass railings with the

belt, effectively trapping me. Thus secured, he began to remove my dress; I lifted my hips to help as he peeled the material from my body before tossing it to the ground beside
the tall bed. His hands kneaded my buttocks as he moved
behind me, straddling my legs. I lifted myself up onto my
knees, desperate for more contact. The position left me exposed, and his growl of approval made me shiver.

His hand splayed across my upper back, pressing my chest
into the mattress, then he bent over me and his lips trailed up
along my spine. My exhalations were panting bursts, hands
gripping the leather restraints tightly. His teeth scraped over
the taut skin of my backside, and I couldn't stop the moan that
forced its way through my lips. My body quivered, wanting
more, but Jeremiah took his time. Hands caressed my hips,
kneading the globes of my backside, then his thumbs ran down
along the cleft toward my weeping entrance.

I surged forward when he parted the tender flesh, my frantic panting a staccato in the quiet suite. He breathed on me, a
hint of what was to come, then lips and a hot tongue unerr-
ingly found my throbbing opening. I keened, my cry bouncing off the wall behind the bed, as he ran his tongue along
the tight ring before pushing in farther. One hand stroked
through my folds and my entire body quaked uncontrollably.

He stayed there for a while as I moaned and thrashed.
"Please," I begged repeatedly, although for what I didn't
know. Perhaps release from the delicious torture, perhaps for
more. Probably both.

His only reply was to chuckle and to continue the onslaught
of pleasure.

When he finally inserted a finger, I pressed against it, desperate for more. He controlled everything, but where he rubbed inside only served to heighten the sensation. Fluid flowed down my thighs, and I was almost crying from the unrelenting intensity.

He pulled away suddenly, then twisted me around so I was lying on my back. I stared up at a savage face as he forced my knees apart, looped his arm under one knee, then slid his hard length deep inside me with one sure stroke. I arched my body and closed my eyes, breath stuttering in my throat at the sudden invasion. The belt kept my arms restrained as he pounded me into the bed, allowing no retreat from his passion.

"Look at me."

I opened my eyes and stared up into his beautiful, intense face. A hand snaked up my body, winding itself around my throat as his face pressed in close. His hips kept up their thrusting, and the continual flashes of pleasure made it hard to think. "Say my name."

"Jeremiah," I breathed, brushing my breasts against his body. Behind the green lingerie, my nipples ached for his touch. I drew my free leg up to his waist, twisting it across his body and locking my ankles behind his back. His eyes widened, and the thrusting grew stronger.

"Say it again!"

"Jeremiah!" I cried out desperately, the word almost a sob. "Please!"

The hand around my throat tightened, not enough to choke me but enough to cause a rushing in my head. His other hand settled on my breast, pushing the stiff material aside and kneading the tissue, pinching the nipple between his fingers. My hips fell into a rhythm, moving with him, our thrusts taking me higher and higher, almost there but not quite enough. . . .

Jeremiah's hand tightened again, constricting my breathing enough for anxiety to cut through the haze of lust. My eyes shot to his passionate green ones, and I read the same need coursing through my veins. I gave myself over to the sensations, trusting him in this even as my lungs began to burn.

Then he released my throat, and thrust hard, tweaking my nipple. The sudden rush of oxygen and blood flowing through my body overwhelmed me, and with a cry and a shudder I came for the second time that evening. I thrashed beneath him, twisting the leather belt above my head and riding the wave of pleasure.

I wasn't sure how long it took my brain to settle back into the present, but eventually I came back to myself and saw Jeremiah still looming above me. His eyes recorded my every reaction; a hand traced down the side of my face in the first honestly tender contact I could remember. A thumb ran over my lips, and I opened my mouth, pulling it inside and tugging it with my teeth.

It was then, when I saw the answering fire in his eyes, that I realized he was still hard inside me.

He reached above me and released the belt, unwinding it from my wrists. My pinkies were numb and my wrists ached, but I didn't care. Keeping my gaze on his, I reached up and pushed on one shoulder, turning him over to lie on the bed. To my amazement, he allowed me to do so, and I followed him over until I was the one crouched over his large body. He had shed his dress jacket and slacks at some point, but still had his white shirt on with only the top two buttons undone. I straddled his hips, feeling his hardness pressing against my backside, as one by one I unfastened the remaining loops.

I had never yet seen him naked and, despite the languor making my limbs heavy, I was eager to search his body as he'd done mine. I could feel his scrutiny but he did nothing to stop me as I peeled back the white cloth and ran my hand along his hard torso. There wasn't an ounce of extra fat; lines of muscle stood out in prominent display beneath olive skin, and small dark nipples. However, scars marred the perfection: one small white irregular star on one shoulder and smaller lines across his chest and belly. I smoothed my hand over them one by one and saw him flinch, but again, he didn't stop me.

Mine. The possessive thought surprised me. I skimmed my fingers up the line of his abdomen, across his pectorals, then leaned down to study his face. He watched me impassively as I traced the curve of his cheek, down past a strong chin with skin that, while clean shaven, still had a slight sandpaper bite. So very beautiful. Cupping his jaw, I levered myself up using his shoulder, then lowered my hips onto his hard member as I bent down toward his face.

A large hand clamped on my shoulder, and I stopped only inches from his lips. The look in his eyes was difficult to read, a guarded yearning I didn't understand. His hand stopped me from bending down, but nothing halted my hips, which continued their downward travel, taking him inside me. Jeremiah swallowed, his throat moving. I undulated my hips, pulling up then pressing him deeper, and he let out a stuttering breath. The hand on my shoulder loosened, and I continued down, pressing my mouth against his neck, then trailing down toward the star-shaped scar on his chest as I rolled my hips again.

I traced the white tissue with my lips, drawing a finger over one small dark nipple. Up close the scar was larger than I'd thought; the skin around it wasn't as discolored but still puckered from the past trauma. I looked up to see him watching me with that incomprehensible look; his full lips were open, and I desperately wanted to see what they tasted like. Rising over him again, I traced my fingers again down the side of his face. "You're so beautiful," I breathed, my eyes roaming over him.

The longing in his eyes deepened as my eyes fell again to his mouth, then he lifted a hand to tangle in my hair, and brought my mouth to his. Our lips clashed in a sudden hunger; his other hand dug into my hip as I rode him hard, hands stroking his torso.

Somewhere beside us a cell phone vibrated, a persistent distraction. "Sounds like someone really wants to talk to you," I purred, grinning down at him.

"They can call back later," he growled, then thrust his hips up, pressing his hardness up deep inside me. I gasped, all thoughts of the caller flying from my head. He rolled me over onto my back and, teeth finding my neck, he hammered me into the mattress. I gripped him with my thighs, moaning, as he pierced me again and again. My fingernails dug into his shoulders, using his hard body for leverage as I met his thrusts with my own. He tugged my hair, wrenching my head back to look at his face. Desperate need shone bright in his eyes and I felt a moment's triumph when he grunted, surging inside me one last time as he came.

I closed my eyes, and held on to his shuddering body. His weight atop me held me secure and I sighed in contentment. "I . . ."

Love you.

My eyes popped open at the unbidden thought. Horrified at what I'd been about to say, I stared at the ceiling as Jeremiah stirred in my arms, finally rolling off me and onto his feet beside the bed. I swallowed, suddenly breathless—had I really been about to say that?

Silently I moved to the other side of the bed and then fled to the hallway bathroom, bypassing the open area linked to the master bedroom. Locking the door behind me, I stared at my reflection in the mirror, still horrified by my own thought processes.

I'd known the man for, what, two days? Certainly not long enough to declare any kind of affection. Yet those three words had almost popped out, and that shook me up. My hands trembled as I turned on the warm water in the sink and grabbed a wash cloth to clean myself.

I'd never had any real relationships where "the words" had been exchanged. Even as a teen, I'd been too pragmatic to say it in reference to anyone but family. The fact that I'd been poised to let them slip out of my mouth caused more than a little distress.

It's silly to think about that this early, I admonished myself, then remembered my father had always said he'd fallen for my mother the moment he saw her. I swallowed at the memory; my dad had been the romantic of the family, my mom the more practical partner. I'd taken after my mom; I was always more inclined to look before I leaped, but this whole situation was foreign territory.

There came the sound of knocking, startling me out of my reverie. Poking my head out the door, I heard it again coming from the entrance to the suite. Glad for the distraction, I grabbed a robe off the nearby hook. Slipping it over my body, I padded to the door, peering through the small peephole. A uniformed hotel worker stood there, holding something in his hands I couldn't quite make out. Curious, I opened the door a crack. "Yes?"

The man gave a small bow. "A gift for Mr. Hamilton and guest," he said in flawless English, presenting a bottle and two champagne flutes.

My eyebrows went up and, not knowing what else to do, I took them from the servant's hands. He gave another little bow, then backed up a step as I closed the door. I turned into the suite, paused, then opened the door again. "Do I owe you anything for . . . ?" The man had already disappeared, however, so with a shrug I shut and locked the door again, carrying the bottle and glasses into the bedroom.

Jeremiah sprawled in a tall chair, frowning at the phone in his hand. When he saw me, his expression cleared and, to my surprise, a small smile spread across his lips. My heart skipped a beat; he was so beautiful, it was hard to believe he was all mine.

For now. I frowned at the pessimistic thought. Reality always intruded at the worst times.

He extended his hand. "Come here." When I padded over and took his hand, he said, "Kneel."

I did as he said without thinking, lowering myself to the floor. His hand stroked my hair as I settled to my knees. A part of me wondered why I obeyed him so readily; I wasn't a card-carrying feminist but I did have my pride. Somehow though, allowing him control gave me a measure of peace I hadn't felt in a long time. I'd been so burdened with my life that, in a way, this felt like a vacation. Seeing the approval in his eyes also made it worthwhile, although the practical side of me refused to delve too deeply as to why. "Who called you?" I asked.

"Nobody important, or they would have left a message," he answered, then gestured to what I held in my hands. "What's this?"

"A gift, apparently."

He reached down and took the bottle and glasses. "Good champagne," he said, examining the bottle. "Must be from one of the patrons tonight."

I stared at the bottle, wondering how he knew it was a good vintage. "I've never had champagne before."

Jeremiah gave me a surprised look. "Never?"

I shook my head. "I only ever had sparkling cider as a youngster, and when I was old enough I never got invited to functions that served it."

"Well, then." Taking the flutes and bottle in one hand, he helped me to my feet then steered me with a hand on my back toward the suite's kitchenette. "At least your first taste will be an expensive bottle."

I watched in amusement as he unwound the wire cage from the lip, then he pointed the bottle toward the wall and popped the cork. Taking the two flutes, he filled them just below halfway before handing me a stem. "Drink."

The pale yellow liquid fizzed in the glass, looking no different from the sparkling fluid I'd always grown up with as a kid and young adult. Curious, I took a sip, then wrinkled my nose at the bitterness, the liquid making bubbles on my tongue. A second sip did little to endear me to the expensive drink. "Ugh, I'm not cut out to be a lush."

Jeremiah laughed, and the sound startled me. He seemed more relaxed and open, and for the life of me I couldn't understand what had happened. The look he gave me of almost boyish amusement had my heart doing flip-flops. Does the man realize how gorgeous he is when he looks at a girl like that?

"Perhaps it is a bit of an acquired taste." He swirled the liquid lightly in the glass but continued to watch me.

I flushed at his perusal, then kicked myself. *Take some initiative, girl,* I chided myself. "Have you ever had a body shot?"

It was his turn to look startled; his eyebrows shot nearly to his hairline. "Have you?" he countered, and seemed unsurprised when I shook my head. Amusement lit his face and I watched him in wonder. His mood had turned almost playful, not at all the brooding, domineering man I'd seen so far. The challenge in his eyes, however, stirred the rebel in me because I met his gaze with an eyebrow quirk of my own. Holding his eyes, I leaned my head back and tipped my glass over my chest, the fluid splashing onto the robe and down between my breasts.

My audacity had the desired effect. Jeremiah's eyes darkened and he reached out, pulling me back into his arms. "You are quite the tease," he said, plucking the glass from my hand and lowering his lips to my neck.

My belly cramped, and I flinched, but tried not to think much about it. Jeremiah's lips trailed down my neck toward the expensive liquid coating my breasts, but when my stomach twisted a second time, I gave a little gasp, my body bowing forward. The amusement vanished from Jeremiah's face as he pulled me upright. "What's wrong?"

His harsh voice demanded an answer, but I had none to give. "Don't . . . feel good," I managed, then stumbled toward the kitchen sink. I barely made it there before retching, unloading the meager contents of my stomach into the basin. My legs were turning to jelly and I was having difficulty keeping myself upright, even while bracing myself against the marble countertop.

I heard the sound of breaking glass behind me, and I looked to see a dark stain on one wall, the remnants of the champagne flute and its previous contents drifting to the floor. Jeremiah grabbed a nearby phone as I retched again. "I need a doctor in this suite immediately," he barked, then my legs gave out and he dropped the phone on the counter to catch me as I fell. "Lucy, stay with me."

My stomach heaved, clenching and twisting, and I cried

out. A hand smoothed my suddenly damp hair back from my face as I shuddered, moaning, no longer in control of my body. I felt myself being lowered to the ground, and Jeremiah's blurry silhouette came across my field of vision.

"I need a doctor now!" A rushing sound filled my ears. Jeremiah's voice was dulled as if coming through water, but I could hear the frantic note in his words. Then my body stiffened, muscles constricting almost painfully, and the world went dark.

13

I was eight years old the first time I got the flu. It was bad, enough so that I had to be rushed to the hospital. While I can't remember much, I do remember vividly the aches and pains as my body struggled to rid itself of every last vestige of the foul disease.

Waking up in that hospital room felt similar, like waking from a painful dream. Eyes still closed, I turned my head to the side, the simple movement making me dizzy and nauseous. At my moan there was a commotion next to me, then a strangely familiar man's voice said, "Get the doctor."

Why was that voice familiar? Who . . . Thinking made my head hurt so I gave up for a while, trying to keep as still as possible. After a moment the nausea subsided and I cracked open one eye, then the other.

I was in a well-lit room, the bright fluorescent lights above like knives in my skull. Figuring for the time being it would be better to keep my eyes closed, I listened as several people filed into the room.

anything he wants • 129

"Ms. Delacourt, my name is Doctor Montague. I'm going to need you to open your eyes."

"Hurts," I mumbled, my tongue sticking to the roof of a dry mouth. I tried opening my eyes again and it was a little better this time. The room and its occupants were fuzzy. The tall figure beside my bed leaned in close and shined a light in my eyes. I flinched but the pain from before was already subsiding and he only did a few sweeps before pulling the penlight away.

"How do you feel?" The doctor spoke very good English but I could hear the slight French accent beneath his words.

"Like I've been hit by a bus," I said softly. "Am I still in Paris?"

"*Oui,* you were brought here soon after your little incident."

"Where's Jeremiah?" I struggled to pull myself upright, ignoring the explosion in my head and the doctor's restraining hand. "Is he okay?"

"He's been coordinating with French officials on investigating what happened," a different voice stated. "Discreetly."

It took me a moment to recognize the familiar form beside the bed. I barely made out Ethan's bald head through blurry vision. "So he wasn't . . . ?"

"No, he wasn't poisoned," he replied, correctly guessing my unspoken question, and I let out the breath I was holding. "He's been going through various channels to try and find the culprit. I sent word that you're awake; he should be here any moment."

Hearing that Jeremiah was okay and on his way eased a burden inside my chest. The doctor handed me a glass of water as I glanced toward the clock, then the dark window. "How long was I out?"

"Three days," Ethan replied, and I coughed on the water I'd just swallowed. The big man shifted. "We didn't know how it would end up. Lucky for you, Jeremiah has some medic training."

"I almost died?" My words were a whisper and I found it difficult to come to grips with the idea.

"You were a very sick woman, Ms. Delacourt." The doctor took my cup and set it beside me on the table I finally saw clearly. "If not for the resourcefulness of Mr. Hamilton, we would not be having this conversation."

I stared at my hands for a long moment, emotions all jumbled together in my head. "I'm tired," I murmured, sliding back down the bed.

"Before you sleep," Ethan said, stepping toward me, "I'd really like to ask you a few questions about the man who brought the bottle to your room."

Everything in me went cold. "You think he was the one who . . . ?"

"That's what we're trying to find out."

The familiar deep voice made my heart leap. Jeremiah peered at me from the doorway, face inscrutable. He walked into the room and stood at the foot of the bed, and I thought I saw relief in his eyes before he glanced at the doctor. "How is she?"

"Awake, and that is a good sign. I'd like to keep her a little longer for observation."

Jeremiah nodded at the doctor, who returned the nod

and silently left the room. Fear settled over me like an oppressive blanket and I blindly reached for Jeremiah's hand when he took the empty spot beside me, not caring who saw the action. Someone tried to kill me. The very thought made my heart race.

"What do you remember about the man who delivered the champagne?" Ethan asked as I clung to Jeremiah's hand.

"He was ordinary," I said, then winced at the phrase. Way to be unhelpful. "He was white, dressed like a hotel employee, and had medium-brown hair and brown eyes I think."

"Hair and eye color can be changed," Jeremiah interjected. "What about facial features? Any scars or moles?"

Thinking made my head ache but I closed my eyes anyway, trying to recall the brief glimpse I'd had of his face. A few moments later, a picture emerged in my mind. "He had kind of deep-set eyes, thin lips, and was a couple inches taller than me. Um, I think he had a mole on his left temple and a scar on his chin, but I don't know how much of that might've been makeup."

Jeremiah's and Ethan's gazes met briefly and my heart sank. I had probably just described half the country.

"What did he sound like?" Ethan asked after scribbling notes on a small notepad.

"He spoke English really well. I thought he sounded American." Frustrated, I thumped my hand on the mattress. "I don't know. He seemed like a normal hotel employee and I didn't think to look that hard." A thought occurred to me. "What about the security cameras? There has to be something on them."

Both men shook their heads. "We already checked," Jeremiah said. "Whoever it was knew exactly where even the hidden cameras pointed. We never got a face shot."

I slumped in the bed. "Is there anything I can do to help?"

Jeremiah's phone went off, and he pulled it out to check the screen. "I need to take this," he said, pulling his hand free from my grasp. "Ethan, see if you can find an artist to draw what she remembers. I'll be back."

Tears pricked my eyes as I watched him leave the room. *Silly girl,* I chided myself, blinking hard, *he still has to do his job.* It still hurt to have him gone, however; there was security in his presence that I didn't feel with a simple bodyguard.

"You know, this whole deal hit him pretty hard."

I looked over at Ethan, wiping my leaking eyes. The bald man wasn't looking at me, too busy typing into his phone, but I could still sense his attention. "What do you mean?"

He didn't answer for a moment, intent on his phone, then clipped it to his belt and looked at me. "How long have you two known one another again?"

The question felt like an interrogation and I frowned. "A few days, why?"

Ethan grunted. "He's pulled out all the stops trying to find out who did this. I haven't seen him this motivated in a long time. Even when we were in the military, or there were threats on his life now as CEO, he wasn't this driven for answers."

My mouth dropped open. "Really?"

Ethan shrugged one shoulder like it was nothing. "When we were in the army, we were involved in some dangerous missions, but to hear him talk, such things were par for the course. Even now, given the cutthroat business he does, he's received a lot of threats from all quarters. In fact, just after he agreed to sponsor my company, someone tried to shoot him outside his building." Ethan snorted. "Jeremiah had already broken the man's wrist and taken the gun by the time I got close."

"What happened next?" I asked when Ethan trailed off, looking at his phone again.

"Nothing. He told me to find out who was behind it and let him know, then got on a plane for Dubai. Didn't seem worried in the slightest." Ethan peered at me. "Maybe it's because you got hurt on his behalf, he tends to be rather protective of people in his employ or care. Either way, Celeste has taken over business operations while he focuses on this manhunt and tries to keep the press from getting wind."

"So, the person on the phone just now . . . ?"

"Was probably one of his contacts. If he didn't want us to listen in, it was probably one that I don't approve of. Either way, he's gone to extremes on this one."

Jeremiah chose then to come back inside, stowing his phone in his pocket. I got my first glimpse outside the hallway and saw two men dressed in black, standing on either side of the entryway before the door closed again. Even has guards posted at the entrance. How much trouble are we in?

"I have the boys looking for an artist now," Ethan said. "Hopefully we can get someone up here within the next few hours."

"Good." Jeremiah moved to my bed then frowned down at me. "You should be resting."

"Who was that on the phone?" I asked bluntly. When his eyes narrowed, clearly annoyed with the question, I persisted. "If it has something to do with me then I should know. Who tried to kill us?"

Jeremiah glared at Ethan but the big security expert once again had his eyes fixed on his phone, deliberately ignoring our conversation. "I'm not sure yet," Jeremiah finally said. "I gave them the description you provided and they're hopeful. Now, rest."

My body demanded I follow the order—I'd been fighting to stay awake anyway, but I still struggled to keep awake. "You won't leave?" I asked, pushing myself deeper under the sheets.

His eyes softened a bit. "I'll be nearby," he promised, and at his words I finally closed my eyes, letting my exhaustion overtake me.

I stayed in the hospital for three more days under observation. The doctor seemed optimistic about my recovery, but I felt weaker than a baby. Needing help to do simple things like walk proved frustrating and I was determined to do it on my own. After I slipped and nearly fell trying to get myself to the attached bathroom, however, Jeremiah ordered that I have constant help available, whether by nurses or bodyguards.

Most of my days were spent sleeping, but it quickly grew boring staying in the hospital bed. When I mentioned this to Ethan, the hulking bodyguard who was an ever-present fixture in my room, a brand-new tablet, still in the box, appeared beside my bed soon afterward. The device gave me something to do with my spare time, and I spent most of it researching my new boss.

I'd joked before that I only knew the Wikipedia version of his life, but as it turned out that's all the rest of the world knew too. There were articles on him that mentioned his time as an Army Ranger, talked about his charity work, and went into detail on his business ventures, but I knew all this already. The media threw out words like "mysterious" and "enigmatic" when they described him, and the words seemed appropriate given the lack of any in-depth information through nearly all channels. Articles on the corporate changeover after his father's death were similarly shallow, mainly analyst predictions on where the company would go under new management, on whether a man who had minimal business education could really take over for the tycoon Rufus Hamilton, and so on.

By day three of my stay I was walking on my own again, just in time to leave the hospital. Our exit felt like something out of an espionage movie: I was shuffled to the basement garage by the bodyguards and carefully packed into a waiting limo that I assumed would take us to the airport. Jeremiah watched over everything, never leaving my side, even maintaining a possessive grip around my shoulders as we drove out of the parking garage.

I dozed through most of the trip, using Jeremiah's shoulder as a pillow. I awoke once an indeterminate amount of time later to see we were no longer in the city but didn't think anything of it, nodding back to sleep until the car finally stopped. Jeremiah shifted under me and I lifted my head, gazing blearily out the window. Grasslands surrounded us, the tall weeds waving in the wind. *This definitely isn't the airport,* I thought, rubbing my eyes. "Where are we?"

Jeremiah didn't answer the question, merely edged toward the door as it was opened from the outside. "Come find out," he said, taking my arm to help me out of the car. Nearby stood a building that looked vaguely familiar, and below the wind I thought I heard the rhythmic wash of ocean waves. There were other cars parked nearby and a few tourists milled about in the chill air, but the grassy hills seemed barren of much else. Sleep still fogging my brain, I struggled to identify where I was, the whole area familiar to me somehow.

Several men in dark suits were scattered around the area and one black man came jogging up to us. "The place is secure, sir," he said, and Jeremiah nodded. I peered curiously along the rolling hills, seeing a few memorial stones jutting from the earth but nothing that jogged my memory. It wasn't until I saw both the French and American flags waving high above the building's entrance, however, that I finally realized where I was.

"You brought me to Utah Beach," I whispered in stunned surprise. The historical site, only one of numerous coastlines used for the World War II Normandy invasion, was something I'd only seen before in pictures or on television with my father. The smell of the water unmistakable, the ocean, difficult to see through the winter haze, was directly behind the building. Speechless, I looked over at Jeremiah, my eyes filling with unshed tears. I'd only mentioned the location once, and had been certain he'd forgotten our conversation, but this was proof he actually had been listening to me.

Jeremiah took off his jacket and slipped it around my shoulders when I shivered. "You mentioned this was someplace you wanted to visit." He looked uncomfortable and edgy, and I wondered if it was my tears. "They have a museum with artifacts from the invasion itself. We can also go down to the water if you're up for it."

His voice was gruff and his demeanor short, but I'd grown used to it and didn't care. Happiness suffused me at the sight of a place I'd always dreamed of visiting. The wind off the water was chilly, cooling the already frosty winter air; the sky was overcast and looked like it might spit snow at any moment. The small photo my father had kept on the mantel didn't do it justice; the site was massive and sprawling, perhaps too much for my current state but, oh, I wanted to see it all!

Emotion choked me up suddenly, and I slipped my hand around Jeremiah's fingers. He stiffened and I saw him swallow, then his fingers relaxed into mine. "Help me inside?" I asked, burrowing myself deep inside his coat.

His gaze softened as he peered down at me, then he lifted my hand to his lips. "I'd be honored."

Looking around at a place I'd only seen in pictures online, I found myself tearing up.

14

We didn't stay at Utah Beach nearly as long as I would have liked. Jeremiah never left my side as I pulled him from one exhibit to the next. I felt myself weakening after less than an hour so asked to go down to the beaches before I faded completely. He obliged me but cut the trip short after I stumbled twice and was shivering uncontrollably from the chill air despite the multiple layers of clothing I wore.

Jeremiah promised me I could come back again when I wasn't as sick or it wasn't so cold, and I believed him.

I slept nearly the entire plane trip back to New York, waking only when we touched down at the airport. True to his word, Jeremiah never left my side as we moved quickly through airport security to the waiting limo, which pulled out to parts unknown, at least to me. I rested my head on Jeremiah's shoulder as his hand moved around to my inner thigh, holding fast. There was nothing overtly sexual but I could feel the possession in his grip and didn't mind at all.

When I saw the beautiful large homes through the windows

of the limo, I lifted my head to stare at the passing scenery. Partial sunlight from the overcast day reflected off the water nearby, and we passed a marina with large sailboats and more than a few yachts. "Where are we going?" I finally asked.

"The Manhattan loft is too public to keep secure. My family home in the Hamptons allows much more security until we get to the bottom of this mess."

Jeremiah growled the last part of his reply and I swallowed, reminded of what was at stake. Turning my attention to the passing houses—no, mansions or estates were better descriptions—I tried not to think about how weird my life had become.

Few of the palatial homes we passed had any similarities to one another besides their size, not in terms of architecture, property, or grandeur. I'd never been to this section of Long Island or any of the more affluent sections of New York, but had heard it described by friends growing up and had seen pictures on TV and the Internet. Many homes along the coastline had piers leading out into the water with large entertainment areas that looked like parks, with green well-manicured lawns dotted with tables and chairs. Despite the obvious wealth in the area, many of the older estates along the water had a homey and well-worn feel to them, light and happy—so different from the big city only a couple of hours away.

The property our limo turned into was no less grand yet more forbidding than its neighbors. The small army of guards at the gate who made us roll down the window didn't make me feel any better, but Jeremiah seemed content with the security. "Is it always like this?" I asked as the big gates drew open.

"I had Ethan bring in nonessential personnel from his security business to watch the premises. Most of them are ex-soldiers so they know what to watch for."

"Oh," I said faintly, unsure how to respond. So he does have an army. "That's, um, great."

The driveway, while not long, was lined with hedges and trees that obscured the estate. It curved to the right and I sucked in a breath at the sight. My family had been middle class, and our home had been nice if not large. So the fact that my old house was a quarter the size of the building before me took my breath away. I could feel Jeremiah's gaze on me and felt I should say something, but I couldn't think of what. The house reminded me of an English castle, all heavy stone and ivy. The residence was blocked off from neighbors by trees and thick brush, but the grounds extended past the house down toward the water. Behind and to the side of the house, I could see a few smaller structures that I assumed accommodated the army surrounding us. The ground dipped sharply toward the water, and a boathouse jutted horizontally from the small hillside out over the water.

An expensive red car was already parked near the main entrance, and beside me I heard Jeremiah give an annoyed sigh. The limo stopped behind the car and as our driver moved around to open our door I saw a slim, blond woman step out of the other vehicle. "Who's that?" I asked.

"Family."

The grumbled word held a wealth of meaning but Jeremiah was already exiting the car before I could ask for more details. He helped me out of the vehicle as the blond woman made her way toward us. She was older than I'd first thought, although it was hard to tell her exact age; her lips looked too full and the skin of her face looked artificially tight and stretched. Only the semiloose skin on her neck and prominent collarbones, courtesy of a superthin frame, gave away her maturity.

"Darling, it's so lovely to see you." The woman opened her arms and embraced a stiff Jeremiah, who didn't return the favor. "The men up front said you were on your way so I waited. Would you believe they wouldn't let the Dashwoods in? They were so looking forward to a tour of the estate."

"The Dashwoods are not on the approved guest list." Jeremiah's voice was polite but strained, as if he was reining back his temper. "What are you doing here?"

The chilly reception didn't seem to faze the woman at all. "I told you, darling, I was merely giving the Dashwoods a brief tour of the estate. They were so looking forward to it and I think you hurt their feelings by turning them away. Perhaps now we can call them back?"

My presence hadn't yet been noticed, which was a relief. The woman was dressed to the nines in a tailored blouse and skirt that matched her shoes and small purse perfectly. I, on the other hand, wore wrinkled and travel-worn clothing, and I'd lost enough weight in the hospital for them to sag on my frame. I hadn't cared how I looked until this moment, so I tried to keep myself as invisible as possible. I'd grown very adept at the skill; our move from Canada to upstate New York my freshman year of high school had been tough, leaving me struggling to rid myself of an accent I never knew I had. I'd always been more of a loner anyway; blending in with large groups was just easier since I never had a flair for being in the spotlight.

Jeremiah sighed at the other woman's statement. "This isn't your house anymore."

The argument sounded old, and the woman shrugged it off. "Nonsense, darling, I'm still allowed to visit the old place from time to time." Her gaze turned to me, taking in my haggard appearance, and her eyes chilled. "Really, Jeremiah, must you bring your bits on the side to the family home? What if the press were to see her?"

My jaw dropped open at her words and my hands curled into fists, indignation spreading through my body. That bitch! I was so angry my mind couldn't think of anything to say that wasn't cursing or didn't lead to some kind of physical altercation.

Even Jeremiah was annoyed by the implication, stepping forward as if to shield us from each other while I fumed, my body tense. "That's enough, Mother," he snapped.

His words sent a jolt through me, and I stared between the two, incredulous. *This shrew is his mom?*

The woman sniffed in irritation, rolling her eyes at the reprimand. "Well, then?" she asked after a brief pause, looking annoyed. "Aren't you going to introduce us?"

Jeremiah looked like he'd just bitten into a lemon but his manners prevailed, even if he didn't like it. "May I present

Ms. Lucille Delacourt, my new assistant. Lucy, this is my mother, Georgia Hamilton."

"Back to this charade again?" The condescension in his mother's tone was palpable.

Jeremiah didn't seem inclined to belabor the point, but I was suddenly unafraid to give the woman a piece of my mind. I opened my mouth to defend myself as the woman in front of us rolled her eyes, then inspiration struck and I plastered a smile on my face. "Hello," I said sweetly in French, laying on the false charm. "You should know that your lips and boobs look like they were done by the same doctor, except he got them backward."

Georgia blinked, obviously surprised. "Ah, you're from France?"

My grin widened as I realized she had no idea what I was saying. "I can see why your sons both have issues," I gushed, gesturing toward her immaculately matching ensemble. "It's a wonder you're still allowed here if this is what he has to put up with every visit."

"Lucy will be helping with the French segments of the business," Jeremiah interjected smoothly as his mother's eyes narrowed in suspicion. He slanted me a look but I couldn't keep the self-satisfied grin off my face. "I've hired translators too long and need someone in-house who speaks it fluently."

I kept the smile on my face but glanced at Jeremiah. *Could he be serious?* I wondered, then discarded the thought. It's probably another ploy to derail his mother. That would, however, be the kind of job I'd love to do. Perhaps we really can mix business with pleasure.

"Ah, well." Georgia smoothed her already impeccable clothes with thin hands. "I still think you had a total peach with that Russian girl, Anya. Started out a bit naïve perhaps, but she cleaned up nicely with a little help from yours truly. Such a shame when you let her go."

Naïve? I snorted. That was not a word I'd use to describe Ms. Petrovski. Jeremiah, however, seemed to disapprove of the conversation's new direction; a line formed between his brows as he frowned at his mother. Georgia merely shrugged, seemingly oblivious to her son's displeasure at the change of topic. "A pleasure to meet you, my dear," she said, but her face didn't seem too pleased. "Perhaps we can do lunch?"

Not on your life. I gritted my teeth, somehow keeping the smile in place as Jeremiah wound his arm through mine. "If you'll excuse us, I must show Lucy to her room."

"Won't you call the Dashwoods first and apologize? They were quite put out."

"Good day, Mother." Jeremiah ushered me toward the door, no more interested in staying with the woman than I was. There was a frustrated sound behind us, then I heard the car door slam as we entered the huge wooden doors leading into the building.

When I stepped inside the house I wasn't sure what to expect. The walls were lined with wood paneling and the sparse pieces of furniture were similarly dark, but the high ceilings and pale walls kept the atmosphere from being too dour. A large staircase twisted up on both sides of the entrance, and light streamed in from the opening beneath the balcony, leading into the rest of the house. Past the stairs and through the opening was a huge kitchen with dark wood cabinets and a large island in the center. The living room was set off by a large television, easily taller than Jeremiah, along the far wall. The back wall was almost entirely lined with glass, leading out onto a large patio overlooking the ocean.

The view took my breath away, but beside me Jeremiah growled in annoyance. "Why is that glass clear?" he said, holding my arm to keep me from entering the room.

"Sorry, sir," one of the men behind us said. "Your mother requested it this way."

"This is no longer my mother's house. Turn it on."

A second later, the view to the ocean disappeared, the glass fogging suddenly. Startled by the change I tensed, but Jeremiah harrumphed and led me into the room. "Smart glass," he said, answering my silent question. "It uses electricity to make the windows opaque. I had it installed throughout the house for privacy."

I'd never seen anything like it before. While I missed the view, the light still scattered through and lit up the room. Across from the TV room was a dining area with a giant dinner table and chairs; beside the table was a fireplace with a large mantel. The tall wall above it looked empty and I wondered what used to hang there.

"Anything else, sir?" Ethan asked, and when Jeremiah shook his head the security detail faded back toward the front door, leaving the two of us alone.

"It's beautiful here," I breathed, looking up at Jeremiah. "This is where you grew up?"

"One of the places." Jeremiah stepped into the kitchen as

I looked around the open living space. "Do I want to know what you said to my mother?" he asked after a moment.

I smiled at the question. "I made a few keen observations, nothing more," I replied, shooting him a sly grin. When he didn't return my smile, merely nodding in response, some of my pleasure diminished. "I promise, I didn't say anything too rude," I added more soberly, not wanting to offend him. This was his mother, after all.

"She can be difficult at times, but it wasn't always like this." He stared off in the distance, momentarily lost in thought. "Keeping house for my father, having to live with his tyrannical dictatorship . . . I think that's why she took to Anya so much; the Russian girl reminded her of who she used to be." Abruptly he switched gears. "Are you hungry?"

Thrown off balance by the sudden subject change, I thought for a moment and then shook my head. "Do you cook? With a place like this, I'd think you would have your own chef."

"My parents did employ a chef when I was growing up, but I found it a waste." He checked inside the refrigerator and the pantry, grunting in approval, then looked back at me. "How do you feel?"

I yawned and stretched. "Tired." I'd slept a lot on the plane but it still didn't seem like enough. Watching Jeremiah and thinking about bed, however, made a shiver go through my body that had nothing to do with the poison. *Hmm, perhaps I'm not as tired as I thought.* He had changed out of the suit and dress attire I normally saw him in sometime during the flight, and now wore a pair of expensive jeans and a white button-down shirt. When I'd seen him in the ensemble for the first time, the change had been a shock but a pleasant one; the way his body filled out the denim made my mouth water, and my hands itched to touch him.

"Let me show you up to your room then." He laid a hand on my back and escorted me out of the room toward the staircase. I leaned against his body as we went up the stairs, winding my arm around his waist. He felt stiff beneath my touch, unresponsive, and I looked up to see him staring straight ahead, a frown deepening his brow. Confused, I pulled my hand back and was disappointed to see him relax. *What's going on?* I wondered, baffled by his response. I thought I'd finally started to understand him, but now he was like a stranger again.

The bedroom he led me into was large by any standard, with a king-sized bed and attached bathroom. All the windows had the same opaqueness and I realized the smart glass I'd seen earlier ran the entirety of the house. Something gave me the impression this wasn't the master bedroom; while spacious, the room lacked the grandeur I would've expected for the master suite. It was on the tip of my tongue to ask what my status was during my stay—was I a guest, or would our arrangement be an open secret?—but as he settled me into the bed, something told me I'd be sleeping alone. Reaching out spontaneously, I grabbed his hand and brought it to my lips, laying a kiss on one thick knuckle.

He stiffened at my touch, freezing for a moment; I thought I saw a flash of yearning race across his face, but if I did, the moment was fleeting. Gently pulling his hand from my grasp, he pressed me back onto the bed. "You need rest," he murmured.

I need you. The thought made my mouth turn down in disappointment. He seemed reluctant to touch me, which hurt more than I thought, but I was tired. Perhaps this was his way of making sure I slept?

Taking a deep breath to relax, I snuggled beneath the covers and closed my eyes, hoping my worries about Jeremiah's actions wouldn't keep me awake. As it turned out, my body did need more rest and before Jeremiah had even left the room, I was out like a light.

15

The sun shone through the nearby window, and I woke feeling more refreshed than I had since my disastrous run-in with the poison-laced champagne. I stretched under the covers before pulling them aside to stand on the carpet. At the end of my bed lay a towel and robe as well as a sleek gray suitcase I assumed was mine, but my stomach rumbled, reminding me I'd turned down a meal before bed. Deciding to skip the bath for now, I padded down the stairs, hoping to find Jeremiah.

Unfortunately it was Ethan who sat at the foot of the stairs, perched atop a barstool that looked out of place in the entryway. He stood as I made my way to the bottom floor. "Good morning."

"Good morning," I replied cautiously. Unsure of what to do, I made my way around him and headed for the kitchen, but didn't see Jeremiah there, either. Sunlight shown in through the clouded glass and I frowned. "What time is it?" I asked.

Ethan looked at his watch. "It's oh-nine-thirty hours."

I blinked at him in surprise. "Wait, it's nine thirty in the morning?" At his nod I asked incredulously, "How long was I asleep?"

"Approximately sixteen hours."

No wonder I feel good. Blowing out a quick breath, I looked inside the refrigerator. "Where's Jeremiah?"

"He's chasing down some possible leads. Left the compound about two hours ago."

I shot him a glance, setting a carton of milk on the counter. "He left you in charge of me then?" At Ethan's nod, I swallowed down my disappointment and headed to the pantry. *Don't be silly, he probably didn't want to wake you when he left.* Coupled with the standoffishness from the previous day, however, I was confused about things. I wanted desperately for someone to hold me and tell me everything was all right.

Except that everything was not all right, a fact I was having trouble coming to terms with. *One problem at a time, Lucy,* I told myself, pulling open a pantry door.

A few minutes later I was munching on some cereal I'd found, staring at my new bodyguard who was reading a gun magazine. He appeared to be ignoring me, but every so often I'd see him touch the microphone in his ear and knew he was listening to the men outside. I watched him for a few minutes, then pointed my spoon in his direction. "Your wife told me you and Jeremiah used to be Army Rangers together."

Ethan grunted, not looking up from the magazine. *Another man of few words,* I thought, remembering the first limo ride in France and how silent he'd been then, too. Remembering I'd

seen the large man limping when we'd first met, I tried another tack. I gestured toward his lower body. "How'd you
hurt your leg?"

"Mission went sour."

"Were you with Jeremiah?"

"No, it happened after he left."

"Why did he leave?"

"Father died."

Getting answers from the bald man was like pulling teeth,
but he was talking so I persisted. "What did Jeremiah do
with the Rangers?"

"Sniper."

My eyebrows shot up. Really? I digested that bit of information for a minute, munching on cereal, then asked, "What
happened when he left?"

The big man was quiet for a moment; I matched his silence for a moment, hoping to ride him out, and finally he
answered. "Pissed off a lot of people."

My jaw stopped working, and I swallowed my food. "Why?"

"He left. Found a loophole or put pressure on the right
people to get a full discharge. Most people thought he was selling out, abandoning his post. It's tough, becoming a Ranger,
and he just gave it up."

"What did you think?"

Ethan glanced up at me. "I made my opinion known to
him well enough."

"So you didn't like the idea, either?" I asked, guessing that's
what he meant.

He hitched a shoulder, eyes back on the magazine. "He

gave up a life many dreamed of having, abandoning his squad. Yes, I had some thoughts on the matter."

"So how did you become head of security for him?"

Ethan sighed and set the magazine on the counter, then turned to face me. Despite his scowl he was answering my questions so I tried not to feel guilty about my persistence. "After I had my accident, Jeremiah shows up at the hospital. Offers me a job if the army doesn't want me anymore. I tell him to get the fuck out and he leaves. Lo and behold, a few months later I get my discharge papers and Jeremiah shows up again, offering me a chance at the business we used to talk about starting when we retired."

"Your security business?"

Ethan nodded. "Jeremiah funded the initial costs but I hope to buy out his portion soon enough."

"Why leave the partnership? Don't the two of you get along?"

Ethan shrugged. "He has bigger fish to fry and I'd rather be in business for myself."

That seemed to conclude any more on the subject but I was still curious. "What was Jeremiah like back then?"

"Younger." At my droll look, a hint of a smile twitched one corner of the man's mouth. "He felt the need to prove himself constantly," Ethan continued, thinking. "He always wanted to be at the forefront of everything, so it came as a surprise when he settled on being a sniper. It helped him, I think, to hone his patience." Ethan cocked his head to the side. "He was never the life of the party but he did know how to relax.

Since his father's death, though, I don't think he's been given much time to do that."

In for a penny, in for a pound. I was getting my questions answered so I might as well ask what else was on my mind. "What about Anya? How did they come together?"

His eyes narrowed and he peered hard at me. I chewed another mouthful of cereal, trying my best to appear innocent. "I probably shouldn't be telling you this," he muttered.

I just munched on my food, giving him an expectant look. It took a minute but he finally rolled his eyes and answered. "Jeremiah had some big Russian deal going down and he needed someone to translate, both for written and verbal communications. Anya fit the bill and became his new personal assistant, moving the previous one to a management position."

"So were they . . ." An item? I couldn't bring myself to say it outright and wasn't sure how much the big bodyguard knew about my relationship with my boss. I colored at his probing look, reaching and pouring more cereal even though I was already full.

"Their personal relationship wasn't any of my business. I could tell she carried a torch but he was impossible to read. Either way, when he found out she was sneaking secrets to his brother, Jeremiah fired her and threw her out. That was probably close to three years ago now."

"What was she like?" I couldn't help but ask.

"Young. Inexperienced. 'Fresh off the farm' like my grandma would say. Smart though, and fluent in two languages.

Jeremiah actually found her in Russia and brought her over here, but once he kicked her out she was on her own."

Poor Anya. Despite the blond woman's arrogance now, I felt bad for the poor displaced young girl. Maybe she got what she deserved, but it was harsh nevertheless. "What about Lucas? Why did Jeremiah call him Loki?"

Ethan shifted, his frown deepening into a scowl. "Loki is the rotten vine on the family tree, and that's saying something. Fucking waste of space, if you ask me."

The sudden vehemence in the bald bodyguard's voice surprised me. Wow, tell me how you really feel. "Is Loki a childhood nickname, or something else?" I persisted, wondering if I had pushed my luck bringing up the obviously volatile subject. "What happened between him and Jeremiah?"

"Besides Loki becoming everything Jeremiah and I once stood against?" Ethan growled. "His problems with Jeremiah happened before I left the military, but the little shit stole thirty million dollars from the company right as Jeremiah took over, then fled to parts unknown."

I blew out a breath. That's a lot of money. "What did he do with the money?"

"Hell if I know—probably started buying weapons." At my confused look, Ethan shrugged. "Loki is the name he goes by now, chose it himself as far as I can tell. I guess his old name sounded too posh to use. He's an arms dealer, makes his money selling weapons to countries that want to blow others up."

My spoon clattered in my bowl as I stared, dumbfounded, at the large man. Ethan's thunderous expression was intimidating and he looked like he wanted to say more, but when he saw my shock his jaw tightened. "I shouldn't have said anything," he muttered, grabbing the magazine again. "Those weren't my secrets to tell."

My brain meanwhile was having a hard time wrapping itself around the facts. I danced with . . . an arms dealer? The sarcastic blue-green eyes popped again into my mind's eye, the familiar and beautiful face marred by a scar across one cheek. *What have I gotten myself into?*

There was a click as the front door opened and Ethan shot to his feet, startling me. He relaxed almost immediately, and a second later Jeremiah walked through the entryway and into the kitchen. I smiled, relieved to see him, but my happiness dimmed when he barely spared me a glance.

"Any luck?" Ethan asked.

Jeremiah shook his head, lips thinning. "I've made inquiries," he said. "I should know in the next day or so."

Ethan frowned but nodded. "I'll be outside then if you need me."

I watched Jeremiah as Ethan strode out of the room. "You look tired," I said, tilting my head to the side.

"I'll be fine." Jeremiah blew out a breath, then looked at me. "How are you?"

"Better." I gestured at the empty bowl in front of me. "Got my appetite back."

He nodded, then his gaze zeroed in on my rumpled clothes. "I left you some bath supplies and clothes at the foot of your bed."

"I saw that, thank you. I was going to shower after I had

breakfast." I shivered, suddenly nervous—I had little experience with outright seduction—then looked up at him through my lashes. "Want to join me?"

He went rigid, hands curling along the edge of the countertop. I saw the fire in his eyes, then to my surprise he shook his head. "I have things I need to take care of before the morning's over."

I hadn't expected his denial, and even though I knew he had every right to say no, the rejection stung. He's busy, someone's trying to kill us plus he has a big business to run.

"Let me help you upstairs."

His hand wrapped around my upper arm but I dug in my heels. "What have you found out so far?" I asked, looking up at him. Jeremiah pursed his lips, looking annoyed—whether at my defiance or the situation at large, I couldn't tell. *Damned if I'll let him see me cry,* I thought furiously, staring defiantly into his eyes.

"Nothing yet," he said, tugging on my arm. "Let's get you upstairs."

I pulled my arm from his grip. "Thank you, I can manage fine on my own," I said with as much dignity as I could muster. His subtle rejection, combined with the previous night's dismissal, left me annoyed and determined to do without his help. I'd barely taken a step up the stairs, however, when Jeremiah grabbed me and swept me into his arms. I squeaked, latching on around his neck, then frowned as he carried me up the steps. "I could have done this, you know," I said, trying not to sound pouty.

"You're my responsibility," he said, taking the stairs two at a time.

Yay, I'm a "responsibility" now. I snorted. "You sure know how to make a girl feel good."

"It doesn't matter as long as you're safe."

I rolled my eyes but tightened my grip around his neck. While he wasn't always the most romantic sort, I did feel safer with him. "Maybe later you can give me a tour of the grounds?" I said as we reached the top of the steps. "I'd love to go down by the water."

Jeremiah shook his head. "Until we figure out what's going on, you're to stay inside the house."

My jaw dropped. "I'm under house arrest?"

"There are too many places outside that are accessible from long-range. Until I can figure out a way to mitigate those risks, you're staying inside these walls."

His tone brooked no argument, which automatically made me want to rebel. I tried however to see it from his point of view. He used to be a sniper so he'd know all about long-distance dangers, and while the thought of someone watching my actions through a scope was disconcerting and more than a little frightening, the prospect of being a shut-in rankled. "What if I wore a bulletproof vest?" I asked. "Maybe a Kevlar helmet? Do they even make those?"

My request made him snort what might have been a small laugh. He set me down outside my room door, and gently directed me inside. "Go shower. The house is yours, but no going outside." He brushed an errant strand of blond hair behind my ear, fingers running along my jaw. "I need you safe, that's all that matters at this point."

I tried to lean my face into his hand, aching for his caress, but he pulled away his hand and stepped back. Giving me a curt nod, he turned and left me standing in the doorway, silently fuming. *This makes no sense,* I wanted to rail at him, *you're the one the assassin is after yet YOU get to traipse all over the grounds!*

The shower was quick and did little to calm me down. I slung the robe around me, wrapping my head in a towel, and headed downstairs again, only to be brought up against another large guard at the base of the steps. I hadn't expected strangers inside the house and wrapped the robe tightly against me as his gaze turned upward. "Where's Jeremiah?" I asked.

"He had business outside, ma'am. We'll be down here if you need anything."

Swallowing, I nodded jerkily then fled upstairs for clothing.

16

After two days in the gorgeous mansion, I was going stir-crazy.

There was only so much a girl could do inside and, while the house was large, I'd exhausted its mysteries. Well, as much as one could with only their curiosity and the Internet. I watched television, surfed the Internet, and tried to keep myself as busy as a house arrest would allow. I was hyper-aware of everything going on around me, always expecting some armed bandit or assassin to barge through the door, and it was exhausting. Worse yet, nobody would tell me what progress if any was being made. Jeremiah more often than not was absent from the house, and the bodyguards weren't talking, so I was on my own. It felt illogical to resent my captivity since it was for my own good, but I found small ways to rebel, even if only in my mind.

There was one bathroom window that wasn't barred or fogged, looking out over the side of the building across a well-manicured landscape. I took my showers there every morning to peek outside, feeling silly for the thrill the small defiance gave me. The window looked out toward the ocean butting up against the rear of the property, with a boathouse sitting near the water's edge attached to a long pier. There was usually a guard in view, and a gardening truck with a small group of workers arrived every other day to make sure the grounds stayed gorgeous. I longed to go down by the water, maybe dip my toes off the pier, but invariably I'd remember Jeremiah's words about long-distance sniping and would close the window in fear. That emotion more than anything kept me imprisoned inside the house and only added to my bitterness.

That didn't mean, however, that everything was boring.

I had free rein of the entire house, with the exception of Jeremiah's office. Eager to learn more about my employer-slash-lover, I made my own tour, noting everything I could find. There were surprisingly few personal effects, with no pictures of family on the wall or mantel. While beautifully decorated, it could have been anyone's palatial mansion. Considering the history I'd been told about the house, I would have expected something unique, yet never found anything that tied it to the Hamilton family.

Until day three, when I found an old painting at the back of the master bedroom closet.

The picture was large, almost as tall as me and framed with a thick, heavy wood. I muscled it out of the large closet and leaned it against a nearby wall facing the light, then took off the covering sheet. At first I thought it was an actual photograph, blown up to nearly life-size, until I noticed upon closer inspection around the face and hair the subtle, telltale sign of brushstrokes. I didn't immediately recognize the face staring at me, although I could see a resemblance to both Jeremiah and his brother, Lucas. The man was young and wore a suit and tie, no different to my untrained eye from any today, and appeared to be about the age of Jeremiah.

The artist, whoever he was, was a master of his craft, capturing the haughty domination in both the eyes and face of the subject. As I stared into the face captured forever on the canvas, I finally realized with a shock the man's identity: Rufus Hamilton, the former patriarch to the Hamilton family and Jeremiah's father.

"What are you doing?" a sharp voice came from behind me. I jumped at the voice and twirled around to see Jeremiah standing framed in the doorway, eyes fixed firmly on the painting. He moved farther into the room but didn't approach, as if the very sight of the portrait repulsed him.

I started to stammer out an apology, then an idea struck me and, nervous at being caught, I blurted, "Did this used to hang in the dining room?"

The question was a diversion, an attempt to dodge any possible wrath coming my way, and I could tell from his reaction I'd succeeded. "Why aren't there any family photos in the house?" I asked when he didn't answer. "You grew up in this house, surely there are some mementos from—"

"I had them taken down when I acquired the property." Jeremiah's voice was curt, his demeanor stiff. He finally turned his gaze to me. "I preferred not to have the reminders of my childhood."

"Really?" The answer seemed so foreign to me, but I knew my upbringing had been radically different. I'd met his mother, and from all I'd heard about his father, Rufus, Jeremiah's life hadn't been all sunshine and roses. Still, it was hard for me to grasp. "You don't have *any* happy memories of this house?"

Jeremiah's mouth twisted cynically as he eyed the painting. "My father didn't like fun unless it was only to impress others. Trips to this house were more for business than any kind of pleasure, usually to court new clients." He snorted. "Rufus subscribed to the old-school style of parenting: children were to be seen and not heard. We . . . weren't always accommodating."

I tried to imagine a younger Jeremiah, but found it difficult. If Lucas was anything like now, I'm sure he made himself heard. Jeremiah though . . . "What was your childhood like?"

The question was impertinent and probably too personal; I wouldn't have been surprised if he hadn't answered. So it surprised me when he replied, "Very structured. You knew your place, or faced dire consequences. Rufus was older when he married my mother and had children; I honestly think my mother didn't know what she was getting into. He had his idea of the perfect family that would look good on paper, and controlled everything about it with an iron fist." He lapsed into silence, staring hard at the picture beside me. "My brother, as you might suspect, didn't always play along. Eventually, when I was in high school, Lucas seemed to straighten out his antics and genuinely learned how to run the business."

There was a fondness in his words that intrigued me.

"You idolized him, didn't you?" At Jeremiah's severe look, I quickly amended my statement. "Your brother, Lucas. Did you look up to him?"

Indecision warred on his face as he debated whether to answer my questions. I wondered how much information I could get out of him before he clammed up again. How much exactly did the world know about the Hamilton family dynamics? Am I encroaching on sacred territory? It was on the tip of my tongue to retract the question when he finally answered. "Lucas shielded me from my father in ways I didn't understand until I grew older. He and my father clashed while we grew up, often when he stepped in to distract Rufus from giving me my punishment for some infraction or another. As we grew older and he moved away for college, then life, I lost that barrier but by then I could take care of myself."

"So when you found out about the money . . ." I said slowly, and watched his mouth purse into a thin line.

"I won't deny it hurt like hell." He raked a hand through his hair, tousling the carefully combed waves. "At first I didn't want to believe it, but the financial records led straight to him and I was forced to go to the board with my findings. By then, however, he'd already fled the country, not bothering to defend himself, which damned him in the eyes of all those involved."

I stepped forward to comfort him then paused halfway, not sure what to do. "What sort of clients did your father entertain here?" I asked instead.

"The really lucrative ones, those he wanted to impress. I remember one man, a retired Air Force general, my father was trying to wine and dine. He spent more time answering questions from me about military life than with my father. The interruption didn't go unpunished; my car was "mysteriously" impounded and certain privileges revoked, but it didn't matter. Less than a year later, I signed up for the army without my father's knowledge, one final fuck-you to the old man." He gave a harsh laugh. "Guess he still managed to one-up me in the end."

I crossed the remaining space until I was standing in front of him. Spontaneously, I threw my arms around his waist, pulling him tight in my embrace. The thin material of his shirt was soft against my cheek. "I'm sorry your childhood was rotten," I murmured against his body, wishing I could somehow hug away the pain and memories. "Maybe you can start to make some happy memories now . . . it's not too late."

Jeremiah stayed silent, and I peered up into his face. He was gazing down at me, head cocked to one side, and a hand came up to caress my face. The slow burn in his eyes, a kindling of desire, made me realize how closely I pressed myself against him. Just as in the airplane, I found myself moved around and pressed up against the wall, Jeremiah's beautiful face looming above me. A telltale bulge pressed against my belly and I sighed, raising my face for a kiss.

Only to have him step back, moving out of my arms. "I can't," he murmured, eyes on the ground beside me.

I blinked, confused. "Why not?"

He looked frustrated by the decision as well. "I don't want . . ." he started before pausing. "Anya . . ."

"Anya," I repeated sharply, aggravated by the connection. What did she have to do with this? I crossed my arms over my chest, trying to stamp down the jealousy tugging at my heart. "Did she and you have a thing?"

The words hurt to say, but the pain in my chest eased when Jeremiah shook his head. "No, we were never an item. But you remind me of her, how she was before everything happened." He stopped again, clearly flustered by the line of conversation. Then the mask slammed down, ironing out his face into the stony expression I always saw. He drew himself up straight and indicated the painting with his chin. "Please make sure that gets put back away."

I watched him walk out of the room, the whole conversation leaving me wondering what other secrets he had.

On my fourth day of captivity, I was walking by Jeremiah's office when I heard his voice coming from inside. Since our cryptic conversation the day before, I hadn't seen or talked to the man, and nobody would tell me what was happening with the investigation. Determination bubbling up in me, I pushed open the door without knocking, barging into the office. It was immediately apparent we had a guest at the house, although I hadn't heard anyone come inside. The red-haired woman sitting in front of the big desk turned to look at me, and my eyebrows shot up as I recognized Celeste, the chief operations officer for Hamilton Industries. She seemed surprised to see me as well, and looked between myself and her boss seated behind the desk.

"Can I help you?"

Jeremiah's voice was stiff as he addressed me, his gaze disapproving of my entrance. Both helped stiffen my resolve and I lifted my chin in bravado. "I'd like to know when I can go home." I'd meant to ask about the investigation but Celeste's presence threw me off. She was the first woman I'd seen on the grounds since I'd met Jeremiah's mother. Her confusion, whether over my presence or at the situation in hand, was a welcome balm—at least I wasn't the only one uncertain about what was going on in this household.

"We can speak later, Ms. Delacourt." The cell phone on his desk vibrated and he snapped it up, coming to his feet. "Excuse me, ladies," he said, stepping around us and out the door. I was left gaping at the space he'd just been occupying.

"Do you have any idea what's going on?" Celeste asked. She sounded indignant, sharing my frustration about the state of affairs.

I could only shrug and shake my head. "What do you know?" I asked, trying to gauge her knowledge of the situation. Perhaps she knew something I didn't.

"Nothing, except Ethan won't let me out of his sight." The redhead threw her hands up in frustration. "He's set a constant security detail on me but wouldn't tell me why. Jeremiah left me in charge of everything, too, and I've been scrambling to keep up." She turned an irritated look to me. "You've been here the whole time?"

I nodded. "He doesn't even want me to leave the house."

The redhead's eyes narrowed shrewdly. "Do you know

anything about what's happening? I swear, I hate it when Ethan and Jeremiah go all alpha male, it makes me nuts."

"No kidding." I snorted. "There's overprotective, then there's just plain rude." Her words confirmed my suspicion that she didn't know about the poisoning but I wasn't sure how much to reveal. The temptation to tell all was strong, even if only to have somebody on my side. Unfortunately, the opportunity was lost as Jeremiah stepped back through the door, followed closely by Ethan.

"Remi, tell me what's going on," Celeste demanded. "I'm fielding all sorts of requests for meetings and appointments with you, and have nothing to tell these people."

"Do you need help doing your job?" Jeremiah's voice stayed cool as he cocked his head to the side, staring at the redhead. "Should I reassign some of your duties to other officers?"

Pride stood out on the other woman's face. Clearly the idea of delegation didn't sit well with her. Finally she pointed a finger at the billionaire. "You have the rest of the week, then I need answers," she said, glaring as if daring him to disagree with her terms.

Jeremiah's nod seemed to mollify her and Celeste turned to leave. She shrugged off Ethan's arm on her shoulder but the big man didn't seem to mind, hovering over her as they left the office. The door clicked shut, then I turned to face Jeremiah, only to see him already watching me. He was as difficult to read as ever so, taking a deep breath, I stepped around the desk so I was beside him. "Please tell me what's going on with the investigation."

I hadn't meant to word my request as a plea. Celeste had been more stern in her demand for information and part of me wished I was more like her. However, I saw a faint softening in Jeremiah's eyes, and a large hand reached out to brush a strand of hair from my face. My breath caught as his fingertips skimmed my jawline, cupping my neck just below the chin. Immediately I melted, pressing against his touch.

Only to once again have it taken away. Unbalanced, I put a hand on the desk as Jeremiah stepped back, eyes suddenly hooded. "It's my responsibility to keep you safe," he said, his voice cold as he turned back to his desk.

Anger spread through me. "I could walk right out those gates and you can't stop me." That statement finally got his full attention. Jeremiah rounded on me, face stormy, but I refused to back down. "You've made me little more than a prisoner in this house," I continued, "you won't tell me anything, and I'm sick of it."

"You signed a contract stating you would do as I said," he growled, face ferocious. "You're not leaving this house."

I took a step back and he followed, then I stiffened my spine and glared up at him. "That contract also stated I could terminate my 'employment' at any time. If you won't let me know what's going on, I'll quit and walk right out those gates down there."

Point made, I turned around to leave the office. I hadn't taken more than a step, however, when the room spun and suddenly I was pushed against a wall. The impact didn't hurt but it did startle me, and I looked up with wide eyes at Jeremiah's face. Gone was the stoic CEO; I'd poked too hard and the beast had reared its head. He towered above me, the grip on my arms like steel, but the outburst seemed to have calmed something inside him. The fire still burned deep in his eyes, however, as he caressed my face again. "I've been trying to resist you," he murmured, eyes following his fingers across my skin. "Being close to me is toxic, and you were caught up in that. The right thing would be to forget you, get you someplace away from me. . . ."

My heart melted. *Don't leave me, please,* I thought, not caring to look too deep into my sudden swell of emotion. As his thumb skimmed along my lips I reached out and took the pad between my teeth, running my tongue along the hard skin. He sucked in a breath, his grip on my arm tightening, and his Adam's apple bobbed as he swallowed. My gaze dropped to his mouth, memories of his lips and tongue on my body making my breath stutter.

"I'm no gentleman," he growled, eyes tracing the lines of my face. His hand lowered toward my breasts, but he clenched his fist instead, stopping short of touching me. "I look at you and all I see is how easily I can break you. You almost died once because of me and . . ."

I shrugged my arms away from his grip, and to my surprise he released me. Jeremiah's eyes clouded and I knew he thought I was rejecting him, but before he could step away I cupped his face with my hands. "Do you want to know what I see?" I said softly, staring into his eyes. My heart twisted at the yearning I read there. "I see an infuriating, beautiful man who's had every dream he ever dared imagine ripped to shreds by life. I want nothing more than to make it all better, but that's beyond my ability." I caressed his cheek with one thumb, then reached down and brought his knuckles to my lips. "I promised to give you anything you want and I meant it," I continued, raising his hand to my lips before letting it rest below my neck. "Believe me, I'm tougher than I look."

Jeremiah swallowed, staring at the large hand that wrapped itself around my throat. He adjusted his grip higher and I tilted my head back, not breaking eye contact. I kept my hands at my sides this time as he studied the contrast between his hand and the soft pale skin of my throat. When he finally raised hungry eyes to mine, an answering fire lit inside my belly. "Take me, sir," I murmured, and literally saw in his eyes the moment my words finally broke down the last of his resistance.

He swept me up in his arms wordlessly and carried me out of the office, padding silently down the hall to the large bedroom nearby. He set me down beside the bed, then shut and locked the door behind us. I watched silently, awaiting his command, as he turned back to me. "Remove your clothing and kneel beside the bed."

Relief rushed through my body, leaving me giddy and excited. My mind flashed to the first time I heard his voice, the command and power that resonated in every word. He could be reading the dictionary and I'd get wet, but when his eyes regarded me as they were now I positively burned. Holding his gaze, I slowly unbuttoned the shirt I was wearing, shrugging it off my shoulders to fall into a loose pile behind me.

My pants were next, the loose fabric pooling around my feet as I stepped out of them.

Jeremiah gave me a once-over, then shook his head as I moved toward the floor. "All of your clothes."

My heartbeat sped up but I complied, reaching around behind me and unclasping my bra. I pulled the straps from my shoulders, hands trembling as I exposed my breasts to his gaze. Liquid heat unfurled in my belly; I could almost feel his eyes caressing my body, which responded to his obvious desire, quaking with need. The cool air across my already hard nipples made my breath catch as I removed the thin flap of fabric from my breasts and let it fall to the ground beside the discarded shirt.

Swallowing hard, I hooked my thumbs through the top of my panties and slid them down my thighs. Jeremiah made an appreciative noise as my backside rose in the air so I continued the movement, almost touching the floor with my fingers before stepping out of the thin material. When I straightened he was watching me, the approval in his eyes a glorious shock to my system. "So beautiful," he murmured, and I flushed with pleasure.

He moved over by the nightstand and, reaching behind the wooden piece of furniture, pulled out an expensive-looking black paper bag with handles. There was no writing on the side to indicate what was inside, and I watched curiously as he set it on the small table. "Hands and knees, on the bed."

My eyes widened, my breath catching in my throat. The position would expose me completely to him, leaving me at his mercy. Nudity in the presence of another was still a new concept for me but Jeremiah's look allowed for no argument. Limbs stiff, I climbed onto the tall bed but kept myself facing him. The thought of exposing the most intimate bits of myself to his open perusal was still too much—my whole body flushed just thinking about it—but he seemed pleased with what he saw. He rattled the bag. "Care to guess what's inside?"

The contents had a solid sound, but my mind blanked on me. "Lingerie?" I hazarded, even though I knew it was much more than that.

Jeremiah smiled, a small quirk of the lips that made my insides flutter. *He really is beautiful like that,* I thought as he reached into the bag and began pulling out items. "These were purchased with you in mind," he said, setting them one by one on the nightstand.

My brain refused to comprehend what I was seeing at first until he pulled out leather cuffs and set those aside on the bed. I stared at the black leather for a moment, then at the plastic items spaced out over the top of the wooden stand. Oh, my God . . . My sexual experience was limited, but while I couldn't name most of the items laid out in front of me, I had an inkling as to how they'd be used.

Jeremiah picked up a slim dark plastic item and a small container of clear lube, then moved around the bed behind me. "Eyes forward," he ordered when I half turned to keep him in sight.

Trembling with uncertainty, I looked forward again. Not knowing what would happen left me apprehensive but part of me was breathless with anticipation. Since I had met Jeremiah I'd seen and experienced things beyond my wildest dreams, and something told me this would be no different. I still jumped when his hand rested on my backside, however, and heard the low rumble of his laugh. So sexy.

"You're so beautiful," he murmured, his hand stroking down my legs then back up the inside of my thighs. "I enjoy having you at my mercy like this."

Slick fingers pressed against my folds, gliding over my throbbing entrance, and I surged forward in surprise. Another hand grabbed my hip, steadying me as the fingers continued to slide down and around in a way that left me panting. One finger dipped inside, pressing around the tight walls of my opening, and a loud moan escaped my lips.

Jeremiah chuckled again, then his thumb moved up toward my other hole, smoothing over the entrance. He had played there before so I half expected it, but the surge of heat I felt as he pressed against the small strip of skin between the two openings shocked me. The pressure felt good in its own right, not necessarily coupled with any other touching. Jeremiah's thumb circled the small puckered hole before pushing inside and I moaned again, confused by my response but no less turned on.

The slick finger disappeared, then something blunt and hard took its place, pressing firmly inside. I whimpered as it stretched me, moving slowly but inexorably deeper into my body. There was very little pain as Jeremiah made certain to move in tiny increments, but the pressure the object created was foreign. It seemed like an eternity before he finally stopped, the strain uncomfortable but not painful. I chanced a glanced backward and saw him admiring his handiwork. He saw me looking and, one corner of his mouth lifting ever so slightly, he motioned with one finger for me to turn back around.

"You've never done this before, have you?" At the fervent shaking of my head, he chuckled. "I teased you before, but I've been waiting to get you and this sweet ass alone."

My breaths came in pants as he spread the cheeks of my backside. I trembled, uncertainty warring with desire. The sensation of my fluids trailing down the inside of one naked thigh made my body flush in embarrassment, but I heard Jeremiah breathe deeply. "God, the way you smell," he growled, fingers digging into the skin of my hips. That was all the warning I had as his face dipped down to my exposed core, mouth and tongue moving through the sensitive folds.

Releasing a shocked cry, I surged forward, barely catching myself on my elbows at the edge of the mattress. I had nowhere to go: fall forward and off the bed or push backward into that incredible mouth. Jeremiah's hands on my thighs gave me little room to maneuver, however, holding me steady as lips and tongue and—oh, God!—teeth sucked and nibbled the sensitive flesh. One hand left a quivering thigh, then fingers pressed inside my weeping entrance, stroking all the right places to leave me a shuddering mess.

The plug in my butt shifted, barely a small bump, and I tensed at the strange sensation. It was foreign enough to be felt above the pleasure, but didn't detract from the experience. The second time it moved I realized the movements were deliberate as Jeremiah rotated the hard plug, but the fingers moving inside me and the tongue nibbling on my inner thigh kept me from noticing much else.

The mattress behind me lifted as Jeremiah stood and moved around to my side of the bed. I laid there, panting, on my knees and elbows and trying to calm my quaking body. His hand stroked my head then down my back, and I noticed the hard bulge in his pants before me. Mind still foggy, I reached out with one hand and massaged the tip through the cloth, feeling the length and girth of his member. Jeremiah shuddered at my touch but didn't move, his hands dancing along my spine, so I grew bolder. I unclasped his pants and drew down the zipper, then reached inside and pulled him free.

His fingernails scraped up my back as I leaned in and drew my tongue lightly across the bulbous tip. Jeremiah groaned and it was all the encouragement I needed; I leaned forward as far as the bed would allow and sucked him into my mouth. The angle didn't allow me much room to maneuver but I did my best, sucking on the head and running my tongue along the rigid length. Jeremiah's hands returned to my head, thick fingers fisting in my hair. I ran fingers between his legs, cupping and massaging the heavy balls, and was pleased to hear another sharp intake of breath from Jeremiah above.

Part of me was horrified by my wanton behavior, but at that moment it was impossible to want anything else. My body still burned for his touch; every movement reminded me of the object still inside me, stretching my body to accept him. My core ached, desperate for contact, and I snaked my free hand between my legs, leveraging myself on my elbow.

Jeremiah stepped back, his member leaving my mouth with a soft pop, then he delivered a sharp smack to my backside. The spank stung and I flinched in surprise, pausing all movement. "Did I give you permission?"

Unsure how to answer, I drew my hand forward again but Jeremiah raised my head so we were eye to eye. "Were you about to touch yourself?"

The total control in his words, his gaze an implacable request for an answer, made my body clench in need. "Yes, sir," I whispered, knowing instinctively that to lie wouldn't go well.

He nodded, acknowledging my answer. "Did I give you permission?"

"No, sir," I whispered. A delicious dread flowed through my body as he nodded again and released my face, then moved around to the back of the bed. His hand trailed along my backside, lightly passing over the plug again as if to remind me of its presence.

"What should I do to someone who disobeys me?"

Fingers skimmed over the warm flesh still smarting from the spank as if to help me with the answer, but I couldn't speak. To tell him to spank me was beyond my power, but the idea was a powerful and surprising turn-on. I wasn't into pain—even the light spank was way outside my comfort zone—but somehow the idea of being punished made me squirm in anticipation. Two of the items on the small table beside the bed were a paddle and a suede many-fingered whip with a braided handle that looked surprisingly soft. The black and red leather contrasted in a way that grabbed my attention—it was almost pretty, a silly opinion perhaps given its intended use as a whip. When Jeremiah's hand hovered over the paddle I tensed, then relaxed as he settled his fingers around the small whip. "You like the flogger?" he murmured, faint amusement lacing his words.

Flushing, I looked away only to have him lift my chin so I was facing him. "I don't want to see you ashamed of being curious." He stroked my cheek with one thumb. "I know you're an innocent and I'll be gentle, but my goal is to please you and for that I'll need your help. So tell me, does the sight of the flogger turn you on?"

I nodded but Jeremiah shook his head. "I need to hear you."

Agreeing verbally was difficult. I swallowed hard, taking a deep breath, before whispering, "Yes, sir."

"Good." He picked up the flogger and snapped it across his arm. The leather strips made a loud crack against his flesh and I tensed. What was I getting myself into?

"Close your eyes."

I did as I was told, heart racing as a blindfold settled across my eyes. Trembling, suddenly apprehensive, I held myself still as Jeremiah moved back around the bed behind me. The urge to tear off the thin strip of cloth from my eyes was strong, but I imagined the punishment for two slights in a row would be much worse than a simple flogging. *Listen to yourself,* I thought, *this is absurd! Why would you allow this man to touch you like this, let alone spank—*

The first crack of the leather against my backside carried little force, but still managed to surprise me. The second lash stung a bit more and landed closer to my sensitive apex. I clenched my muscles, trying to protect my exposed bits from the tool.

"Keep your knees apart."

Oh, come on! The urge to resist rose up but I beat it down, determined to see this through. Relaxing my body proved more difficult but I forced my muscles to loosen, balling my hands into fists to relieve some tension. The object inside me no longer seemed as obtrusive, or perhaps I was starting to get used to having it there. Either way, the whole experience was proving a lot to take in at once.

Two more cracks of the whip, and when the last one landed across the exposed, sensitive flesh, I yelped. There was a stinging pain but I knew no damage, which allowed me to withstand the next three lashings. By the time the last one fell, I was panting, my backside and thighs stinging. Jeremiah didn't seem inclined to hold much back and I knew my fair skin would show marks from the leather.

A hand smoothed along the tender skin, tracing the burning lines with a soft touch. "Seeing my mark on you pleases me." He laid a kiss on the small of my back. "I have another surprise for you."

I waited, unsure what was coming, then felt something thin wrap around my hips. A small but firm piece of what I assumed was plastic nestled against the tender bud between my thighs, held firmly in place by the straps around my hips. When it suddenly began to vibrate, I gasped.

"I thought you might like this," Jeremiah said, trailing one hand down my damp thigh. "This one is only meant for your clit; I have a larger one that stimulates everything at once but it would get in the way of what I plan next." He held my hips secure as I bucked and trembled, sparks of pleasure flying through my body. "God, you're so fucking sexy."

The bed dipped behind me but I barely noticed, too caught in the sensations rolling through my body. When something nudged against my weeping opening, parting the folds as if asking permission, I pushed back with a breathy moan. The blindfold left me little else to focus on but the pleasure, and I needed him inside me. Jeremiah obliged, pressing his hard length inside my tight entrance. With him filling me I again noticed the sensation of the butt plug, the foreign object creating pressure against my inner walls.

"God!" Jeremiah leaned down over me, his naked torso— When had he taken off his clothes?—pressing me into the mattress as he thrust hard and fast. I welcomed the powerful stabs, a very different pressure building inside me and demanding release. Moans escaped my lips and my hands fisted in the covers, holding me steady as Jeremiah pounded into me from behind. He nudged my knees wider, changing the angle, and hit something inside my body that left me a panting mess. "Pl-please," I stuttered, the word more moan than word. The orgasm I so desperately needed was close; it would only take the right push to . . .

Lips pressed between my shoulder blades, tongue dipping to taste the skin. His hand reached around and pressed the small vibrator hard against my core. "I want to feel you come," he murmured, his voice thick with passion, and I rocketed over the edge with a loud cry, my body exploding with sensation. The orgasm wrung out what little energy I had left and I laid my forehead on my hands, panting.

Belatedly, I felt Jeremiah pull out, then heard the crinkle of a condom wrapper. He finally removed the plug, and before I could understand what he meant to do I felt the blunt tip of his erection against the tight ring of my anus, gently seeking entrance. I squirmed, suddenly uncertain even as I quaked with the aftershocks of my orgasm.

Jeremiah's fingers skimmed down my sides, sliding across the soft flesh of my breasts and down over my hips. "I've dreamed of how your ass would feel around my cock," he murmured behind me, laying a kiss on my shoulder. "I promise to make it good, please . . ."

The raw need in his voice touched a curiosity within me, and I relented as he pushed through the tight barrier ring. In the darkness of that blindfold, there was only sensation. Jeremiah's heavy breathing matched my own, and the obvious pleasure he derived from this small taboo touched an answering fire still ablaze inside me. There was no pain, only a strange and new pressure, but when he made a small roll of his hips, the sudden sensation made me press back against him, hands curling around the edge of the bed.

Jeremiah hovered above, solid arms on either side of my body keeping him from crushing me. I reached out blindly and put my hand over his, and he laced our fingers as his thrusts picked up. His pleasure was my goal but I found myself also into our actions, the foreign sensations melding with the earlier pleasure. His hands tightened around mine and he grunted, forehead falling to my back as he shuddered and came silently.

There was an immense satisfaction in giving such a powerful man this kind of release. *I wish I could see your face*, I thought as he sat up, pulling himself gingerly from my body. I stayed where I was for a moment, basking in the afterglow, then collapsed sideways onto the mattress. Parts of me were deliciously sore, especially when I moved, but I stretched contentedly anyway. "That was incredible," I breathed, closing my eyes and laying my head against the pillows.

"Was?" Jeremiah sounded amused by my statement. Still trapped by the blindfold, I heard but couldn't see a curious clinking noise, then I was twisted on the bed and my arms stretched above my head. Before I could protest, thick cuffs surrounded my wrists and with a *snikt* I heard them secured to the headboard. My mouth dropped open in shock, then Jeremiah lifted one eye of my blindfold. My glare only seemed to amuse him. "You threatened to leave before," he said, letting the blindfold snap back into place. "This will keep you here where I can protect you. In the meantime, however, I can think of a few ways we can take advantage of this.

"Care to find out?"

17

The afternoon bled into twilight, then night, and Jeremiah proved exceptionally attentive. When he finally did release me from my cuffs, I didn't try to run, caught up in the sensual storm he created and never let die. The billionaire proved nearly insatiable, and I had little choice but to rise to the challenge. Four times that night he woke me, intent on delicious torment, and four times I collapsed afterward, spent. The fifth time, it was I who woke first, taking my time beforehand to watch him as he slept. In slumber he relaxed, his face outlined by the light streaming in through the opaque window. I traced a feather touch along one brow, pausing only when he stirred. So beautiful, and all mine.

For now.

How a man like this would ever notice me was beyond my comprehension, yet here he lay, a feast for my wandering eyes. The soft sheets covered only up to his stomach and I drank in the sight of his beautiful body, marred only by the small white lines of scars barely visible in the low light. Seeing them, knowing what he must have been through to get them, made my heart squeeze painfully. Knowledge about his life in the military was one thing, but these scars were a testament to the fact that he'd fought and was wounded, a reminder forever of the missions he went on and the danger he must have faced.

I traced the sparse line of hair leading down his abdomen and saw, with some satisfaction, the sheet below his belly rise as he grew hard again. Slithering down the bed, I pulled the sheets carefully over my head, then bowed my head over his body, licking the heavy tip before drawing him into my mouth.

Jeremiah's hips rolled, pressing up toward my mouth. Emboldened, I put my hand along the base and stroked upward, then followed it back down with my mouth. He grew harder and I smiled, bobbing my head over him. Whatever inhibitions I may have once had were thrown out the window, at least for tonight.

A hand threaded through my hair and I heard a low groan above me. I placed my hands on his thighs for leverage as I took him deep, and felt him arch up into my mouth. Then hands pulled me free, taking hold of my shoulders and twisting me sideways until I was lying on my back with Jeremiah above. He stared down at me, any hint of sleep erased from his beautiful face. I could feel the desperate need in his movements as he opened my legs with one knee, stabbing deep with little preamble.

Throwing back my head with a gasp, I clutched at his back, fingernails digging deep, as he moved over and inside me. Muscles still sore from the night's overindulgences protested but I didn't care; I wrapped my legs around his waist and begged for more as he thrust hard inside me. His mouth crashed down on mine, all passion and no finesse, and I rose to meet him, arms twining around his neck. Our coupling this time was short and fast, but the orgasm that rocked us both at long last drew us down into sleep.

When I finally awoke the sun was high in the sky and I was alone in the bed. I stretched, arching my back and noticing the leather cuffs still attached to the headboard. The sight made me smile, a reminder of what happened only hours before. There was definitely some discomfort from the previous night's antics and I hobbled into the bathroom, drawing a warm bath and giving my sore body a chance to soak. I took my time getting ready, allowing myself a bit of pampering and using the extra time to let the water wash away some of the soreness and aches.

My tummy was ultimately the one that dictated it was time to head downstairs, so I dried off and got dressed, putting my hair up quickly in a plastic clip before heading out. I heard voices downstairs and, curious, went to see who the new guest could be. There was nobody in the entryway at the base of the stairs however so, shrugging, I headed toward the kitchen, making a beeline for the refrigerator.

"I took the liberty of looking you up, Ms. Delacourt."

I almost dropped the milk from my hand at the unexpected voice, whirling to face the woman who'd spoken. "Mrs. Hamilton," I said, her cold scrutiny making me feel as though I'd been caught stealing. "I didn't realize you'd be here."

Her lips flattened into a hard line as she looked me up and down. "Women of your economic stature have a tendency to throw themselves at my son. He usually has the presence of mind, however, to see through their wiles." She sniffed in derision. "You're not even that pretty; at least his previous assistant had that going for her in the beginning. Tell me, do you have something on him?"

My jaw worked but I didn't know what to say. "Excuse me?"

The older woman rolled her eyes. "I see no other reason why my son would associate with you. Both parents dead, barely middle class. You may know French but you appear to have none of the credentials to run any form of business. Did he get you pregnant?"

The brazen question shocked me speechless. Anger built up inside me but I could do little under her condescending stare other than move my jaw soundlessly. The cold scrutiny in her gaze offended me on every level but I couldn't begin to put my jumbled thoughts into words. My hands curled into fists—I wanted nothing more than to knock the smile off her sanctimonious face—but a lifetime of good manners kept me rooted in place. "I'm not pregnant," I finally managed to retort, but the answer didn't begin to articulate what was burning through my mind.

"Ah, so just a bit on the side." The older woman *tsk*ed, shaking her head in disbelief. "To think he'd bring you here to the family home. Ms. Delacourt, if you have any sense or class, you'll leave this house immediately. Given the type of girl you are, however, I probably shouldn't hold my breath."

"Enough, Mother."

I was an instant away from throwing the milk jug at the self-righteous woman, and while Jeremiah's presence didn't alleviate that desire, it did manage to distract Georgia. The older woman's face reset itself into a pleasant expression when her son walked through the entryway, but neither Jeremiah nor I were fooled. "You said you were leaving," he said in a cold voice that seemed to wash right over the older woman.

"Oh, I am, darling, but I saw your lovely assistant and stopped to chat."

"Lovely assistant," my ass! My hand had all but crushed the plastic handle of the milk container. I wanted to scream at the odious woman, but all I could do at the moment was stay in place, shaking and trying not to cry in frustration.

"Please leave, Mother." Jeremiah's tone was firm but tired. "Before I have to bar you from entering permanently."

She waved him off. "Oh, pish posh, you wouldn't do that. I raised you in this house; it's as much mine as yours. And besides, you know I only want what's best for you because I love you."

The statement made me snort in disbelief, but a glance at Jeremiah's weary expression told me this was an old argument. "Do you have any respect at all for your son?" I asked.

Georgia shot me a snide glare. "Stay out of this," she snapped. "You have no idea . . ."

I slammed the milk container down on the marble counter, the plastic making a popping noise as it crumpled. "Your son owns this house and allows you to visit at your pleasure, yet you walk all over him as if he's still a child. I know what good parenting looks like, and you don't deserve his obvious loyalty."

Georgia's face contorted into a snarl. "You little bitch," she muttered, turning toward me and lifting a hand as if to slap me. Then Jeremiah was there, his hand around his mother's wrist, holding her steady. I kept my chin high, indignation burning a pit in my belly, meeting the woman's hateful glare.

"I won't have you insulting my guests in my house," Jeremiah said, voice low and angry, his words again capturing his mother's attention. "Andrews," he called, and a young guard trotted into the room. Only then did Jeremiah release his grip on the woman's arm. "Please escort my mother to her car and make sure she exits the compound safely. Inform the gate she's only to be allowed onto the grounds from now on with my approval."

"Keep your hands off me," Georgia snapped as the young bodyguard tried to take her arm. "Your approval? Jeremiah, be reasonable, this is silly." Her son, however, stayed silent as she was escorted, protesting loudly, out of the kitchen. I heard the front door open and close, then silence reigned through the house.

I blew out a breath. "I'm sorry for telling off your mother," I mumbled, lifting up the milk jug in my hand. The base had a large dent in the plastic but thankfully nothing was broken.

"She can be difficult."

His reply was simple but held a wealth of meaning. "Still, she's your mom," I continued. "Probably wasn't my place to say anything."

The awkwardness wasn't how I'd hoped to spend the morning, but the matriarch's presence had soured everything. No longer hungry, I put the milk back in the refrigerator, then followed Jeremiah out of the kitchen. "Have you learned anything yet?"

"Nothing."

The reply was curt and, frowning, I dug deeper. "Ethan mentioned you had some other sources, did they have any—"

Jeremiah rounded on me. "What did he tell you?"

I blinked, surprised by his sudden change of mood. "Nothing," I replied quickly, then frustration welled up. "The exact same nothing that you told me. I don't know what's going on with the investigation except that I almost died and now I'm stuck here."

Jeremiah's lips pursed. "We're dealing with it."

"Dealing with what? Nobody will talk to me!"

He raked a hand through his hair, taking a deep breath. "I promise you," he said in a low voice, "we will find out who tried to poison you. Once the threat is neutralized, you're free to leave."

I pointed to the entrance nearby. "You leave through that door every day, but make me stay inside?"

"Someone could be trying to kill you."

His words rang with truth, but didn't match what I had seen so far. "I'm not the target," I shot back, matching him glare for glare. "You said so yourself. I'm not asking you to paint a target on my back and set me loose in the world, I just want some answers."

"Dammit, Lucy!" For a split second he looked ready to burst, a savagery in his eyes I'd never seen before. The sight shocked me, but as quickly as it happened the emotion disappeared; the gates came down over his features and once again he was the stoic CEO I knew. Thought I knew, I amended, startled by what I'd seen.

"I promised to take care of you." His low voice was even and calm like normal. "I only ask that you don't ask any further questions for your own protection. When it's safe, you can leave."

Defeat bloomed through me, making me want to rip out chunks of my hair. Jeremiah turned his back on me and marched outside, closing the front door lightly behind him. Fingers rigid, I ran my hand through my hair, unsettling the clip so that it clattered to the floor, but I couldn't care less at that moment.

The frustration was overwhelming. I tried taking deep breaths but nothing calmed the sudden swell of anger at the situation. This house was my prison, and Jeremiah had become my warden. The opaque window glass might as well have been bars; the technology trapped me inside as surely as any iron or other metal shield. I hadn't seen the outside since arriving except through that tiny bathroom window, and the absurd thought that I might be stuck like this forever propelled me across the living room to the back wall of windows and the door leading outside.

The handle to the door leading onto the patio was cool in my grip. Before I could talk myself out of my actions, I turned the knob and opened the door, peeking out over the landscape and ocean less than a hundred yards from the back of the building. . . .

Only to shut it immediately, overwhelmed by fear of who might be lying in wait for me.

A sob wracked my body, and I clapped a hand over my mouth to stifle more from coming. *Stop being such a ninny,* I admonished myself. *If Jeremiah can do it every day, so can you.* For a moment, I hated him for putting the idea in my head that I, too, could be a target. I'm nobody; there's no reason for anyone to come after me. The stress of my situation, however, finally caught up with me, and I held tightly to the wall as I tried to get a grip on myself. It took several deep, shuddering breaths before the sobs subsided, leaving me spent and all the more desperate to leave. *I need to get out of here or I'll go crazy, that's all there is to it.*

I'd been so sure that alarms would sound when I opened the door, but when I turned the handle and pressed forward, there wasn't a peep from the house. No Klaxons rang out, signaling my escape, and part of me was disappointed I'd waited so long. *So much for security,* I thought drolly. Somewhat reassured I wouldn't immediately be caught, I cracked the door farther and peeked outside. No bodyguards were visible and the doorway was a direct route down to the water and boathouse I'd seen every day through the small upstairs window. The property was lined with tall trees, obscuring the neighbors' view of the compound. The midday winter chill clung to the air, and there were no boats visible on the ocean before me. My death grip on the doorknob wasn't getting me anywhere, however. Now or never.

Steeling myself, I strode out the door and made my way down the back patio steps toward the boathouse, gait jerky and nervous. I looked back and saw I'd forgotten to close the living room door but knew if I turned around I wouldn't find the courage to leave again. It felt incredible to be outside again and, at that moment, I didn't care if any guards saw me.

The boathouse was even more interesting up close. What I'd thought was only a shack was really a two-story building, following the contour of the shoreline with the lower floor exiting out onto a pier that stretched out over the water. The upper floor was at ground level; stairs along the side of the building took you down to where the boats were kept, but I didn't see anything in the swirling water. As I drew closer I noticed the upper floor looked like a small living quarters although, given the condition of the exterior, I hazarded a guess that nobody had lived there for a while. The boat-house's construction was different from that of the house, much older and more worn down, the aged quality giving it a rustic feel the elegant mansion lacked. While it looked sturdy enough, the elements had done a great job stripping away the paint and finish to the wood; green lichen covered parts of the floor and wood siding, poking through the remnants of paint lingering on the surface.

I'd barely reached the planked walkway of the building, the old wood sagging softly beneath my feet, when a bell rang out from somewhere within the compound. My heart skipped a beat at the sound, and I ran the last few steps to the boat-house before me, looking for an entrance. Glancing back, I saw three guards running toward the mansion I'd just left, splitting up and disappearing around the corners.

Were they looking for me, or an intruder? The idea the killer could be on the grounds paralyzed my mind, and I mentally kicked myself for my reckless rebellion. *Stupid, stupid! What on earth were you thinking?*

A quick scan of the boathouse revealed a nearby entrance and I hurried toward it, seeking somewhere safe to hide. The door was unlocked and I pushed inside, closing it swiftly after me. I laid my head on the wood, watching through the window as more guards appeared around the open door I'd just vacated in the mansion. Disappointment bloomed in my belly. *I'm going to be in so much trouble,* I thought, suddenly guilty.

From the corner of my eye I saw something move, and before I could react a hand clapped over my mouth. I screamed, or tried to anyway, as I was dragged back from the window by strong arms. I kicked over a wicker chair and a lamp in my struggles, but my assailant didn't release me. I kicked backward but my feeble attack was deftly avoided. *Oh God,* I thought miserably, despair washing over me, *I'm about to die, aren't I?*

Jeremiah, I'm sorry . . .

"Fancy meeting you in a place like this," said a jovial voice behind me. "I really was hoping the next time we saw one another it would be under better circumstances."

Shocked, my struggles ceased as I recognized the voice. "You really need to learn a few new defensive maneuvers," my assailant continued. "You're easy to predict after a while. Now please don't scream, my dear, I'd rather the wrong folks not discern our location."

The hand around my mouth lifted and I stayed silent, unsure what to think. His grip on my arms, pushed high up my back, didn't stray an inch. "Am I about to die?" I whispered, heart in my throat.

"That all depends on how quickly my little brother arrives." A smooth hand crept up my torso to encircle my neck, pinning me back against his body. "Care to make any wagers?"

18

I trembled in his arms, casting about for a weapon. Once upon a time, the boathouse had been occupied. Furniture, much of it half hidden by sheets, dotted the floor. At some point, however, the living space had been converted to storage, and numerous items dotted the dusty room, including several which were tied to the high ceiling. There was nothing close by for me to use, however. "Are you the one who's trying to kill Jeremiah?" I asked, stalling for time.

Lucas chuckled, the laugh shaking us both. "While I probably have better reason than most to wish for such a thing, I'm afraid I'm not your man."

Confused, I leaned my head back to look at him. Lucas was shorter than his stockier brother, such that my head lay atop his shoulder, but his grip was like iron. The man's gaze was placid, and his lips curled up into a smile at my perusal. "Surprised? I may dislike my little brother, but I'm not interested in his death. Indeed, I've been doing everything in my power to prevent it."

"Then why are you here?"

He laughed again, then dipped his lips close to my ear. "Maybe I missed you."

Butterflies exploded in my stomach. "Liar," I muttered. Knowing he wasn't going to kill me made me suddenly realize the intimacy of our position, and my body's betrayal irritated me.

"Most definitely." His cheeky response made me roll my eyes. "Or perhaps I know who you're looking for."

I twisted around to look at him. "You know who's after Jeremiah?"

"Perhaps," he repeated, his smirk widening.

My lips pursed in annoyance. Infuriating man. "They're going to find us soon," I said, glancing out the window. "You should let me go," I cautioned. "People might get the wrong idea."

"If I know my little brother, they already know exactly where we are." He gestured at the ceiling. "There's more than likely a camera or three in the rafters above us, watching our every move." Lucas kissed my cheek, and I flinched away in surprise. "Should we give them a show?"

Irritated by his innuendo, I struggled again but was held fast. "If you had information, why not come through the front entrance like a sane man? Why do all of this hiding and sneaking?"

"It's more interesting this way. My brother can be anal about his security; it's fun showing how easy it is to circumvent." He shrugged. "Besides, my brother would be more likely to call the authorities than let me inside and hear what I have to say."

"Like he won't do that now anyway," I muttered, and Lucas gave a small chuckle. The boards beneath our feet began to quake, and the heavy thump of boots pounding against the boards outside the boathouse shook the old structure.

Lucas merely adjusted his grip, shuffling me between himself and the entryway. "Showtime," he replied, seemingly unconcerned, as the door into the boathouse crashed open. Guards poured in and surrounded the two of us, and my heart skipped a beat as guns were trained on us. I didn't see Jeremiah among them, however, and a shard of disappointment lanced my heart. Lucas merely heaved a sigh. "Looks like Jeremiah's no longer fighting his own fights," the gunrunner added.

The distinctive clicking noise of a handgun being cocked was easily recognizable, especially when it came from directly behind us. Lucas quickly let me go at the sound, hands lifting as I sprang away to see a gun being held against the sarcastic man's head.

"Give me one reason why I shouldn't kill you."

There was death in that voice as Jeremiah appeared behind Lucas, his eyes blazing with a savagery that took my breath away. The obvious height difference between the two men had never been more apparent; Jeremiah seemed to tower over his older brother, the muscles in his arm bulging against the business shirt he wore. The black gun was trained on Lucas's temple, Jeremiah's knuckles around the grip white with strain.

I looked between the two men. Surely Jeremiah wouldn't . . . Not his own brother . . .

Lucas froze, hands up on either side of his head. "Familial loyalty?" Lucas answered lightly, his light words belying the strain I saw in his face. From the sound of his voice he might have been talking about the weather, but the eyes locked on me were bleak.

"Not good enough." Jeremiah pressed the gun harder against his brother's temple, and Lucas closed his eyes.

"No!" I blurted out, heart racing. I moved around until I was beside the two men. "He came to help us, Jeremiah. He knows who's after you, don't kill him!"

The billionaire didn't look at me but I saw the gun tremble against Lucas's head. The bodyguards near the door lowered their own weapons but didn't move to help, leaving the brothers alone. My throat froze, suddenly terrified at what I was about to witness, then Jeremiah lowered his gun. He grabbed Lucas's arm and twisted it behind the other man's back, and only then did the bodyguards move in. "Take him to the house," Jeremiah said, voice low and tight.

The bodyguards took Lucas from Jeremiah, snapping a set of handcuffs around his wrists. The older brother didn't put up a fight, seemingly content with the way things were going, but the guards still clustered around him as if he was dangerous. I moved to follow them, when suddenly a hand grabbed my arm, bringing me up short. "Not so fast," I heard Jeremiah growl.

I thought that I had seen him angry before, but I'd never seen him like this. There was real fury in his eyes, directed at me, and I knew I had messed up royally. "Jeremiah," I said, trying to apologize, only to cut myself short when I saw his free hand ball up into a fist.

"Do you know what I've done to protect you?" Gone was the total control I had always seen, and in its place was a ferocity that looked alien on his face. When I tried to move, the hand around my arm tightened and I tensed, stopping all movement.

"The girl didn't know I was here," Lucas said from across the room. His rapt gaze watched our confrontation keenly. I became aware that the guards were also watching us, having paused in the doorway, but again made no move to help.

"I said, take him to the house!" Jeremiah roared, and I watched in disappointment as the guards shuffled out through the door and back toward the house, leaving me alone with Jeremiah.

I tried to stay calm, even though the heat I felt from him was overwhelming. When the door clicked closed he released my arm, but as I moved away he followed my retreat, stalking me across the room. My hip finally bumped up against a table, then I backed into a wall with no other means of escape. He towered over me, fists clenched at his sides, and I tried to quell the sudden misgivings in my chest. "Jeremiah, I'm . . ."

"Do you realize how much danger you're in?" A scowl twisted his face but he didn't move a muscle to touch me. "Why did you leave the house?"

"Because the assassin is after you, not me?" I hadn't meant for the statement to be a question, and from the look on

Jeremiah's face it was the wrong answer anyway. "Look, I'm really sor—"

I was pinned to the wall suddenly, the hands on my shoulders pressing me back against the wood. Squeaking in surprise, I turned wide eyes on Jeremiah and saw him blink, a small frown furrowing his brow. The anger was still in his voice, however, as he said, "You saw his face at the hotel. Do you have any idea what that means to a man who lives his life in the shadows?"

I'm sorry, I wanted to say, but Jeremiah's dark look quelled my courage to speak. The hands on my shoulders trembled, Jeremiah's beautiful face contorting in his struggle for control. He bowed his head, and to my surprise laid his forehead against mine.

"You could have been killed," he rasped, the words piercing my heart. "I've done everything I can to keep you safe, gone to people I swore I'd never contact again—all for you. Why did you leave the house?"

Heart twisting, I raised my hand to cup his face but he lifted his head, turning a suspicious gaze on me. "Did you know my brother was here?"

I drew back, stung by the accusation. "Of course I didn't." Frustration bubbled up at his disbelieving look. "I don't know anything about what's going on, thanks to you," I snapped, glaring at him. I slapped his chest in frustration, the movement doing little to make him retreat. "How would I even get information like that while under constant surveillance? You lock me away in that house, guards watching my every move. You don't tell me anything you're doing, lecture me about staying safe without telling me anything, and expect me to meekly go along with it—"

"Goddammit," Jeremiah roared, startling me into silence, "I can't have your death on my hands!" Wild desperation came into his eyes as his hands left my shoulders, framing my face without touching my skin. "I promised I would keep you safe, then you go and pull something like this."

I watched in wonder as a myriad of emotions played across his face. Despite learning to read his normally subtle body language and limited expressions, the sudden passion on his face struck me dumb. His own battle for control was obvious; he reached out to caress my neck, then checked himself, as if afraid to touch me. "My family destroys outsiders who get too close; I've watched it happen to my mother, Anya, and countless others." He swallowed. "Maybe I don't deserve happiness, but you do, and I'll get you through this." One finger caressed my cheek. "I'm not a good man," he murmured, staring at his hand fisted near my chest. "I should never have brought you into this. I almost got you killed, and now I need to see you safe."

The pain in his eyes, revealing emotions that were always kept bottled inside, made tears spring to my eyes. I tried to touch his face again but he grabbed my wrist, holding it beside my head. "You can't do this again," he ground out. "We don't know who is after us or what means he has available to get close."

My heart shattered into a million little pieces. Trembling, I searched for a way to show my remorse. "I'm sorry for leaving the house."

"Sorry isn't good eno—" Jeremiah retorted angrily, then stopped as I lowered myself to my knees. He released my wrist and stepped back, everything about him going still as he stared down at me. "What are you doing?" he finally said.

I'd never felt so helpless in my life, sitting there at his feet. I had no idea how he'd react, but somehow I knew he needed to be in control, the emotions coursing through him too much to process. "Asking for forgiveness." I swallowed, then added, "Sir."

The remaining wildness in his face drained away but he still hesitated. I stared at his feet, no longer having the courage to watch his face. He still wore the expensive business pants but instead of the dress shoes to which I'd grown accustomed, he wore a pair of rugged black boots. I wondered if they were the same ones he'd worn while in the army, but didn't feel that that moment was the right time to ask.

The silence stretched, making me nervous. I stayed where I was, praying I hadn't made the wrong move. My biggest fear was his rejection, so relief shot through me when he finally said, "Stand up and raise your hands over your head."

Swallowing again, I did as he ordered, my eyes moving toward the ceiling. A line of rope hung down from a large roll of cloth above me, likely an old sail, and my heart skipped a beat as Jeremiah wrapped the rope around my wrists. "Hold still," he said, then fished around until he found a small piece of cloth nearby. He snapped it once to remove debris, the sound making me jump, then tied it around my head to cover my eyes. The world plunged to black, and when he tightened the rope above so it lifted me to my tiptoes, I gave a small gasp.

"So, you want to be punished."

I whimpered, heart racing, but didn't negate his question. Despite the heavy boots, he was surprisingly silent on his feet; I cast my head around blindly, trying to find him, then started as I felt his breath on my neck. "What should it be?" he murmured, fingers sliding along my raised arm. "Should I spank you for your disobedience? Whip you? What kind of punishment would teach you not to court death?"

My mouth worked silently but I didn't respond. Somehow, given his current state of mind, I doubted he'd be gentle with me. I remembered the flogger he'd used on me the previous night and, despite the current situation, felt an answering heat unfurl in my belly. *Now is not the time for this!*

"Perhaps a different form of punishment is required." His hand left my arm and unsnapped my pants with deft fingers. They dropped to my feet as he grabbed one leg behind the knee, lifting it high and to the side until I was balancing on one foot, holding the rope around my wrists for support. My face flushed, realizing how I had to look exposed like this. All the underwear I had was of the sexy variety, something I secretly appreciated but that made unexpected moments like this awkward.

A finger slid across my panties and I jerked against my bonds in surprise. "You're wet," he said, his tone such that I couldn't tell what he was thinking and longed to see his face. He let go of my leg, then hooked his thumbs around the band of my panties and slid them down to my ankles. My face burned as he undid the buttons of my shirt, pulling it open to reveal my torso. Rough hands skirted the edge of my bra, then slid beneath the thin material as he spoke. "Perhaps nipple clamps; they can be painful. Is that punishment enough for you risking your life?"

Fingers wrapped around my nipples and I tensed, waiting for the pain, but he only fondled them a bit then let go, leaving the bra displaced and my breasts exposed. A perverse disappointment jolted through me and I stifled a sigh. *I don't like pain,* I thought, but the avowal seemed weak even in my mind.

The rope jerked up again, until only the tips of my toes scraped the ground. Muscles stretched in my arms and my wrists burned, but I clamped my lips together and kept silent. I thought I heard the whisper of footsteps behind me as another hand smoothed over my backside. "Should I take you anally? You seemed to enjoy it yesterday but unprepared it can be very painful. Is that punishment enough for playing fast and loose with your life?"

A hand cracked against one cheek and I flinched, the movement swinging me around. I scrambled for purchase, my panties falling to the ground as Jeremiah disappeared again but I couldn't stop the slow twirl of the rope. Another spank across the same cheek made me spin faster, butt burning.

"Should I use my belt on you?" he asked, voice tight again. The sound of a buckle being loosened came from nearby. "Would that keep you from any more foolhardy attempts like this? Answer me!"

"I'm sorry," I replied, earnestly meaning the words and not just because of his threats. I remembered the desperation on his face, the loss of control when I was in danger, and my throat tightened. "I'm so sorry."

"You're sorry, what?"

"I'm sorry, sir."

"What are you sorry for?"

Hurting you. The pain on his face, the rage when he'd confronted his brother, the surge of emotion, was what I regretted most. I knew, however, that wasn't the answer he wanted. "For disobeying you and putting myself at risk." At the last minute I barely remembered to add, "Sir."

Hands grabbed my hips and hauled me forward against a hard body, knee moving in between my knees. Taken by surprise, I instinctively opened my legs and was hauled up until I was straddling his hips. I felt a moment of probing against my naked core, then he plunged inside and I gasped.

"I promise you," he growled, punctuating every other word with a thrust of his hips, "you'll feel every one of those punishments if you ever do this again."

I tightened my legs around him as one big hand moved to my back, holding me still as he rammed into me. The sheer power of each deep stab bounced me into the air; there was little pain, but because my body had been preparing for a much harsher punishment, every nerve ending was alive and on fire. His hands dropped to my backside, squeezing and parting the twin globes for deeper access, and I exploded. The orgasm took me by surprise, my body bucking and twisting as he continued his assault.

Our movements had dislodged the cloth over my eyes and, panting, I looked down to see Jeremiah watching me, his face strained by his own desire. The raw hunger in his eyes seemed more than just sexual, and the sight stabbed through my heart. I wanted to kiss him, caress his beautiful face, but the bonds held me aloft, keeping me from giving him any comfort. *Maybe this is my punishment,* I wondered, feeling the loss keenly in my gut. How oddly appropriate. Then he shuddered beneath me and the moment passed, and we both took a moment to come down from that stunning high.

Holding me tight against his body, he reached up and effortlessly untied the knot from around my wrists. My limbs felt boneless as he set me on my feet. I wobbled, bare feet scraping against the wood floor. His grip was gentle, so different from only a moment before when everything had been quick and rough, but as soon as I was steady he let me go and stepped away. "Get your clothes on and I'll take you back to the house."

Jeremiah turned away before I could get a good look at his face; disappointment churned in my belly at the subtle snub but I set it aside, dressing myself quickly and following after him. He had moved toward a far wall, and as I approached he pulled aside a thin rug covering a pair of rings in the door and hauled open a trapdoor in the floor. The hinges didn't make any noise as the hatch swung open. "This will take us to the house."

I stared wide-eyed down into the darkness. Steep concrete steps led down into the underground passage, and a chilly damp wind blew from somewhere at the other end. "Is it safe?"

"This is how I came in here unseen. It's safer than going outside, at least until we figure out who's behind all this."

Still I balked. "Why do you have a trapdoor to the boathouse?"

Jeremiah's lips thinned but he answered, "There were incidents in my childhood that necessitated . . . additional measures. My father was a paranoid man, but in some instances he had good reason to be afraid. The house has a panic room and this exit in case of an emergency, but we've never had to use either since he died." He held out his hand. "Come on, Lucy," he said, his voice gentler than before, "let's get you to the house."

I took his hand tentatively, still unconvinced whether it was a good idea, but nevertheless took that first step down into the dark passageway.

19

I found out very quickly that I didn't like secret passages.

There was little light along the narrow tunnel. We passed lightbulbs spaced several yards apart but only two worked along the entire corridor. The main light came from a flashlight phone app, reflecting dully off the slick wood floor. I kept a firm grip on the back of Jeremiah's shirt to keep from slipping on the rotting planks.

The passageway's proximity to the ocean left everything covered in moisture; I didn't dare touch the walls glistening in the low light. The tunnel was warmer than aboveground and humid, a cloying darkness I was desperate to escape. It seemed to go on forever, the walls pressing ever closer. Right as I was readying myself to push Jeremiah aside and flee the rest of the way, we came to a stop and the light shone up at a trapdoor above. Jeremiah twisted a metal ring and pushed, but the door didn't budge. He heaved at it twice and it finally ripped free, making a sound like wood splitting. There wasn't much light streaming in from the new room, either, but definitely more than in the dark tunnel, which was a welcome relief.

"Climb up," he said, and I noticed a metal ladder against the far wall. The chill from the rungs bit into my hands as I scaled the short distance into the new room. There was a marked difference in the temperature and ambient humidity as I realized we were back in the house. I had only a moment to recognize the kitchen pantry, shelves lined with cans and packaged goods, before the door was wrenched open. Blinded by the sudden light, I gave a surprised squeak and raised my hands in surrender as three guns were pointed in my face.

"Stand down" came Jeremiah's order from below. After a moment's hesitation the guns were lowered, and I sat back on the floor, my feet still inside the hole. The guards stepped back as Jeremiah pulled himself from the dank opening. I scooted sideways to make room, not trusting my jelly-legs after that scare, but Jeremiah lifted me effortlessly to my feet and escorted me from the tiny room.

The living room and kitchen were full of people, mainly guards, so Lucas stuck out among the group. He was flanked by two men, and as I came into view he gave me a once-over. I thought I saw relief flash across his face briefly before the smirking mask settled back in place.

Jeremiah fixed his brother with a glare, striding toward the smaller man. "If you don't tell me what you—"

"Archangel."

Jeremiah paused. "What's Archangel?"

"Archangel isn't a what, but a who." Lucas shifted uncomfortably, a petulant look on his face. "Can't we lose the cuffs?" he asked, rattling the thin chain. "My poor shoulders can't take much—"

"Lucas," Jeremiah growled, cutting off his brother and ignoring the request, "who is Archangel?"

"An assassin, and a very good one at that. Pricey as well." He rolled his eyes. "Contrary to what you may think, I wasn't the one to hire his services; I even tried to warn you as soon as I heard about the hit."

"When?" Jeremiah asked sharply.

"The night of the charity gala in France. I tried to call your cell but there was no answer." Lucas snaked a look at me, a twinge of regret in his eyes. "I should have left a message but instead I decided to contact you directly. By the time I reached your room, however, it was too late."

Jeremiah spoke first, his voice suspicious. "The caller was a blocked number."

"A hazard of the profession." Lucas's lips rose into a smile that didn't quite reach his eyes. I got the impression the grin was an automatic response, an oft-used professional mask, because something flickered in his eyes and the smile disappeared. "I decided to contact you directly but I was only a minute behind the medical team dispatched to your room. I saw you raging about and knew something had happened."

That bit of information got Jeremiah's attention. "You were there?"

Lucas nodded once somberly. "I knew you wouldn't believe me if I approached you then and didn't want to cause a scene—in the state you were in, you would have throttled me—so I stayed back." Lucas snuck a look toward me. "I apologize for not being faster."

"I'm alive." As far as forgiveness went, the words were a paltry expression of gratitude, but I saw another brief flash of relief across his face. My mind was having trouble equating this man with his chosen career; I couldn't see Lucas as an arms dealer. I guess even bad guys can have a heart.

"What about Archangel?"

Jeremiah's question recaptured Lucas's attention. "He's new in the professional circuit but rapidly working his way up. I know of at least twenty confirmed hits but am certain there are dozens more. The man uses any tools necessary for the job. He's good enough to leave no evidence, even so far as to hack surveillance cameras." He jerked his chin toward me. "She's the only one who's seen his face and lives to tell the tale."

I went cold. "So he really is after me now, too?" I whispered. The room suddenly spun and I clung to a nearby countertop for support.

A frown flickered across Lucas's face and he took a step toward me, but Jeremiah was already there, an arm around my shoulders pulling me close. I appreciated the much-needed support and gave Jeremiah a smile, even as Lucas was held back again, the guards on either side grabbing his arms.

"Who hired him?" Jeremiah asked, his eyes on me and not his brother.

"It doesn't matter, only that the assassin's coming after you."

The nonanswer drew Jeremiah's full attention. "You don't know, or you won't tell me?"

The deadly note in the billionaire's voice shivered through me, but Lucas merely shrugged it off as if he heard similar threats every day. Maybe he did in his line of work, I thought as Lucas replied, "We can worry about that after the fact."

"We can worry about it now. What are you hiding, Loki?"

Consternation flickered across Lucas's face at the use of his other name. "I wish you wouldn't call me that," he said, the jovial mask slipping for a moment.

"Why not?" Jeremiah shot back. "It's your name, isn't it?"

"That name was given to me, I didn't create it myself." Indecision creased his face, as if he wanted to say more, explain what he meant, but Ethan chose that moment to come into the room. If the bald bodyguard noticed or cared about the increased tension in the room, he gave no indication. "We have a visitor."

Jeremiah's lips thinned at the interruption. "Who is it?" he asked.

Ethan glanced over at Lucas. "Anya Petrovski."

I was watching Lucas when Ethan spoke, so I saw the spasm of anger move across his face. He saw me looking and tried to cover it up, but his eyes still burned with emotion. *Just like his brother,* I thought. *It's all in the eyes.*

"There's no need to involve her," Lucas said, his voice smooth and dismissive. If I hadn't grown so accustomed to reading Jeremiah's stoic expression, I might have been taken in by the words. "She's probably here to plead my case to you, which is entirely unnecessary."

I glanced up at Jeremiah and saw him studying his brother through narrowed eyes. "Would she know anything about this?"

Lucas snorted. "Definitely not, other than the fact I came here to warn you."

He sounded flippant and uncaring, but Jeremiah seemed unconvinced. He turned back to Ethan and said, "Leave her car outside the gate. Search both it and her thoroughly, then bring her to the house."

Ethan nodded and whispered instructions to a nearby guard, who then disappeared from the room. For all of a second, Lucas's lips pursed and his eyes flashed, then the jovial mask slipped back into place. "I do love drama," he said, his lips turning up into a tight smile.

"What is the meaning of this?" came a woman's voice from the entryway, her strident tones bouncing off the wood and stone. Lucas's smile froze, eyes widening as his head snapped around toward the voice.

Jeremiah glanced at Ethan, jaw tightening in annoyance. "Why isn't she gone?" he demanded.

"She hadn't left the gate yet when you ordered the lockdown," Ethan said just as Georgia Hamilton swept into the room. She was flanked by two more guards who faded back toward the front door, escort duty done. The older woman fixed her eyes on Jeremiah and marched straight up to him angrily. "What is the meaning of this?" she snapped, glaring up at her son. "You throw me out of my own home, send your police force to escort me off the property, then force me back in when I'm obviously not wanted?" She drew in a shaky breath, covering her mouth with the knuckles of her hand. "Haven't you any concern for my feelings?"

The overwrought performance was sublime but, given my experience with the woman, I couldn't dredge up any sympathy for her imaginary plight. Nor, apparently, could Jeremiah, who replied coldly, "Rest assured, Mother, you'll be gone from this house as quickly as we can manage."

Annoyance wrinkled her nose briefly, then the waterworks started. "How can you dream of keeping me away from my . . ."

"Well, hello, Mother. Did you miss me?"

Lucas's snide words stopped the older woman in mid tirade. Clearly shocked, she turned around to stare at her elder son, who stood glaring at her from the center of the room. "What is he doing here?" she demanded, all traces of her previous grief disappearing in an instant.

"Lovely to see you, too." Gone was the professional nonchalance Lucas had maintained throughout the conversation with Jeremiah. Sarcasm now laced everything, the bitter sneer across his face angled toward the thin woman who'd just entered the room. The scar on his cheek stood out as the skin around it darkened in repressed anger.

Georgia looked as though she'd bitten into a lemon as she rounded on Jeremiah. "Don't listen to anything he says," she spat. "He's nothing but a liar and a cheat."

Lucas threw his head back and barked a laugh, then bowed toward his mother, a mocking smile on his face. "I learned from the best. Inherited from both sides, in fact."

Puzzled by the exchange, I looked up at Jeremiah for some clarification but he, too, seemed confused. "What's going on?" he demanded.

"Nothing," Georgia said, then lifted her chin and squared her shoulders. "I'd like to leave now as it appears family means little in this house."

"Oh, Mother, no. Please. Stay." The sarcasm dripped off Lucas's every word, but the woman merely crossed her arms without looking at her elder son. A cruel smile tightened Lucas's face but the wounded look in his eyes didn't quite jibe with the expression. "Wouldn't you like to know what happened to that thirty million dollars I was accused of stealing?" Lucas asked. "Surely curiosity has been eating away at you about how I spent it."

Georgia flinched ever so slightly, the sign little more than a momentary purse of her lips. "I don't need to hear this, it's not my business," she said, sniffing in disdain and pivoting toward the entryway. "When your little argument is over, I'll be in my car."

"Stop her." Jeremiah's command was immediately obeyed as the two guards along the doorway closed ranks, blocking the exit. Georgia squawked in outrage but Jeremiah ignored her, his attention on his brother. "I don't like secrets," he said, voice low.

"Yet you've helped perpetuate one for almost eight years now." Lucas never stopped watching his mother, even when she refused to return the favor. His eyes were a cauldron of emotions, flickering and changing so fast it was difficult to decipher any one in particular. "Come now, Mother, should I tell him or would you like to do the honors?"

Giving an irritated groan that sounded childish coming from the older woman, Georgia turned her back on her elder son. Suddenly realizing that she had an audience scrutinizing her every move, she smoothed her features and waved her hand airily. "I don't know what you're talking about," she said, rolling her eyes. "Now if you'll excuse me . . ."

Lucas's eyes narrowed at the display, then he turned to Jeremiah. "Have you ever wondered where Mother gets all her money?"

The question seemed to startle Jeremiah. He gave his brother a long, hard look before turning to glance at his mother. I followed his gaze and wondered what he was thinking. Georgia Hamilton wasn't a good actress; she avoided everyone's eyes, her head swiveling from one exit to another as if pondering which one would get her away quicker. Finally, she met Jeremiah's look and rolled her eyes. "Come on, you don't actually believe him, do you?" she snapped.

"Believe what?" Jeremiah looked between his family members, confusion mixing with annoyance. Neither his brother nor his mother seemed inclined to do more than glare at each other, so he raised his voice and asked again, "I'm not to believe what?"

A cell phone rang, the sharp sound piercing the tense atmosphere. Ethan melted out of the room as the answer to Jeremiah's question hit me like a ton of bricks. *Oh, my God.* "Your mother was the one who stole the money."

I hadn't meant to vocalize my thoughts, it was only a theory, but the words electrified the audience. Georgia rounded on me. "That's absurd!" she snapped. Her face contorted in anger. It was an odd sight to behold, as many of her features had been deadened by Botox injections and their near-tranquility didn't match the obvious rage in her eyes. "What would you know anyway? You're just the trollop my son brought home."

"Wasn't that how you, too, started out?" Lucas practically cooed as my hands curled into fists. "Didn't Father find you in a Vegas dance hall? Come now, Mother, projecting your issues on her doesn't forgive you your own sins."

A spasm of pain cracked across the older woman's face at the memory, which she tried and failed to conceal. "I don't need to hear this," she repeated bitterly, but much of the fire had gone out of her words.

She turned away, only to have Lucas block her path and snag her arm. Despite the cuffs around his wrists, he held her firm. "Do you know what you've done to me, Mother?" he murmured as she turned and glared. He leaned in close, their gazes locking, but neither seemed willing to budge first. "Do you know what your lie reduced me to?"

I stared at them, still shocked by the revelation, then looked up at Jeremiah. He was as still as I'd ever seen him, and it was difficult to tell what he was thinking. Part of me wanted to know more about Georgia—had she really been a Vegas showgirl?—but now was definitely not the time for questions. *There's so much about this family I don't know.*

"Don't blame me for what you chose to become," Georgia spat, glaring up at her elder son.

"How was anything that happened to me my choice?" Even from several feet away I saw his body trembling as he released his mother's arm, his hands curling into fists. "Everything I was, everything I had, was locked up in this company. Then that was taken away, I was accused of stealing thirty million dollars, and I took the only option available to me that didn't include jail time."

"Selling weapons to the highest bidder?" Jeremiah interjected in a wooden voice. "That was your only recourse?"

Lucas blinked at the interruption, then stepped away from Georgia. He looked shaken, his eyes hollow as he looked back at his brother. "It didn't start out that way. I needed to get out of the country and a man I once considered a friend needed a skilled negotiator to broker a deal on some cargo. I didn't know until I was in the air what that 'cargo' consisted of or, I swear, I'd have walked into the jail myself."

Georgia snorted. "And you want to lay the blame at my feet?"

"Take some responsibility for what you've caused," I said, unable to contain myself anymore. Every face in the room held varying degrees of disgust and astonishment at the older woman's behavior and words but nobody was willing to speak out.

She rolled her eyes and casually inspected her nails. "The reason doesn't matter. He is what he made himself—I'm not the one who should live with the shame."

I sputtered, unable to control my own anger. "He's your son," I exclaimed. "They're both your sons! Don't you care for them at all?"

"Of course I love them," Georgia snapped, giving me a haughty glare. "Keep your opinion out of matters that don't concern you."

I wanted to throttle the sanctimonious bitch but at her words Lucas's face shut down. "You're right, Mother," he said, chin coming back up. I recognized the moment his familiar mask snapped back into place. He gave the woman a tight-lipped smile even as she ignored him. "We each have to live with our own mistakes, don't we?"

Jeremiah finally stepped forward. I laid my hand on his arm and felt him tremble, the emotional upheaval locked deep inside. His attention was focused on Lucas, who had visibly retreated from the conversation, locking himself behind a familiar wall of congeniality. "Brother . . ."

"Do you know our mother is shopping around a biography about the Hamilton family dynasty to various publishers?" Lucas said, interrupting his brother. The sudden color in her cheeks betrayed Georgia's anger, but he continued. "An insider's look at our family dynamics, from our dear departed father to the current leader of the family business. She, of course, is the beleaguered heroine in this tale of drama, wealth, and corporate espionage. Reportedly the bids for the book were up close to seven figures before every last editor pulled out." At Georgia's shocked look, Lucas waggled his fingers. "You're not the only one with industry contacts willing to help you screw somebody over."

"What are you talking about? This is absurd. . . ."

"*And*," Lucas continued, his haunted smile widening, "she's also selling access to her billionaire son. If a businessperson can't gain an audience with the CEO, why, he or she can be an impromptu 'guest' at the family home, conveniently timed to run into the new head of the family. All for the right price, of course."

"This coming from a man who sells weapons to dictators and scum of the earth for them to use against innocent people?" The color on Georgia's cheeks was high as she glared down her nose at her elder son. "You dare come in on some high horse, spouting this load of lies, after what you've done?"

"At least I don't hide what I am," Lucas murmured, parroting his mother's arrogant stance.

Georgia rounded on Jeremiah. "Tell me you don't believe this drivel," she demanded, hands on her hips.

Jeremiah's gaze, however, was intent on his brother, ignoring his mother completely. Lucas didn't flinch from the probing look. "You can prove this?" Jeremiah asked finally.

"I can," Lucas replied as their mother huffed in outraged affront.

"You take his word over mine." Georgia gave Jeremiah a disappointed look whose sincerity, given her previous outbursts, rang hollow.

Does she even realize how she looks to everyone? I wondered. Judging by the way she ignored the guards and other occupants of the room, I highly doubted it. The woman seemed locked inside her own little world; the opinions of others didn't matter. What a horrible way to live your life.

Jeremiah stepped forward until he was standing in front

of his mother. He leaned forward, and while I couldn't see his face I did see Georgia flinch away. "I swear, Mother, if what he says is true, I'll—"

"You'll what?" she challenged. "Throw me out? Cut me off? Do you really think you're the first Hamilton male to make those threats to me?" Georgia snorted. "How do you think I stayed married to your father all those years? Good looks and charm? No, I always had something over him—it was the only security I had." She met Jeremiah's glare with one all her own, but the color had drained from her face, leaving only cosmetics to give her any color. "I knew that old bastard wouldn't leave me a red cent when he croaked, but how was I supposed to know he'd go so soon? You two thought I was no different from your father, and maybe now that's the truth, but I knew for certain the only person I could rely on was myself."

"So you threw me under the bus." Lucas's statement wasn't quite a question, but it was obvious he wanted answers.

Georgia blanched, as if the impact of her actions had only then occurred to her. Her mouth moved silently for a moment. "It was never supposed to go this far," she said finally, voice low. She fiddled nervously with her purse, grabbing a tube of lipstick and a small mirror, but her hands were shaking too much to apply a new layer. "That bastard father of yours didn't leave me a dime; in fact, he managed to tie everything I thought I'd secreted away into Jeremiah's inheritance. I knew there was no way my sons would take care of me. Don't think I haven't noticed how you act around me," she added as an aside to Jeremiah. "Barring me from my own home, acting as if I'm an infant. You're just as bad as your father, assuming I can't take care of myself."

The accusation jolted Jeremiah, but Georgia continued. "Everything happened so quickly. I managed to find the will and read enough before the lawyers came to know I'd been screwed. Over thirty years I'd been with that bastard, bearing his children, overlooking his infidelities, playing my part as the dutiful Stepford wife, and he left me nothing. I helped run some nonessential committees, the ones Rufus felt perfect for my distinct lack of any useful talent. Each had been allocated a certain amount of funds which combined equaled just over thirty million dollars." She lifted her chin. "So I took it."

"And left me taking the blame?" Lucas demanded.

"I didn't think that far ahead," she snapped. "I knew I was on borrowed time, so I spent as much as I could. Turns out it was tougher to get rid of the money than I thought, at least without attracting too much attention. By the time I found out you were the prime suspect—I didn't bother to participate in the investigation for obvious reasons—you'd already fled the country, and I still had a sizable chunk of money left. So I kept it."

Lucas put his hands over his heart. "I feel for you, I really do."

"Can the bullshit, Lucas. I messed up, plain and simple." She turned to Jeremiah. "Now what?"

"Yes, Jeremiah," Lucas added. "What do you want to do about these new developments?"

The CEO didn't seem in any condition to talk, still obviously startled by the turn of events. I had no advice to give, only tightened my hold on his arm in silent support. *What a horrible choice*, I thought, sympathy pouring through me as Jeremiah looked from his mother, tapping her foot impatiently, to Lucas, who stood quietly with raised eyebrows and obviously expected an immediate answer.

Then the front door burst open and a familiar woman's voice shouted, "Lucas!" Every head turned toward the sound, and a moment later a disheveled Anya Petrovski stumbled in through the entryway door, flanked by two large guards. Gone was the dressed-to-the-nines beauty from the ball; very little makeup graced her face, and the elegant clothes were rumpled and disheveled as if she'd just thrown them on haphazardly. Her hair was pulled back in a loose ponytail, and while her natural beauty still showed as plain as day, her features were less severe, making her appear younger and more vulnerable. Her eyes quickly scanned the room and it was obvious the moment she found Lucas that he was all she was interested in.

Lucas, however, eyed the girl coldly. "I told you to stay away from me," he said, voice devoid of emotion.

His reaction toward the woman surprised me but Anya endured his scorn. She was babbling in Russian, back stiff and face stoic, but tears had pooled in her eyes at Lucas's icy rebuff. The Russian beauty moved toward him until he held up a hand to ward her off. "I'm sorry," Anya finally moaned in English, her eyes haunted.

"I told you I never wanted to see you again," Lucas growled. His glare was frightful to behold—in that instant he looked and sounded very much like his brother, and Anya quailed.

This wasn't the haughty, annoying woman I'd met before; the desperation and pain in her tone bled through, even if the exact meaning remained a mystery. I exchanged a look with Jeremiah, who looked as baffled as me. What was going on?

Lucas pointed at Jeremiah. "He's the one you should be begging for forgiveness," he said, voice dark, but Anya continued speaking to him in Russian. She kept clutching the Orthodox cross I remembered hanging from her neck at the gala in Paris, pleading with a stone-faced Lucas to no avail.

"Why is she here?" Jeremiah finally asked. At his words Anya grew quiet suddenly and seemed to withdraw in on herself, looking at the floor and wringing her hands.

Lucas gave the blond Russian a look of contempt. "You were wondering before who hired the assassin to kill you?" Lucas jerked his thumb at the cringing beauty, giving his brother a tight smile.

"Surprise."

20

At first, I didn't understand what he meant. The whole room was silent for a moment, then Jeremiah snapped his fingers and pointed toward Anya. Immediately the two men who had escorted her into the building each grabbed an arm, holding her firmly in place. Only then did Lucas's meaning sink in, and I gasped at the revelation.

"Anya hired the assassin." The words, summing up my own confused understanding of the situation, came from Jeremiah. Incredulity crept into his voice, as he repeated it as a question. "Anya hired the assassin?"

"Never cross a Russian," Lucas replied, rolling his eyes and sighing. "It seems as though the truth of that saying extends beyond my current profession."

"I did this for you," the blond woman said to Lucas, struggling to free herself from the guards' grip. "I thought this was what you wanted!"

"What I wanted?" Lucas sneered at Anya. "You did it for yourself—don't try to lay blame at my feet."

Anya eyed the bodyguards around her but kept speaking to Lucas. "You said you hated him, that you wished——"

"I never wanted him dead," Lucas roared, and Anya flinched.

"You always talk about him," she persisted. She slipped into Russian for a second then caught herself. "When you drunk, you always talk about how you wish to go home . . ."

"And killing my brother will get me my place back?" Lucas barked a laugh. "Anya, you're not a stupid woman, all evidence to the contrary in this situation aside. Look at me!" He spread his arms. "Thousands of people are dead at my hands. Maybe my finger wasn't on the trigger but I provided the bullets, the guns. I'm covered in blood—how can I come home after what I've done, what I've allowed to happen?"

Anya's chin trembled as my own heart constricted at the man's obvious pain. She crooned something softly in her native tongue and reached out to Lucas, but he slapped her hand away. "Don't flatter yourself, my dear." His cold fury sliced through the air, designed only to inflict pain. "I never loved you. Why would one have any affection for a clever tool?"

The blood drained from Anya's face as she gaped at Lucas in disbelief. "You said . . ."

He waved a hand through the air, rolling his eyes. "Words mean little, you should know this. Your usefulness, as well as my patience, has run out. I no longer need your drama." Lucas regarded her coldly, then made a shooing motion with his hand. "You can go away now."

Wow. I watched the scene, uncertain anymore what to

think. As much as I'd detested the woman when I'd met her in France, my heart went out to her now . . . which was silly, given the fact that she'd done so much to hurt us. But at that moment, I had trouble believing that the woman would do such a thing.

Anya drew herself upright in a facsimile of her previous pose but the devastation in her eyes was terrible; the backbone of steel and attitude that had sustained her was gone, broken by his words. A single tear worked its way down an ivory cheek. "I give you everything," she whispered brokenly in a thick accent. The fingers where she gripped the ornate cross around her neck were pale and trembling. "I become anything you need, do things that shame me and my family, all for your love. Now you tell me it was a lie?"

I remembered Ethan telling me that Anya was a simple country girl when Jeremiah hired her to help with Russian translations. Looking at her now, I didn't see the haughty, condescending beauty at the party, but a young girl thrown into a world against which she had no defenses. The way she clung to the necklace, a symbol of the religion to which she obviously still clung, made my heart ache for her. *Is this where I'm headed?*

"We Hamilton men corrupt anything we touch." Lucas gave Anya a pitying look. He spared me a glance before continuing. "You were caught in the crosshairs and that was unfortunate."

"This is not how it was supposed to happen," she whispered. "He said this was what you wanted, that . . ."

She trailed off, but in the dead silence her words carried

through the room. "Who said?" Lucas and Jeremiah both replied, echoing each other.

At that moment, several things happened simultaneously. The lights all went out in the large room, casting odd shadows from the muted light streaming in through the window. I had time to realize the glass lining the back of the room, which had stayed opaque for the last several days, no longer hid its view of the ocean behind the house, then it struck. There was a small *pop* and Anya toppled forward onto the floor, a stunned look on her face. Then I was suddenly grabbed and flung sideways into the kitchen, pressed behind the tall marble-topped island by a heavy body. Something whistled past my head, the air singing with its closeness. I gave a startled shriek as a jar of flour on the counter behind me exploded.

The room erupted into motion as people scrambled for cover. Guards dove toward the kitchen or the entryway foyer, piling through the narrow passage. There was another *pop* and a young guard tripped, falling motionless to the ground. He was dragged through the doorway by his comrades, disappearing from my view.

"What's going on?" I asked, heart threatening to tear from my chest.

"Sniper."

Oh God. I trembled against Jeremiah, who pulled me tightly against his body. I heard a loud *thock* inside the island and jumped, but no bullet exited on our side. Beside us one guard broke from his position by the door and headed toward us. Another pop sounded and he spun around, landing gracelessly on his back half inside our cover spot. Surprise and fear flashed briefly in his eyes before his face went slack, and the sickening realization I'd just watched somebody die was almost too much to bear.

"Breathe," Jeremiah ordered, and I let out the air I hadn't realized I'd been holding. He edged sideways and checked for a pulse in the guard's neck, then grabbed the small earpiece and microphone. "Ethan, report."

"Somebody sabotaged the electrical system, including the backup generators." Ethan's voice was tinny and faint but I was close enough to Jeremiah to hear. "We're working to sort that now. What's the situation in there?"

"A sniper has us pinned in the kitchen," Jeremiah bit out. "We need that glass back as cover to get out."

There was a pause, then, "Roger that. Randy says ETA on the power is two minutes."

Jeremiah cursed, dropping the comm onto his lap. "Two minutes," he repeated, and I nodded. "Might as well be forever."

"Visiting with you is always such a pleasure, brother."

Lucas's voice was light and Jeremiah's head whipped around to glare, but the scarred man wasn't even looking at us. All his attention was on Anya, still lying prone in the middle of the floor, clutching her bleeding belly and moaning softly. Lucas had somehow managed to overturn the thick coffee table and one chair as cover, but neither afforded him much protection. Anya reached one arm toward him, sobbing softly as her other hand clutched the gunshot wound in her belly.

"I'm coming, baby." Lucas made a quick in-out movement

with his head, peeking very briefly from cover, and an instant later a bullet tore a hole into the wall behind him. He cursed, then cast about and grabbed a pillow nearby. "This would really be easier without the cuffs, brother," he called out.

Jeremiah dug around in his pockets and tossed a small keychain across the room to land behind the coffee table. "What are you doing?" he asked.

"Probably getting myself killed," replied Lucas, quickly unlocking his cuffs. He paused to take a deep breath, and looked over at Jeremiah. "Wish me luck," he added, then tossed the pillow sideways into the open area beside him. It exploded, sending bits of stuffing flying everywhere, but Lucas was already moving, grabbing Anya and pulling her toward his hiding spot. Another *pop* through the window and Lucas hissed, but he was back behind his barrier and managed to pull Anya with him behind the long table. Two bullets in rapid succession struck the wood table Lucas hid behind with loud *thocks*, but neither appeared to make it through.

Careful to stay hidden, Lucas moved to inspect the wound in Anya's stomach. From the bleak look on his face, I could tell it was bad. Anya sobbed softly, one hand fluttering over her belly while her other hand held tight to Lucas's arm. Out in the entryway, Georgia's screaming reached truly operatic levels. "Mother, be quiet!" Jeremiah shouted, and instantly the screaming stopped. I wondered if it was fear for her life or that of her children that had the woman in hysterics, but right then wasn't the time to consider that.

"Stay with me, Anya," Lucas murmured, removing his shirt and carefully pressing it over the wound.

"I'm sorry," Anya whispered, bloody hand fluttering weakly through the air. Tears tracked down the side of her face into her hair, and the bleakness in her eyes was heartbreaking. "I should have known, I never wanted . . ."

"Shh, don't talk. You're going to be fine."

The lie was obvious; even from this distance I could see the amount of blood pouring from the wound and the increasing pallor in the Russian woman's face. "I never should have listened to him, I only wanted you to be happy. . . ."

"You're going to be fine," Lucas grit out, but the reality of the situation was increasingly apparent in his desperate gaze. His hands left the blood-soaked shirt against her belly to cup her face. "Who told you to do this? I need a name, Anya, stay with me here."

She didn't answer him as her breathing grew labored. Her body grew slack, her free hand falling to her chest. "I gave you everything," she whispered, exhalations coming in uneven gasps. "Don't forget me."

"Anya," Lucas said, smoothing back her hair, "stay with me. Hey, you never took me to that little town you were from. What was its name again?"

Anya, however, didn't seem to hear his question, her pallid face growing slack. "Everything," she repeated, eyes staring off into nothing. Her hand slipped from the Orthodox cross below her neck, and she drew in a rattling breath. "I sold my soul. . . ."

Lucas's face contorted. "Anya, stay with me. Anya . . ."

But she was gone.

Lucas's breath came out in a ragged hiccup, then he pounded the tile floor with a bloody fist and let out a string of curses. A bullet smacked into the wood behind him but he didn't flinch. All the masks were gone, and I saw the profound defeat in his scarred features.

In death, Anya's pallid body looked so small and young. I'd never wanted to see the woman dead, even when I had seen her at her worst. Learning about the young girl she'd once been, then seeing her crying on the ground, had erased my residual bad feelings toward the woman. Her final words had been a sucker punch to the gut, and I could only imagine it was worse for Lucas. Maybe he deserved it. The thought was unkind but I couldn't help but wonder what he'd asked the Russian girl to do on his behalf, manipulating her obvious feelings for him no matter whether or not they were reciprocated. Does love mean so little to this family?

The lights in the kitchen flickered as the electricity came back on, but the glass lining the back of the house remained clear. "Get that safety glass on," Jeremiah barked, holding me tightly against him. A second later someone flipped the switch and the glass fogged over again, the ocean disappearing from sight. The sniper, however, wasn't finished; bullets continued to pop through the fogged glass, mostly centered around Lucas's and Anya's location.

Apparently the gunman didn't like being made a fool of.

"Go," Jeremiah said softly, pushing me to my feet and propelling me toward the entryway less than ten feet away. He shielded me with his body as we ran the short distance to the relative safety of the main lobby of the house. Lucas came through not long after us, bloody hands hanging stiffly at his sides.

Georgia was at the far end of the lobby, one guard holding her in place. The frantic expression on her face melted as both her sons came through the door, but she paled when she saw the blood on Lucas. Wresting her arm out of the guard's grip, she moved toward her elder son, jaw moving in helpless shock, only to have him lift a hand to stop her. "It's not mine," he said. There wasn't any emotion in his voice. Anya's death must have burned it out of him, at least for the moment.

Uncertainty marred the older woman's face, as she clearly debated what to do. I wondered what she would do, perhaps try to mend the relationship with a hug, but her personality won out. Her chin went up as the arrogant mask clamped down hard, and it occurred to me the whole family hid parts of themselves from the world as if showing any true emotion would allow others to use it against them. And perhaps that's what had happened in the past.

Ethan came through the front door, flanked by another guard with a cell phone to his ear. "We've got generator power back on but it's going to take a while to fix the mess with the main power lines," he said. "There are three wounded outside, emergency medical is en route."

"We have casualties in here, too, with at least two dead. Get all the wounded upstairs and coordinate to make sure everyone gets attention." Jeremiah put a hand on each of my shoulders, then pushed me toward Ethan. "Take care of her and my brother, there's no time to waste."

"Sir?"

"We need to find that sniper now before he disappears

again." He looked at me. "Stay with Ethan; do whatever he tells you."

I had to force myself to release his arm. The urge to try to hold him back in the safety of the house was strong, but I knew it wouldn't stop him. He needed this, to be back in the trenches hunting the bad guy. That he was the ultimate target didn't matter to Jeremiah, I could see it in his eyes. So instead of protesting, I swallowed my fears and said, "Promise me you'll stay safe."

His manner softened at my words, whether in relief or something else. He kissed the top of my head as the wounded guards were brought inside. "I'll be back for you, I promise," he murmured, then headed out the door.

"Take them upstairs," Ethan ordered, and the remaining guards moved up the staircase with the wounded.

"Great," Lucas muttered, staring woodenly at the floor, "I have Captain America babysitting me. Whoop-de-freaking—"

Ethan spun around in front of me, his fist exploding across Lucas's face, sending the man to the ground in a crumpled heap. "I've wanted to do that for years," Ethan said under his breath.

I stared down at the scarred man in dismay. "Did you really have to do that?" I asked, moving forward to see if Lucas was okay. "He wasn't any threat . . ."

A hand wrapped around my head, clapping a cloth over my mouth. Startled, I struggled, opening my mouth to scream but instead breathing in a sickly sweet aroma. Almost immediately the room spun, and I heard Ethan mumble a soft

"I'm sorry for this" as my legs gave out and I was lowered to the floor.

I've heard that phrase too much tonight, was my last thought before losing consciousness.

My dream was weird: I couldn't tell, even within the context of the subconscious fantasy, whether I was flying or falling through the air. Clouds whipped past me, the ground far away like I'd only ever seen from inside an airplane. Something was in my arms, perhaps the reason for my descent, but I wasn't afraid. The ground drew ever closer, yet I felt entirely content with the whole situation, although I had no idea why.

The real-world feel of somebody rummaging through my pockets popped me out of the dream state. Sudden vertigo made my head swim, remnants of the dream perhaps, before I realized I actually was moving and that I was lying on my side. My hands were tied in my lap in front of me, my feet were similarly bound, and I was precariously perched across the backseat of an unknown car. When I tried to sit up, I also discovered that I was tied down by seat belts, the thick straps pulling me back onto the warm leather.

A man sat in the driver's seat, working with a phone in his thick hand. Figuring he didn't know I was awake yet, I surveyed my surroundings, blinking away the grogginess. Everything was covered in black leather, the textured, expensive type, and it smelled brand-new, but the car itself was unfamiliar to me. The backseat was narrow, with very little leg room—I stayed curled up to keep from bumping the sides of the car—so I guessed it was a sports car of some kind. The whine of an engine used to fast speeds confirmed that suspicion but didn't give me any other details. I turned myself to peer up through the window to the overcast skies outside. The leather squeaked beneath me, attracting the driver's attention, and my heart skipped as I recognized the familiar face. "Ethan?"

He turned back around, staring at the road. He tossed the cell phone onto the passenger seat and I realized it was mine, the replacement Jeremiah had given to me after I broke mine in Paris.

"The girl is awake?"

My eyes widened when I heard the other voice. I peeked around at the passenger seat in front of my head but nobody else was in the car. The voice hadn't come from any one direction, and Ethan didn't seem surprised although his jaw did tighten.

"The sedative wore off early," Ethan replied. His voice was gravelly, angry, as if he didn't want to respond.

My cell phone on the seat in front of me burst into sound, visibly startling Ethan. "What is that?" came the disembodied voice, annoyance creeping into its unctuous tone.

"The girl's phone." Ethan picked it back up and looked at the screen. "It's Jeremiah," he added flatly.

My heart raced at the name. Chest tight, I bit my lip to keep from crying out.

"Answer it," the voice directed. "Put it on speaker."

Ethan put the call through, then set the telephone down. Before he could say anything, however, I exclaimed, "Jeremiah!"

"Lucy. Where are you?"

Something cold inside my soul melted at his voice. He sounded strong and sure, and I desperately needed the assurance. "I'm in the backseat of a car," I replied, hating the desperate quality of my voice but eager to get out as much as I could. "Some sports car with all black leather. I can't see anything but overcast skies out the window. I'm with Ethan." I stopped, not sure how to break the news about my kidnapping.

My eyes met Ethan's stony gaze in the rearview mirror, then the big man sighed. "I'm sorry about this, Jeremiah."

"Ethan?" he growled. Perhaps if I could see Jeremiah's face I could decipher the emotion I heard hanging on that simple word—surprise, rage, betrayal, disappointment—but for now there was only the word and the demand for answers behind it.

"They have Celeste." Profound regret tinged the big man's voice, and I saw his mouth turn down.

Jeremiah cursed. "When?"

"I don't know but I got the call while you were arguing with your family. You know I'd do anything to protect her."

"So you set this up?" Even over the phone, the rage in Jeremiah's voice bubbled over. "You let three men die because—"

"No," Ethan exploded, "that was not me. I didn't know anything until that call, and the lights went out before I was off the phone. I swear to you on whatever honor I have left that I had no part in that attack."

"You ask for trust after kidnapping my—" Jeremiah cut himself off, then asked, "Where are you going?"

"To make the trade."

"Goddammit, Ethan!"

"You'd do the same for her, don't bother denying it." Ethan glanced back at me, then gave a harsh laugh. "This whole thing is just like Kosovo."

There was a pause at the other end of the line, then Jeremiah growled again, "Goddammit, Ethan . . ."

"When this is over, don't blame Celeste. This is all my decision." Ethan picked up the cell phone. "I'm hanging up now. Good-bye, Jeremiah."

"Ethan, wait—"

Ethan disconnected the call, staring at the phone in his hand.

"Throw the phone out the window."

I started at the smarmy voice beside my head as Ethan did as he was told, lowering the window and tossing out the cell phone. I looked up beside my head and realized the voice was coming from the car speakers. Part of me was relieved there wasn't another person in the car with us but I had the sinking sensation I would very soon meet the voice in person.

"What happened in Kosovo?" the voice asked conversationally.

"An informant betrayed us," Ethan replied, voice neutral. "We didn't realize until after the fact that our target had kidnapped the man's wife and family, so he gave us up to save them."

"Did they all survive?"

"No" came the clipped reply.

"Pity, although perhaps a fitting end for his crimes. Betrayal really is the nastiest of sins, wouldn't you say?"

Ethan's knuckles on the steering wheel were white from the strain of his grip, but he didn't reply to the obvious taunt. "What are you going to do with the girl?" Ethan asked after a short pause.

"Kill her, then kill your friend when he comes to save her."

I moaned and squeezed my eyes shut, tears leaking from the edges of my lashes. When I opened my eyes again, I saw Ethan staring at me in the rearview mirror. "And if I don't bring her to you?"

"I kill your precious wife. Hmm, eventually. She really is a pretty little thing, if you like redheads, that is."

Ethan's hands twisted on the steering wheel. "You son of a bitch . . ."

There was a commotion on the other end of the line, then a woman screamed in pain. Celeste. Ethan swerved the car at the sound, bellowing, "Stop it!"

The screaming stopped but the soft sobbing in the background was almost as gut-wrenching. "If you don't want any more marks on your precious wife," the voice stated, no longer amused, "you won't call me any more names. Are we clear?"

"Crystal," Ethan growled, but his profile conveyed a bleak hopelessness.

My heart was pounding, threatening to leap from my chest. My breaths came shaky and fast. "Ethan, please," I whispered, throat constricting at the thought of what was coming. *I don't want to die!*

"Shut her up," the assassin said.

I squirmed, desperate to get free, as Ethan grabbed a white rag from the passenger seat and reached back toward me. His long arms found my face easily, but I fought, holding my breath and twisting every which way I could against the seat belts to get away. Ethan had the patience of Job, however, and spots danced along my vision as I quickly exhausted my oxygen supply. I sobbed out a breath, the sickly sweet aroma of the drug trickling down into my lungs, and seconds later I fell back into unconsciousness.

This time, there were no dreams.

21

I didn't know how long I was out this time, but the increased rocking and bouncing of the car was what initially pulled me out of my drug-induced slumber. It wasn't until we stopped, however, that I became fully conscious, the sudden lack of movement jarring me awake. There was the sound of a car door and the clunk of a seat, then my legs were grabbed, their bindings removed. I fought but my struggles were weak and ineffectual as I was pulled from the vehicle and slung over a shoulder. Chill air circulated off the water and I immediately began to shiver, the thin clothing I wore no match for the wet winter gust.

"Can you stand?" Ethan's voice rumbled.

My stomach roiled, nausea threatening to overwhelm me, but I managed a weak "Yes." The world spun again but Ethan was gentle, setting me on my feet beside the car. I staggered, placing a hand on the glossy sports car for support, and forced myself to look around. Seagulls screeched above, their plaintive cries slicing through the air. The ocean surf lapped rhythmically nearby but I wasn't able to see the opposing shoreline with the fog over the water. Factory buildings lined the seaside road, blocking us in. The waterfront road was narrow and hazy, tendrils of fog snaking in over the bumpy asphalt, but I saw another car a few hundred yards away pointed ominously toward us. "Is that . . . ?"

I noticed something from the corner of my eye and glanced back to see a gun in Ethan's hand. My breath quickened but he caught my gaze and shook his head ever so slightly, keeping the weapon pointed to the ground and hidden behind my body. "Where's my wife?" he called out to the assassin, who was still obviously listening from the car.

The door to the car facing us opened, confirming my fears. A slim figure with very red hair staggered out of the vehicle as the door was shut behind her. "Ethan?" Celeste called, her voice tinny over the distance.

"I'm here, Celeste," he called back, and I could feel the tension leak out of his body as Celeste's head snapped in our direction. She staggered toward us, and I could see she was both blindfolded and had her hands cuffed behind her.

"Wait for her to reach you," the assassin said, his oily voice through the car's sound system making my hands curl into fists. I bit my lip as a solid *snikt* came from behind me, no doubt Ethan readying his weapon. My chin quivered and I gritted my teeth, determined to be strong. *Oh, but it's so hard.*

"Perhaps now would be a good time to mention that your wife is wearing a bomb?"

I heard a quick intake of breath and Ethan's grip on my upper arm tightened. The pleased note in the assassin's obsequious voice intensified as he continued, "If you're considering any heroics, the first casualty in this conflict will be your beloved wife. So please put away that gun you're hiding behind Ms. Delacourt or my finger might get a bit . . . twitchy."

Ethan immediately raised his hands in the air, brandishing the weapon he held, then tossed it inside the car. "Almost there, baby," he called out to the redhead. My heart ached for the woman, who was stumbling blindly toward her husband, only able to use the sound of his voice to navigate. Twice she almost fell, a dangerous proposition as her hands were tied behind her back, but she managed to catch herself each time.

"How quickly do you think you can take your wife out of range?" Smug superiority fairly oozed from the car speakers. "Let's play a game: Is the bomb on your wife triggered by radio signal or by cell phone? You get one guess. And don't try to use the car when you escape, I might have that similarly wired to blow." A dark laugh came from the sound system. "How far will you have to go to ensure her safety if this all goes sour, or I decide to be a real son of a bitch?"

Ethan growled, his body vibrating with the sound, but his voice was strong and sure as he continued to call to his wife. Her answering cries were full of fear, and as she came close, Ethan stepped around me and caught her in his arms. I saw a red mark across one high cheekbone and what looked like a small burn on one shoulder, but otherwise she seemed okay. The redhead's loud sob ripped through the tension as the bald man crushed her against his body, kissing the top of her head for a long moment before pulling the blindfold from her eyes and picking her up in his arms.

I knew the moment Celeste saw me because she gasped. "What's Lucy doing here?" she demanded, voice suddenly strong. Her eyes fell to the handcuffs on my wrists and she gave her husband a piercing look, fear giving way to confusion.

"My finger is getting itchy on this button," the assassin's impatient voice came through the speakers, and a dawning horror flowed across the redhead's face.

"No," Celeste blurted out, "you can't leave her here." When Ethan didn't reply but only turned toward a nearby alley, Celeste's protests rose to shrieking levels and she struggled in his arms. The small woman had no chance, however; her hands were cuffed behind her and there was no way Ethan would let her go. I watched them fade into the distance, the man's huge loping strides taking him far away quickly. A detached numbness came over me as I realized I was well and truly alone, and more than likely about to die. How did my life come to this?

Across the way, the driver's-side door opened and a man unfolded himself from the car. He was dressed casually, with only a thin leather jacket to protect him from the frosty air coming in off the water. His slacks flapped lazily in the breeze as he made his way toward me, footfalls from his wingtip shoes growing steadily louder. He wore narrow-framed sunglasses, despite the overcast light, that fit his face well. A detached part of my brain noted he was almost handsome but in a muted way, the "nice guy" who you never really noticed. Given the day's events, I doubted I'd ever forget this man's face if I lived through this.

I stood my ground as he approached, leaning against the

car for support. My legs were jelly, threatening to collapse from the fear, but I faced him head-on and tried to emulate Jeremiah's stoic stare. No mean feat, especially when he finally stopped close enough for me to touch. He examined me silently and I met his gaze, my breaths coming quick, but I was unwilling to back down anymore.

"It's rare I actually meet one of my targets face-to-face," he said finally, quirking one eyebrow. "Of course, it's also rare that they see me and live to tell the tale. Truth be told, I prefer it this way, watching a person's face in those final moments." He chuckled, the sound hollow and devoid of any real mirth. "Of course, you were never a target until you survived my poison. Tricky girl."

The fake smile on his face didn't reach his eyes and sent a shudder through me. His eyes were dead, dark pools that held nothing else beneath. I struggled to keep myself under control, clamping my lips tightly together so I wouldn't make a sound. As determined as I was not to beg, the prospect of dying left me faint and I clung to the car mirror to keep from collapsing.

"Not that I don't enjoy our time together"—he glanced at his watch—"but we have less than ten minutes until the cavalry arrives. Six, if they have a method in place for physically tracking either one of you that I don't know about. These factories are a maze, tough to get through even with a map." The assassin reached behind him and pulled out a black gun, caressing the barrel with his free hand without taking his eyes off me. He saw me watching and shrugged. "It was a blow to my professional ego when both of you survived my poisoning attempt. That won't be a trick I use again, but still, I need to correct my mistakes."

I kept my eyes on his, trying desperately to control my breathing. A dozen scenarios flitted through my head on how to get away: hand-to-hand combat, running away, diving off into the water. In every scenario, however, I lost. Badly. The quiet confidence in his face told me everything I needed to know, that his skills in pursuit of prey were far greater than my skills at fleeing, especially out here in the open. A detached numbness spread through my body as I watched him prepare his weapon. *Is this really it? Am I merely ending up as bait to lure Jeremiah to his death?*

A narrow tube appeared in one of the man's hands, and he casually connected it to the end of the gun, spinning it in place. He cocked his head to one side and studied me. "You're very brave," he commented. "Most targets would be begging for their lives right about now."

I would've done so if I thought it would mean anything. The wind picked up from the water, waves crashing into the wooden supports beneath us, shaking the ground beneath my feet. My own shivering ceased at the realization that I was about to die.

"I prefer it face-to-face like this," he continued, "but most people run away and I have to shoot them in the back. Annoying business, that—almost takes away the dignity and pleasure." He raised his weapon and leveled it with my face. "Don't worry, my dear, you'll see your beloved billionaire again soo—"

Something whistled past my ear and the assassin spun

around, collapsing onto the ground. I stared down dumbly as he thrashed at my feet, grunting in obvious pain and holding his shoulder, then common sense flooded back with a vengeance. I spun to flee but hadn't taken a step yet when a hand grabbed my ankle and I toppled to the ground. I managed to catch myself, skinning my knees for the first time since childhood, but was immensely grateful that Ethan had bound my hands in front of me. I squeaked as my hair was grabbed and I was hauled backward and over the assassin until I was all but lying on top of him.

"That son of a bitch," the assassin muttered, and I didn't know who he was talking about until a small device appeared in his hand. It had two small buttons, one blue and one red, and looked much like an electronic car key. I realized, horrified, that it was probably what would detonate the bomb on Celeste.

"No!" I grabbed his hand, wrestling for the device. Something had obviously gone wrong—Ethan had betrayed him, or the cavalry had arrived early on its own—but it didn't matter; I couldn't allow him to press that button. All I could see was Celeste's panicked expression when she saw me, her cries not to leave me even as Ethan hustled her away, and I couldn't think of letting her die. Not without a fight.

The assassin hadn't expected my resistance, and I'd almost pried the device from his grip before he fought back. One of his arms was all but useless—blood poured from a large wound in his shoulder—so between his wounded arm and my cuffed hands, we were almost evenly matched. I also realized quickly he was using me as a shield against the new sniper and didn't want to compromise that, as he looped one leg around my waist and jerked me down, trying to wrench the controller from my grip.

A flash of triumph shot through me as I snagged the small plastic device from his hand, but before I could throw it into the water nearby, an elbow slammed into the side of my face. Pain exploded through my skull and, stunned, I hesitated too long and his hand was back over mine, trying to pry the remote from my fingers. Ears ringing, I tried to hold on to it but another elbow, this time to my chest, knocked the wind out of me. Dazed, I struggled to breathe and faltered long enough for him to wrest the small implement from my grip. Anger and triumph contorted his face, and I watched helplessly as he pressed the red button.

Nothing happened.

He blinked, then looked down at the controls. His finger slid again over the red button, but whatever he was expecting clearly didn't materialize. "Well, fuck," he said, shoulders slumping in defeat.

I snapped my head back, catching my skull against his nose and mouth. The impact again stunned me, but his grip loosened and I rolled sideways away from him. Our eyes met as his good arm raised up, pointing the gun directly at me.

Then the back of his head exploded, and he collapsed back on the asphalt.

Body quaking, I struggled for breath but couldn't take my eyes off the grisly sight. Hysterics threatened, sobbing breaths forcing themselves from my lips as I pushed myself upright, chest aching from where his elbow had impacted. Tears, however, didn't come; a pervasive numbness overwhelmed me and all I could do was stare at the slack face of the assassin, the hole in his skull, and the . . . the mess behind his head. *I think I'm going to be sick.*

I don't know how long I sat there, staring at the bloody mess before me, before I heard car tires approaching our location. Too numb to move my head, I nevertheless watched dark sedans and SUVs move in, surrounding us on the narrow waterway road. People wearing the familiar dark uniforms I'd seen for nearly a week now exited the vehicles, milling about the scene. None of Jeremiah's people approached me, although one man did gently pick up the remote that had skittered out of the assassin's hand when he'd been shot. As much as I wanted to say something, tell them what it was, I couldn't take my gaze off the assassin's face, the man's expression forever frozen in astonishment.

A *whoop*ing sound drew closer, and I finally turned my head to see a helicopter appear through the fog over the water. A tall man stood on one of the skids, and as it approached the land's edge he leaped off, landing effortlessly and running straight toward me. A long rifle hooked across his shoulders bounced with his loping gait, and when he came abreast of me he fell to his knees and immediately folded me into his arms.

My body shook, the action uncontrollable and fierce, and a sob burst its way out as I finally gave way to the emotions I'd kept bottled inside. I clung to Jeremiah as he picked me up gently, keeping me pressed firmly against his body, and loaded me inside one of the waiting SUVs.

The ride home was quiet, for which I was eternally grateful. Jeremiah kept me on his lap, his hands caressing my back and arms in a rhythmic pattern that helped calm me. There was no demand in his touch; perhaps a touch of possessive protection, but I desperately needed that form of safety. The earlier numbness had worn off but I was too tired to cry or scream. All I wanted was to curl up in a dark room, safely away from society, and try to forget the past several hours.

My brain, however, kept reliving horrible scenes: the guard dying in front of me at the house, Anya's final moments, Celeste's wails as she was carried away to a safety I'd been denied, the assassin's head exploding in a splash of gore. When I'd found a drop of what I thought was blood on one sleeve while in the SUV with Jeremiah, I'd almost gone crazy trying to strip out of the contaminated clothing. Only Jeremiah's deep voice, his hard hands deftly peeling the offending layers from me, kept me from falling into the hysterics in which I so desperately wanted to indulge.

Any hope of solitude, however, was dashed when I saw the vehicles lining the front of the mansion, unfamiliar faces and uniforms standing guard at the entrance. I whimpered when Jeremiah's car door opened, not wanting to be in the middle of yet another circus, and clung to his neck as he carried me out of the vehicle. His lips grazed my ear, breath warm against my skin as he asked, "Can you walk on your own?"

The urge to answer no, to stay safely against him as long as possible, was a strong temptation. I nodded, however, a spark of independence goading me to take control of myself. Jeremiah still didn't release me for several more seconds as we walked through the unfamiliar crowd, then he gently set me on my feet once we were inside the entryway. I teetered for a moment, keeping my grip tight on his arm, but he didn't seem to mind. "Who are these people?" I said finally, clearing my throat. My voice sounded thick to my own ears, likely due to my earlier crying.

"They're government officials, here to take my brother into custody."

Jeremiah's lips were a thin line and I couldn't tell whether or not he approved, but the idea of Lucas going to jail was disheartening. In the lobby, the scarred man was staring at a nearby body bag, a tired look on his face. Lucas's gaze followed the body as two men in coroner's uniforms hefted it up and took it outside, then he looked up at me. Relief flashed in his eyes. "I'm glad you're safe, my dear," he said, giving me a small nod. "There are already too many casualties in this debacle."

"Thank you for your help," I replied, sighing. "I wish it didn't have to end this way for you."

"It was the risk I took in coming here." Lucas hitched a shoulder, one side of his mouth lifting in a smirk. "I appreciate your concern, however. It's . . . sweet."

I frowned, trying to determine whether the statement was a compliment or an insult, and my dilemma seemed to amuse him. "Good-bye, fair lady," he said as the officials in suits tugged him out of the house. "Hopefully we will meet again soon."

Jeremiah stepped sideways, blocking the path through the door. "Brother," he started, but Lucas shook his head.

"Don't. Whether you're apologizing or condemning me, I don't want to hear it. The truth is out and now we each live with the consequences."

The brothers stared at each other for a moment, two matching profiles against the fading light outside. Finally, Jeremiah stepped out of the way, and Lucas was led silently out to the waiting vehicle. I watched, disappointed, as the car containing him and the various officials rolled out toward the main gate.

Jeremiah looked around the lobby. "Where's my mother?" he asked a nearby guard.

"The officials took a brief statement, then said she was free to go, sir."

The CEO's lips thinned very briefly, and he sighed. I frowned; I'd hoped for more from the odious woman, but I guessed the habits of a lifetime were difficult to give up. I put a comforting hand on Jeremiah's arm, then tensed as I recognized another familiar figure walking toward us.

Ethan had a wary look on his face but, to my surprise, he wasn't wearing any handcuffs. Celeste was nowhere to be seen, and while I very much wanted to know if she was all right, I kept silent. "I'm glad you're okay," the bald man said to me.

I moved closer to Jeremiah, suspicion and mistrust echoing through my brain. Despite knowing why he kidnapped me, and the impossible situation into which he'd been placed, I couldn't bring myself to forgive his actions. Seeing him now only brought back memories of a cloth over my mouth, the sickly aroma of the sedative seeping down my throat, and the terror of him abandoning me to my fate.

"Thank you," Jeremiah said from beside me, his arm pulling me tighter against his body. His body remained stiff as he addressed the bodyguard. "This could have turned out much different without your help."

Ethan nodded. "I managed to find a heavy freezer inside one of the buildings. It kept any signal from getting in long enough for me to disarm the bomb around Celeste." His gaze turned to me. "I hear I have you to thank for the extra delay."

Confused, I turned to look at Jeremiah. He helped? How?

"The Kosovo reference," Jeremiah said, answering my silent question. "Our informant on that mission led us into a trap, giving us faulty intel that got several men killed. However, he dialed the new coordinates on his cell phone so we could complete the mission anyway." His powerful gaze never left the bald bodyguard's. "I'm glad the outcome was better this time around."

Ethan shrugged, but his eyes crinkled in a wince. "Celeste isn't happy with how I handled the situation." He glanced at me. "Leaving you behind with that assassin might be the one thing that costs me my marriage."

Part of me desperately wanted to comfort him—I'd seen firsthand how much he adored his wife—but I couldn't get any platitudes through my lips. It was all too fresh, too many bad memories and sensory links to work through before I could ever feel comfortable around the man. I think he saw that because regret etched across his face. "I wish I'd seen another way," he said, eyes on me.

Before I could react, Jeremiah stepped forward. His arm was already moving and his fist cracked along Ethan's jaw with a sickening snap. The bald man staggered back, falling to the ground, as Jeremiah towered over his prone figure. "You're fired."

A protest lodged in my throat as I stared between the two men. Something silent passed between them, then Ethan nodded. "I expected worse."

Jeremiah stepped forward, extending his hand, and helped Ethan to his feet. "You still have my respect, but I can't afford to trust you again." He stepped away. "Get your things from the bunkhouse and be off the property in half an hour; we'll deal with the business end of things later."

Ethan nodded soberly, then turned to me. "For what it's worth, I'm sorry for how I acted."

"Your wife was kidnapped," I replied, surprising myself. "You did what you thought you had to do, and managed to alert the cavalry to rescue me." I struggled to find the words to continue, still conflicted about the day's events. Was I really forgiving the man? "I hope you and Celeste can work things out," I finished lamely, unable and unwilling to absolve him yet. His presence still made me nervous, and I shifted closer to Jeremiah.

Ethan saw the movement and sadness flickered through his eyes. "Take care of him," he told me, the statement a surprise, then he turned and walked back out the door.

I peered up at Jeremiah, who was watching the entryway through which his old friend had just exited. He must have felt my gaze because he turned his head to look at me. My lips parted as I was struck yet again by how beautiful he was, and lifted one hand to caress his face. One large hand slipped up and covered mine, and he placed a soft kiss on my palm that sent sparks through my body. Without thinking, I threw my arms around his torso and buried my head in his chest, tamping down the sobs that threatened to form. *I'm safe.*

And I knew, beyond a shadow of a doubt, that I was irrevocably, madly in love with the man before me. The emotion burst through me, leaving me light-headed at the realization that I was head-over-heels for the hard yet tender man I'd met only a short time before. Even the logical side of my brain, the part that had railed against such a silly notion before, was in silent agreement.

Jeremiah's arm came around my shoulders and he kissed the top of my head just as another guard came through the door. I peeked sideways to see that the younger man looked nervous. "Um, sir . . ."

"Yes, Andrews?" Jeremiah replied, keeping me tight against his body.

Andrews swallowed, seeming reluctant to speak. "Government officials just arrived at the gate," he said finally, placing his hands behind his back and standing straighter. The military stance seemed to give him more confidence. "They're here to collect your brother."

I blinked, confused, then looked up at Jeremiah. His face was blank for a moment, then he began to curse.

Ducking my head against Jeremiah's torso, I hid my smile at Lucas's deception and marveled at the day's events.

22

The restraints around my wrists pulled tight, the cool leather holding me fast. The restraints were supple, designed not to cause any irritation, but I'd had them on all night and most of the morning. There was some discomfort, but I was too caught up in other sensations to really notice. Light streamed through small cracks in the heavy drapes, but the room stayed dark and secluded, the perfect getaway for what we were doing.

Jeremiah's lips traveled up my spine, teeth grazing my naked skin as he moved back up my body. Fingers skimmed over my hips, tracing along the sides of my breasts against the mattress. My breath caught as his knee slid between my legs, and I felt his hard length press along my thigh. A hand smoothed my hair to one side as he rained kisses along my neck and up to my ear, teeth tugging gently at the cartilage. My hips rose in silent supplication; he nipped my earlobe but obliged my need, slipping easily inside me.

I sighed, my eyes fluttering closed. Our lovemaking had

been frenzied and passionate before, but now, hours later, the edge had worn off and it was much easier to enjoy ourselves. Jeremiah insisted I stay bound to the headboard, subject to his every desire, and it never occurred to me to refuse that demand. His authority and domination helped chase away the bad memories; I was safe, secure in his grasp, and focusing on that allowed me to enjoy the pleasure of the moment.

He rummaged for something, hips continuing to move his hard length in and out of me in long sure strokes, then the small vibrator I wore clicked on again. I let out a gasping breath as his arm slid under my waist, lifting me up to my knees. Fingernails skimmed along my back as he thrust harder, and I grasped the headboard for additional support.

"So beautiful," he murmured, hands caressing my back and over the globes of my backside. "Everything about you is a turn-on."

I bit my lip, his words a balm to my soul, and pressed back for more. He surged inside me, drawing a strangled gasp from my lips. Fingers dug into the skin of one hip, an anchor as he thrust repeatedly inside me, our coupling no longer a leisurely affair. I braced myself against the wooden headboard, shameless moans and cries being pulled from my throat. The tiny vibrator, perfectly positioned so as not to interfere with his access, sent waves through my body with each thrust and spiraled me higher and higher toward yet another orgasm. Other toys lay on the table beside the bed: floggers, feathers, dildos, and several items I wasn't sure what to call, but Jeremiah wasn't interested in any playing—no toys were used except the cuffs and the vibrator, both of which were more than enough in my opinion. I was spent and sore, but just as insatiable as the man inside me.

His thrusts became more erratic, a sure sign he was close to coming. My tired body tightened as well, bracing for another orgasm. I felt his breath along my neck, the rough stubble on his chin scraping along one shoulder. His hand snaked between my legs and pushed the tiny vibrator in closer to my body, straight on the throbbing center of pleasure within my folds, and with a strangled moan I came yet again. Every last bit of tension drained from my body, my forehead collapsing on my arms as my body shook, skin tingling from the overabundance of ecstasy I'd experienced through the night.

Jeremiah collapsed over me, spent, his welcome weight pressing me further into the mattress. I didn't mind at all, grateful for the contact. Eventually, he stirred and reached up to unbuckle the cuffs, freeing my wrists from the restraints. I wiggled around until I was on my back, staring up at his muscled torso. My wrists ached but I didn't care, as I ran my hands along his hard stomach and down his arms.

He drank me in with his eyes, his gaze caressing me like silk. Behind his eyes I saw deep yearning, evidence of a hidden need, and love blossomed in my heart. I tugged on his shoulders, pulling him down on top of me, and he came willingly, lying across my body so I could wrap my arms around him. His warmth and hard body made my soul sing, and I closed my eyes as I caressed his back. Being free of the restraints, however, also freed my mind to wander, and even though I didn't want to dwell on certain events, they still rose to the forefront of my mind.

A lot had happened over the past two days, but the most worrying was the investigation into Jeremiah. The government officials who'd arrived to pick up Lucas hadn't been amused to hear he'd escaped, and they also weren't happy to learn about the additional kidnapping drama that had happened the same day. Accusations that he'd allowed his brother to escape paled in comparison to the storm created by the dead bodies. Jeremiah's use of his private helicopter over public land, ironically enough, was the largest issue keeping his lawyers busy. We had, at least for the moment, been absolved of the deaths both on the property and along the waterway, but the violation of restricted airspace could still be enough to land Jeremiah in jail.

Hamilton Industries had also suffered a blow when Celeste had stepped down as COO following her kidnapping. Jeremiah didn't talk about it and I didn't pry, but I'd heard enough from his side of phone conversations to determine that she didn't appreciate being kept in the dark and put in danger, however indirectly. The status of the redhead's relationship with her husband was still a mystery, but I hoped she would forgive him. Time and space had given me a little perspective: Ethan had been between a rock and a hard place, and chose to save the one thing he loved most. I hated to think what I'd do in a similar situation.

In what I considered a comical twist of fate, I was finally performing many of the duties of a personal assistant for

Jeremiah, taking phone calls and messages and helping with day-to-day business activities. It surprised me how much I enjoyed the fast-paced work; Jeremiah forwarded his calls to me and I helped set up his day and keep track of who needed what. To be honest, he threw me into the deep end, sink or swim, but I needed the distraction and I think he knew that. Whenever I slowed down or finished my duties, when I had a free moment to let my brain think of something besides work, I'd invariably flash on an image or memory that disturbed me: the assassin's open wound, Anya's body in that bag, staring down the elongated barrel of the assassin's gun. I'd only managed to embarrass myself once by crying, but with each day the memories became easier to bear. Work, at least, allowed my brain to remain disconnected from the unpleasantness.

A hand slid beneath my head, lifting it from its position buried in his chest. Jeremiah gazed down at me, eyes searching mine. He traced the outline of my brow, fingers light against my skin as he followed the contour of my face down along my jaw and neck. His caresses pulled me from my thoughts and I closed my eyes, giving myself over to this simple pleasure.

"You're thinking too hard," he murmured, his chest rumbling with the words. "Right now, I only want you to feel."

I gave a soft sigh and opened my eyes, my thoughts pulling me out of the moment. "Are we safe?" I asked, pushing my face into his hand and kissing a knuckle. "Do you know who Anya was talking about, who the person was that convinced her to hire the assassin?"

260 • sara fawkes

It was a discussion we'd already had, and I knew Jeremiah was well aware of the continuing threat somewhere out there. Anya's last words before the sniper started firing, mentioning a man she never named, were a dark cloud looming on the horizon. I could feel it casting a shadow over me, but worried more for Jeremiah. He didn't seem to be as intent on finding the mysterious figure as he was on keeping me tied to his bed. I remembered my earlier conversation with Ethan at the hospital, where the former bodyguard talked about the CEO consistently shrugging off all kinds of danger. Jeremiah had already rejected his mother as a suspect, despite the new information and the fact that she fled without a word. His nonchalance toward the potential menace bothered me, and I couldn't tell whether it was confidence or if he was doing it for my benefit—I hoped it was the latter.

"We'll get it sorted out," he replied, kissing my forehead. "I'll keep you safe, I promise."

For a familiar argument, a familiar answer. His patience was frustrating, especially since I wanted answers now. *It's only been a few days,* I admonished myself. *You can't expect immediate results on a case with no leads.* Still, I hated being on the sidelines, unable to help in any meaningful way.

I pushed insistently at one shoulder, and Jeremiah rolled sideways onto his back, pulling me along with him so I was lying atop his body, straddling his waist. Tired as I was, I still raised myself from him, staring down at his beautiful face. He watched me, too, the fire in him cooled for now, his face as open as I'd ever seen. His hands smoothed up and over my breasts, then down to rest on my hips as he waited on me.

Everything in me sang at the sight below me. A girl could live forever and not get tired of this. I traced the lines of his muscles, then leaned down so my breasts pressed against his chest. Skimming his lips with mine in a feather-light kiss, I gave him a half smile as I whispered, "I love you."

"No."

My world stopped. For an instant I thought I was falling, but nothing had changed. I sat up straight, confusion racing through me as I stared down at the suddenly stony expression of the man beneath me. My mouth worked, trying to think of something to say, but it was as though my brain had shut down. Jeremiah's hands circled my waist and, as if I weighed nothing, he lifted me off and to the side, then sat up, swinging his feet off the bed. I blinked, the meaning of what had just happened beginning to sink in, and watched as he stood and picked up his clothing.

I looked back down at the bed, trying desperately to keep my breathing steady. Stupid, so very, very stupid. My fists balled up around the pillowcase as I held in my emotion, trying for the stoicism I'd always seen in his face. "Why?" I asked, unable to think of any other question to ask. There was a small break in my voice at the end of the word, but I forced my eyes up, thankful that I hadn't yet shed a tear.

He ignored me for several seconds, quickly buttoning his shirt, then pulling on his pants without looking at me. Finally he turned back to face me, his face as closed off and emotionless as I'd ever seen. The drastic change from only a minute ago was like a death knell in my heart.

He must have seen the distress on my face because he sat

down on the bed beside me. "I don't think . . ." he started, then paused a moment in thought. "I'd prefer it if we kept any mention of love out of our relationship for the foreseeable future."

"Why?" I repeated, more forcefully this time. I was slowly breaking apart inside, and keeping myself together was becoming more difficult by the moment, but I needed an answer.

Jeremiah studied me, a clinical examination that was void of any of the tenderness I'd experienced at his hands since our meeting. "Let's think about this logically," he said finally. "You've known me for roughly two weeks now. Is that enough time to build any type of emotional attachment?"

He was being rational, voicing arguments I'd used on myself when the *L*-word first popped into my head, and part of me still agreed with him. But with every word he uttered, the cracks in my heart grew wider, expanding and multiplying and going deep to the quick. "I'm not asking you to say the same," I finally managed, but the words tore at my soul.

"Maybe not," he replied, "but . . ." He cupped my face, and I flinched. "Why ruin what we have with platitudes like this?"

Pain blossomed, but I kept my face steady. I'd learned from the best, after all. When I reached out to touch him he stood, perhaps a bit too quickly, and retreated back. Grabbing his phone, he added, "Now that you've been cleared in the preliminary investigation, you're free to leave the grounds for anything. With the police presence being what it is, I think we're safe from any more attacks for now. One of the guards can drive and escort you anywhere you want; just keep me informed as to your whereabouts."

A dull ache spread through me as he walked across the room to the door. There he paused, staring at the brass door handle. I thought for a moment he'd turn around and address me again, maybe explain himself further, but he merely turned the knob and left. The latch closed with a finality that was shattering, had numbness not taken over my heart.

Dimly, I felt myself climb out of the bed and go through the motions of dressing myself in clothes still strewn about the room. Cleaning myself up in the bathroom was almost an afterthought, a delaying tactic to keep from showing myself to the world, but when I finally stepped out of the bedroom into the rest of the house, only silence greeted me. From the day I'd arrived at the mansion estate, the house and grounds had been teeming with people, usually the guards or other staff. Now that the danger was past for the time being, they had returned to their regular assignments, and the sudden famine of souls in the house echoed the painful emptiness within me.

I made my way down the stairs, bypassing the kitchen completely. Food didn't sound good right then; in fact very little sounded good at that moment, so I walked to the front door and peered outside. The air was chill, almost bitterly so. The milder weather we'd had for a while had taken a wintery turn. Snow flurries dotted the ground, but I didn't care that my nose immediately began to sting from the frosty wind. A black limousine sat right in front of the large doors, its exhaust a billowing cloud of steam in the icy air. I couldn't imagine it belonged to Jeremiah. Surely he would have already left; it had been several minutes since he walked out. He'd suggested before that I could leave the grounds. Did he call this for me?

I'd stayed away from public places, keeping to the house and not leaving the estate even after the kidnapping attempt. I remained mindful that there was still somebody out there gunning for us, who was willing to use others to do his dirty work. At that moment, however, staring at the limo, I no longer cared—being shot through the heart couldn't hurt any more than this. I left the house and moved to the car, opening the door and sliding inside. The interior was warm, a marked difference from the outside air, and up near the front I saw the dark head of the driver. "Where to, Ms. Delacourt?" he asked.

"Away from here," I mumbled absently. Realizing the distance sound had to travel, I readied to repeat my answer louder but the car lurched forward, heading for the gates. I didn't bother looking out the windows; instead I just stared at my hands, deep in thought.

What if Jeremiah was right? What if my feelings were premature, too soon to be considered genuine? It was reasonable that Jeremiah would hold off on sabotaging a relationship by acting too soon; there were still too many unknown variables in the equation. At least, that was how the rational side of my brain saw it—a man like Jeremiah must have similar issues with moving too fast.

The limo stopped briefly at the gate, and the guards quickly waved us through. I peeked through the back window, watching the great big gates close again, trying to ignore the squeezing in my chest. And really, it was only one part of our relationship with which he took issue. Such a silly word anyway. Love. I'd seen how he looked at me, the way he touched and held me. *Really, Lucy,* I thought, *do you really need platitudes of devotion?* "Love" is just a word.

Right?

A sob welled up from deep inside, surprising me with the sudden depth of emotion. My hand went to cover my mouth, determined to hold the inexplicable grief inside, but I couldn't stop the shuddering breaths or the tears that abruptly appeared and flowed down my cheeks. It's just a word, I thought again, but the pain wouldn't stop. I knew what love was, I'd grown up in a household where it flowed freely. Wouldn't I have a better idea of what the emotion felt like than Jeremiah anyway?

"Is everything all right back there, ma'am?"

"Everything's just dandy," I replied, my voice thick. Then for an instant it all became too much. "Got my heart broken today," I admitted, "but I'm trying to get through it."

"Ah," the driver responded. "Well, my brother always was an idiot."

I was in the middle of rummaging through my purse for a tissue when the meaning of the man's words sank in. My head snapped up, grief and heartbreak momentarily forgotten, as I stared at the back of the driver's head through the small partition. A hat covered his head, and the mirror was angled in a way that made it impossible to see his face. "Lucas?"

"In the flesh." He pulled off his hat, uncovering dark hair.

When he turned around to look at me, I saw that he wore makeup of some kind, presumably to get past the guards. His skin was lighter, the nose seemed bigger than I remembered, but the prominent scar on his cheek revealed his identity more than anything else. He gave me a quick perusal. "You look terrible."

His words pricked my remaining feminine pride and I sat up straighter, glaring at him through the tears. Focusing on the matter at hand was a great deal easier than the emotional roller coaster. "What are you doing?" I asked, striving for bravado.

Lucas shrugged one shoulder. "Apparently, I'm kidnapping you. I thought you of all people would recognize that fact."

I stared at him for a moment, flabbergasted, then groaned loudly. Slumping in the seat, I leaned my head back against the cool leather, suddenly too tired to think of fighting. Lucas watched me in the rearview mirror but I didn't care; all I wanted was to not think, not remember my last conversation with Jeremiah.

"Let me guess: You told my brother the dreaded *L*-word, didn't you?"

I didn't bother responding to his question, instead staring at the ceiling of the limo. Two kidnapping attempts in one week—I'm a very popular girl. The thought held little amusement, however. I just wanted to be alone to lick my wounds in peace.

Lucas didn't seem the least bit deterred by my silence. "My brother is a fool," he continued. "Any minute now he's going to realize what he's done and . . ."

The small telephone on the dash rang suddenly, startling me. Lucas chuckled. "That's probably him now."

I stared at the phone, torn. Thinking about that beautiful, cold face as I had seen it mere moments ago made my already bleeding heart break more. *Why?* I wanted to scream. This was more than a bruised ego—I honestly needed an answer. None of the last twenty minutes made any sense.

Lucas reached out and pressed a button on his dashboard. The ringing broke off on a flat note, and I gave the dark-haired man a startled but dubious glance. "Don't worry, ma chérie," he soothed. "By now my brother has probably discovered the drugged chauffeur and is mobilizing the troops, so to speak."

Speechless, I watched as he pulled us into another parking area alongside a long white limousine. A driver stood beside the front door, a large scary-looking man with sunglasses and tattoos across his knuckles. Lucas stepped out of the car and walked around to the back door, opened it, and poked his head inside. "Coming?"

My mouth worked soundlessly, still trying to grasp what was going on. "Why?" I asked finally. It was the same question I'd asked Jeremiah and held within it all the same doubts and anxieties.

"Maybe I need your help with something," the dark-haired man said, "or possibly this is because I've finally discovered my brother's weakness." Then his gaze softened as I pressed back into the seat. "Or perhaps I want to help you. I knew what would happen the moment I laid eyes on you." Sympathy flowed from his voice. "My brother holds everything

268 • sara fawkes

inside, while you wear your heart on your sleeve for the world to see. Jeremiah rejected you when you mentioned love. Given that our mother and father are likely the ones to whom he compares the word, is his response so surprising?"

"Is this what happened with Anya?" I asked, looking up into his eyes. "Did he drive her to you in this same way?"

Lucas blanched, the unexpected question hitting him hard. "Not quite," he managed, struggling to compose himself again. "They never had anything more than a business relationship, although I think Anya wanted something deeper. It made my seduction easier . . . but enough of my past. Tell me: Did you ever tell my brother no?"

I flushed, glaring at him, but the sudden truth behind his words hit me like a truck. Lucas must have seen my realization because he continued, "Jeremiah is used to getting his way, and isn't above manipulating others any way he can to achieve his own ends. A valuable skill in business, perhaps less so in a relationship; the thrill of the hunt is what makes the final acquisition that much sweeter. How hard did my brother hunt you?"

As his words sank into my heart, Lucas motioned around the inside of our limo. "This car is being tracked. If we stay here much longer, he'll find us. Once he's here, you'll be his again to do with as he wants. Where's the challenge in that?"

I swallowed, heart still bleeding as a cold ache suffused me. Lucas reached inside, offering me his hand. The look on his face was mischievous but I saw pity and a familiar longing in his eyes.

"Let's make him chase us, shall we?"

Read on for a special bonus story.

DEVIL'S DUE

Sara Fawkes

Lucas knew a deal with the devil when he heard one, but he'd run out of options.

Turbulence shook the passenger cabin and he held tight to the rickety seat, gritting his teeth as the shuddering grew stronger. Crates strapped to the walls on either side of the seats pitched back and forth, secured only by thin straps and frayed netting as worn as the rest of the plane. The seat was no better; it wobbled beneath him like an old roller coaster you couldn't trust to stay on its track. There were no windows to see outside the plane, which gave him a tiny amount of nausea that kept him from any kind of rest.

From the opposite end of the plane came the tinny note of raised voices and barks of laughter. The door of what Lucas assumed was the cockpit opened and a large man emerged, heading down the narrow gap between the seats to the back of the airplane. The plane dropped suddenly, pushing

Lucas's already queasy stomach into his throat, and the big man lurched sideways, one meaty hip bumping hard into Lucas's shoulder. Lucas struggled not to empty the remaining contents of his last meal all over the other man's shoes as the stranger merely muttered a curse in a foreign language and righted himself before continuing quietly to the rear of the plane. The businessman's presence was ignored, and Lucas snuck a peek over his shoulder to watch the large man descend the stairs behind the seats and disappear. Welcoming voices greeted his arrival down on the cargo deck.

Lucas turned forward again, running a shaky hand through his hair. From habit, he tried to smooth his rumpled clothes but to no avail. The expensive shirt and slacks had seen too much abuse in the last twenty-four hours and only a hot iron would make them presentable again. A hollow laugh escaped his throat as he realized he looked exactly as he felt, unkempt and heading toward an uncertain future. For a man who had always had his life figured out and planned, the entire situation felt like a farce.

I made a mistake, he finally admitted to himself, gripping the chair arms again for support. Lucas shut his eyes, trying to find some sense of inner calm, but there was none to be had. *No American prison could be this much of a nightmare.*

He had always prided himself on having diverse contacts, eyes and ears he could rely on for information. That network had proven very useful in navigating the corporate world; he always had facts and figures first, and no news escaped him when it came to business. But nothing had prepared him for the shit storm created by his father's death, and the subsequent disappearance of corporate funds—thirty million dollars' worth of corporate funds, to be precise. Despite the fact that Lucas had been among the first to discover the financial discrepancy, he had almost immediately become the lead suspect in the case.

So you ran. You stupid son of a bitch.

Fleeing hadn't been his first thought. He'd still been reeling from hearing his father's will read, realizing everything he'd spent the past decade sacrificing his life for was being pulled out from under him. The company—all stocks, all properties, *everything*—had been given to his commando little brother: Jeremiah. Jeremiah, who hadn't even bothered to attend Rufus's funeral or wear civilian dress when he came to the lawyer's office. Jeremiah, who now held the future of the entire company in his inexperienced grip.

To rail against the unfairness of the universe was pointless, but goddammit life sucked sometimes.

Forget the company, focus on your own problems. You ran away from an investigation for money laundering. Talk about nailing your own coffin shut.

Any other day, Lucas would have brushed off the "request" by Davos to help with a business venture. The man, while an effective information broker, wasn't someone Lucas would normally trust with anything else. Since their introduction three years before, Lucas had approached the slick European businessman only a handful of times and, while impressed with what he received, always came away wondering at what price the information had been bought. The first time had been to undermine a potential competitor,

blackmail them into dropping out of a lucrative bidding contract. Lucas had expected a scandal, something he could
threaten to take to the press, but he hadn't been prepared
when Davos dropped a folder filled with images of children,
supposedly from the offending bidder's home computer.

The pictures and evidence had been immediately turned
over to the police—surreptitiously, of course—and not used
for blackmail as previously intended: Lucas played to win,
but the uncovered secret sickened him. He had won the contract but the transaction was like a plague, its taint an oily,
murky memory continuing to haunt him long after. Davos's
information had always been good, however, so when the
man approached out of the blue that morning, saying the
police were on their way to arrest Lucas at that moment,
the former CEO had believed it. The Greek man had offered his help, on the condition Lucas perform some business
services in exchange, and in the height of madness Lucas
had agreed.

The nose of the airplane dove again and Lucas held on,
but it continued on its downward trajectory and he realized
they'd reached their destination. Indeed, the men he'd heard
in the cargo deck below returned to their worn seats, reluctantly buckling in and continuing their earlier conversations.
They were a rugged bunch, most covered in tattoos, with
short hair or bald heads, and the craggy faces of those who
worked hard for a living. Lucas, still wearing his expensive
suit that probably cost two months' worth of wages for these
men, was a fish out of water, slowly dying in the current atmosphere.

The landing was as rough as the flight, and the wheels had barely touched the ground when the men were back up and moving. Lucas stayed in his seat and watched as large moving equipment—hand trucks and the like—were unlashed from the walls and pushed to the rear of the aircraft. It wasn't until the plane finished taxiing that Lucas finally unclipped his belt and stood, legs shaky from the long flight. His bladder was filled to bursting but there was no way he could pee right then; he was too tense and nervous, unsure what was about to happen.

The cockpit door opened again, and another man stepped out of the cabin. He towered over Lucas, wearing a black leather bomber jacket and tall boots over his faded pants. His face was that of a boxer, the kind that had seen too many fights, with a thick jaw and an even thicker, more crooked nose, but he held a power that commanded instant respect. His eyes fell on Lucas and the businessman went rigid. The gaze inexplicably reminded Lucas of his father, although Rufus Hamilton had never been this imposing. *The old man is dead,* Lucas thought, *and anyway, you know how to deal with men like this.*

Well, perhaps not quite like this, but it couldn't hurt to pretend he did. Lucas stepped forward, extending a hand. "Lucas Hamilton," he said.

There was a noticeable pause, such that Lucas almost dropped his hand, before the large man returned the proffered grip. "I am Vasili," he said, with a thick Russian accent. He gave Lucas the once-over then cocked his head to the side. "What do you know?"

"I'm brokering a deal of some sort, although Davos never told me the details."

Vasili gave a harsh laugh that did nothing to raise Lucas's confidence. "Your friend has a lousy sense of humor."

"He isn't my friend," Lucas replied in a clipped tone. It irked him to be in the dark, but he hadn't had time to ask any questions before. Davos had given him directions to an old airport in Pennsylvania and little else, other than saying *take it or leave it*. "What do I need to know?"

The Russian's gaze could have pierced glass, and Lucas knew he was being sized up. "You are merely the hand taking the money." Vasili moved toward the rear of the plane. "Come, the client is waiting."

The large man's thick voice was matter-of-fact as he said it, and the words sent a shiver down Lucas's spine. *What have I gotten myself into?* Following the man toward the back, he descended the stairs down to the cargo hold below. The huge rear entrance was already opening, the men who'd ignored Lucas the entire flight moving quickly to unload crates down to the tarmac. Heat radiated through the opening, the sun reflecting off the asphalt bright enough that Lucas had to shield his eyes for a moment, still used to the darkness of the upper cabin. He saw that they were in a small airport but had no way to know their exact location. The sun beat down, the midday rays a balm against Lucas's chilled skin.

Vasili and Lucas approached three men standing beside a white SUV near the exit. Two looked like bodyguards, dressed in dark clothing and keeping a watchful eye on the proceedings. The third was dressed in a flamboyant white suit, matching the vehicle behind him. His hair was a pale strawberry blond, his skin too fair for the sunny weather, but he didn't seem to mind. His expression remained stony as he glanced at his watch. "I expected you almost an hour ago."

The statement was met with stoic silence from the large Russian. After a moment, the other man's eyes flickered to Lucas in keen appraisal. "I hadn't realized you'd be bringing company."

Vasili indicated the blond man and Lucas in turn. "Jan Blomqvist, Lucas Hamilton. Davos sent this man in his place." Vasili crossed his arms, nodding his head toward Lucas. "Do your business with him."

If Blomqvist recognized Lucas's name, he didn't say anything. He signaled one of the guards, who disappeared momentarily behind the SUV, then emerged with a foldout table which was set up quickly between the men. The other guard placed a briefcase on the table, unlocking the case but leaving it closed before stepping back. Blomqvist jerked his chin in its direction. "There is the payment, now I want my merchandise."

Lucas glanced at Vasili before moving forward, cracking the suitcase to peek inside. There was a great deal of money inside, the entire case filled with stacks of twenties, all neatly bound together. Lucas had no idea what to do next but Vasili, looking over the shorter man's shoulder, nodded then snapped his fingers, shouting something in Russian. Immediately, four men hurried over, each holding a plastic case in his arms.

These were set down nearby, with more apparently on the way as one of Blomqvist's guards set one case on the table beside the money, opened it, and pulled out its contents.

The sight of the large gun was like a blow to the guts for Lucas. He suddenly couldn't breathe, could barely do more than keep himself from collapsing to his knees. The already cloying heat became unbearable, and sweat broke out over his skin. *Oh God,* he wondered, *what have I done?*

The guard handed the assault rifle to Blomqvist, who turned it over in his hands. "Very nice," he murmured, running his fingers over the metal. "How many more are there . . . ?"

They were interrupted, however, by the sound of another car crunching toward them. Lucas looked over to see a similar white SUV come quickly abreast of the other, its tires screeching to a halt, then one of its back doors opened and a man was ejected. Blood stained the front of the man's shirt, and when the guards hauled him to his feet it was apparent he'd been beaten. Lucas cringed inwardly, managing to hold his ground, barely, but unable to take his gaze from the man's bloody visage. There was a dazed expression on the other man's face, likely caused by too many blows to the head, but his eyes were wild even as he sagged toward the ground, held up only by the guards' grip.

Blomqvist cocked his head to the side, studying the bloody man. "Where did you find him?" he asked a guard.

"Hiding behind one of the hangars."

"Indeed. Well, his timing is perfect." Blomqvist clapped

his hands together. "I was hoping for a demonstration." He turned to Lucas. "You, come here."

The blood in Lucas's veins ran cold as Blomqvist beckoned the former CEO to approach. A shared glance with Vasili quickly told Lucas that there would be no help from that quarter, so reluctantly he took the few steps toward the Scandinavian. Blomqvist didn't seem to care about the hesitancy, but pulled Lucas beside him, thrusting the large gun into his hands. "Shoot him."

"Shoot who?" Lucas said dumbly, his brain unable to comprehend the command. The gun in his hands felt heavy, its weight giving credence to the command. *No, he couldn't be* . . .

The amusement faded from Blomqvist's face. "I'd like a demonstration of the merchandise," the blond man said. "You will shoot him, or I will shoot you."

The guards on either side of the bloody man released his arms and he collapsed to the ground in a heap. Lucas gripped the weapon in his hands, but couldn't do more than stare down at the bloody man at his feet, struggling to wrap his brain around the situation. *I've never held a gun before.* He doubted the information would be of any concern to Blomqvist, even if Lucas could have made himself speak at that moment.

The cool metal of a gun barrel was pressed against the side of Lucas's head, and the dark-haired man went rigid. "Three seconds," Blomqvist said. "Him, or you."

Immediately bringing the gun to his shoulder, Lucas

pointed the barrel at the man beneath him. His finger curled around the trigger, but he couldn't make himself pull it.

"*Ett.*"

Sweat poured from Lucas's face. *This can't be happening. Please tell me this isn't happening.*

"*Två.*"

The bloody man raised his head, eyes almost swollen shut from the beating. The gun trembled in Lucas's hands, his breath coming shallow and fast. *I can't, I can't.*

"*Tre.*"

Click.

His finger was still tight around the trigger he'd pressed, the gun lifeless in his hands. The fact that he'd actually *pulled* the trigger, however, reverberated through him.

"Hmm." Blomqvist leaned forward and plucked the gun from Lucas's limp grip. He worked the mechanism then pulled out the magazine. "Empty. Well, that's a shame."

One of Blomqvist's guards reached inside the box the rifle came from and pulled out a box of ammunition, which he held out to the Scandinavian. Blomqvist shook his head and gave the gun to the guard. "Do it on the other side of the car."

The guard nodded and they dragged the man, who had begun mumbling, around the big SUV. Lucas couldn't do any more than stare at his hands. Even the sharp report of gunshots wasn't enough to startle him out of his stupor. Blomqvist's gaze bored through his skull and when the blond man snapped his fingers, Lucas raised dead eyes to the Scandinavian.

Blomqvist moved in front of Lucas. "You should smile more," he said, his own lips curling up as if to show him how it was done. "Life is much easier when you smile."

Aware of the gun still in the man's hand, Lucas hitched up first one side of his mouth, then the other. Blomqvist nodded in approval. "See? Easier." He snapped his fingers and his men began loading the crates into the SUVs. One stood near the table as if waiting for something. When Lucas didn't move, Vasili stepped forward and picked up the suitcase of cash.

"A pleasure as always, Vasili," Blomqvist said before getting into his car. Lucas watched, eyes dull, as the vehicles pulled out, leaving behind only the still corpse laid out across the asphalt.

A sharp clap on the back broke Lucas out of his daze, making him stagger. Vasili stared down at him, a thoughtful look on his face as if surprised Lucas had made it through the encounter. "Three more stops," Vasili said, then shouted to his men again.

Lucas didn't remember getting back into the airplane, only that he was buckled in his seat when the engines roared to life once again. He stared at his hands, the ones that had only moments before held the gun. They were covered in an oily sheen, the kind used to keep metallic parts from rusting too quickly. A laugh burbled up but he quashed it down, knowing that if he started he wasn't sure he could stop.

The muscles of his face burned, but his face seemed frozen in that smile. It was a permanent tattoo on his face, a mask to cover the screaming inside.